He crushed her against him praying for time to stand still. He wanted and needed more time for them. He needed to be so deep inside Jillian's heart, that no matter what, her faith in him would be unshakable. But it wasn't to be. The sound of an approaching airplane drew his attention. Harrison ran to the edge of the trees and recognized the plane immediately as their ride. Relieved that he and Jillian were still alive, yet doubtful about the future, he returned to her. "That's our ride."

I'LL BE YOUR SHELTER

GISELLE CARMICHAEL

Genesis Press, Inc.

Indigo Love Stories

An imprint of Genesis Press, Inc.
Publishing Company

Genesis Press, Inc.
P.O. Box 101
Columbus, MS 39703

ISBN-13: 978-1-58571-309-7
ISBN-10: 1-58571-309-0
Manufactured in the United States of America

First Edition 2003
Second Edition 2008

Visit us at www.genesis-press.com or call at 1-888-Indigo-1

DEDICATION

I'll Be Your Shelter *is dedicated to the cop in my life. Thank you for being my shelter when life has gotten tough. Your love and support has seen me through and for that I will always be grateful.*

CHAPTER 1

"Conversation over, gentlemen. My client will answer no more questions until a better offer is placed on the table," Jillian Newman informed the two interrogating officers. "Tell the District Attorney that I will be waiting to hear from him personally. Until I do, don't ask Mr. Reid another question. Do we understand each other?" She gave the two angry men a pointed look. "Now if you'll excuse us, I would like to speak with my client alone—preferably in a room without microphones."

"Ms. Newman, I'll tell them everything," Drew Reid promised insistently. "I didn't shoot anybody and I don't want to go to jail." His handsome young face showed the signs of worry and sleepless nights.

"You're not going to jail, Drew," Jillian assured her client. "Now don't say another word until I have spoken to the District Attorney. You see I used to be married to the DA, so I know how he thinks. I'll be able to secure an agreement from him not to prosecute with the information you're willing to provide.

The problem though, is that you were caught driving the victim's vehicle and for that the DA will demand probation. But for now stop worrying and trust me to get you the best deal that I can." She smiled at the young man whose future was in her hands.

"Yes, ma'am."

Jillian walked into her office an hour later. She deliberately closed the door gently, despite the urge to slam it for all it was worth. The District Attorney's office was trying to ruin a young man's future to please the masses clamoring for an arrest. She accepted that her client was responsible for his actions and for being with known gang members, but the young man had not been involved in the crime. She had called them on it and eventually gotten them to back down. Now they wanted his help without any guarantees. Jillian wasn't going for it. If they wanted her client's assistance, then the DA's office would have to make a few guarantees before any exchange of information were to happen.

She collapsed into her desk chair and allowed the supple leather to support her exhausted weight. Using the toe of her shoe to spin around, she stared out of her sixteenth-floor office window. The sight of the "Magic City" laid out before her always helped to ease the pressures of the day.

It was a typical June day in Birmingham. The temperature warm and the blue sky sprinkled with white fluffy clouds. The statue of Vulcan was back on Red Mountain as a symbol of the city's steel history. Down below on the city street people could be seen taking advantage of the pleasant weather. Some strolled to local eateries while dedicated joggers pounded the pavement. At the moment, Jillian too had the desire to be out there enjoying the warmth, but it wasn't possible. For the time being she had to focus on the case at hand.

Just then the door to her office swung open and in walked District Attorney Josh Williams, her ex. His stride was long and determined. Standing an even six feet, Josh prided himself on the athletic physique that he worked so diligently to maintain. At age thirty-five his striking good looks, honey brown coloring, and taste for designer clothing made him excitingly appealing to most women. At one time, Jillian had been just like those other women, but now at age thirty, time had taught her a most valuable lesson—looks can be deceiving and glancing at Josh now, she wondered what she ever saw in the man.

"Jillian, what game are you playing?" Josh bellowed.

Unfazed by his dramatics, Jillian merely looked at him as she leaned back in her chair nonchalant. "Don't come into my office raising your voice, Josh. Your theatrics no longer work on me."

Josh released a frustrated sigh. He shoved his hands into his pockets as he stared at his ex-wife. More and more these days she was getting in his way and butting heads with him. "Okay, here's the deal. In exchange for a name and address your client gets a year of probation after which his record will be wiped clean."

Pleased with the deal, Jillian smiled up at Josh as she rose from her chair to shake hands on the deal. "Not that I don't trust you, but can I have it in writing?"

Josh returned the handshake and graced her with one of his rare smiles. "Done. You know, Jillian, when you're through defending the riffraff of this world, come see me. I would love to have you working for me."

"Thanks, but no thanks. I like being my own boss."

Josh didn't reply. He walked around her office looking at the various paintings on her wall.

Eventually turning back to her he said, "Do you know what today is?"

Jillian turned and glanced out the window. There was no way for her to forget and she knew Josh had reminded her on purpose. "Of course I do." She looked at him and swiped at the tears that slowly ran down her face.

"My boy would have been five today." He nailed her with a look that spoke volumes.

Jillian knew Josh blamed her for their son's death. She had been driving at the time. "I blame me too, Josh. It was a moment in time that I can't get back."

"Believe me, I know." He continued to glare at her.

"If we're finished, I have work to do before I head over to Faye's for dinner."

"How is your lovely sister these days?" He glanced down on her in that superior manner that he had perfected.

Jillian ignored his sarcasm. The two had never gotten along. "Well, thank you. I'm due over at her place for dinner at seven. I have a meeting in about an hour and files to get through before heading home by five to shower and change for dinner." She shuffled papers across her desk making her point.

"I'm gone then." Josh effectively ended their conversation. "I'll have the papers drawn up and brought over."

"Thank you."

An hour later the intercom announced the arrival of a new client. Jillian met the man at the door and introduced herself. "Have a seat, Mr. Owens." She waved the older gentleman to one of the chairs in front of her desk. His sun-browned complexion was a testament to his years of working in the sun. She returned to her seat and flipped to a clean sheet of paper on her legal pad. "All right, Mr. Owens, why don't you tell me how I can assist you."

The older man wrung his hands nervously as his eyes met hers. The fear in them was impossible to miss. "I work for a construction company that I believe is building with inferior materials. The invoices say one thing, but when the deliveries are made, its a different product altogether."

"Have you spoken to the contractor, or do you suspect him of being behind this?"

The man nodded his head. "He isn't a nice fellow, Ms. Newman. The man is scum and I know he's behind it. He's the only one who orders supplies and he signs all the invoices, so that's why I went directly to the city's building inspector with my suspicions."

"What's the name of the contractor?" Jillian asked with pen poised in hand.

"Harold Compton."

Jillian wrote the name down, then continued to listen as Mr. Owens went on recounting his story.

"When nothing happened, I went to the police and was told that they would look into it. Then yesterday I received an envelope in the mail. There was no return address."

"What was inside?" Jillian encouraged him to get to the point.

The man nervously removed a handkerchief from his back pocket. He dabbed at the beads of sweat forming across his forehead. "Order invoices for last month's supplies."

Jillian frowned confused. "Why would you receive building invoices at home?"

"The invoices possessed my signature."

Jillian nodded while turning the details of his story over in her head. She rose from her desk and began pacing the floor. "They're sending you a message that they know what you've done, and if you persist, it will be you who takes the fall." She returned to her chair. "And the police didn't find anything? No evidence of a report from the building inspector or sign of inferior supplies?"

"Not according to the policeman I spoke with."

Jillian nodded then thought for a moment. "This is what we're going to do, Mr. Owens. You return to work and say or do nothing. Give me a couple of days to check into your story and I'll give you a call as to how we're going to approach this matter. If anything else should come up, more documents or physical threats, you let me know and we'll go to the police together."

"Yes ma'am. It sure is nice to have someone on my side," the man said standing. He extended his hand then left the office.

By the time Jillian looked up from the files on her desk it was eight o'clock and the telephone was ringing. It had taken her some time to clear her thoughts of the new case and refocus on other cases.

"Jillian Newman speaking."

"Girl, where are you? My dinner won't wait forever you know," Faye Bernard scolded her younger sister over the telephone. "How is some man supposed to find you all locked away in that office of yours?"

Laughing, Jillian teasingly responded, "Who said I was looking for a man?"

"Well if you're not, you should be."

"Enough already, I believe we've had this conversation a million times. Look, I'm sorry for ruining your dinner. Why don't you all go ahead and eat without me. We'll just do dinner another time."

"We will do no such thing. The kids are at David's parents, so we adults can have a proper meal with no spills and bubbles being blown into milk." The sisters shared a laugh. "So get yourself over here and be careful."

Jillian replaced the receiver and immediately began preparing to leave the office. She filled her Italian leather briefcase with folders that had to be read before morning. Checking her desk, she was confident that she had everything that she would need tonight. She pushed from her chair standing. A quick survey of the street below told her just how late it was to be downtown. There wasn't a car in sight. Just then a bolt of lightning illuminated the sky. A clap of thunder soon followed. Jillian jumped reflexively. Delaying no longer she left the office for the parking garage below.

Jillian stepped off the elevator with keys in hand as another bolt of lightning ripped across the sky.

Dreading the pending storm, she wished she had told her sister that she wasn't coming to dinner tonight. She quickened her pace. Downtown parking lots were dangerous doing daytime hours and even more so after normal work hours. When she had worked for a large legal firm, she hadn't had to worry about security. The firm provided around-the-clock guards for its building and parking area. But now, on her own, she was just another tenant in the Kelly Ingram Professional Building. She approached her black Lexus sports utility and noticed three well-dressed men involved in a heated discussion, two lanes over. Their voices couldn't be heard clearly, but the hand gestures and body language bespoke of their anger. Sensing trouble, she hurried to the safety of her vehicle. Just as she closed the door behind herself and turned over the ignition, a gunshot echoed in the cavernous structure.

Instinctively, Jillian glanced in the direction of the three men. Blood covered the chest and hands of one man, as he stared in disbelief at the other two men. He soon crumpled to the ground and out of sight. When the two remaining men glanced in her direction and aimed their weapons, all went suddenly white with lightning, then completely dark as the storm took out the city lights.

Jillian didn't wait to see if they would come back on. She seized the opportunity and threw her car in gear. The vehicle jumped from the pressure of her foot slamming on the accelerator. The headlights temporarily blinded the gunmen, as tires squealed and burned. She maneuvered the sports utility vehicle down the winding exit ramp and exploded onto the deserted street below. Thinking quickly, she turned left onto 20th Street and then right in the direction of the downtown police precinct where she eventually came to a stop. It was the only building on the street with lights. The rain was just starting to fall as she got out the vehicle and ran to the door.

"I'm attorney Jillian Newman and I would like to report a shooting," she hurriedly spoke as she approached the on duty desk sergeant. Professionally recounting the details of the evening, she waited as the desk sergeant informed dispatch to send a patrol car to the location.

"Ma'am if you would return to the scene with Officer Powers here." He pointed to a big man, "He'll take down a description of the suspects."

Reluctantly, Jillian agreed to accompany Officer Powers and his partner back to the scene and out into the raging storm. She thanked Officer Powers as he opened the rear passenger car door for her under the precinct overhang. Alone on the back seat, she desperately tried to steady her nerves as she inhaled deeply through her nose. She silently watched as they passed block after block of downtown buildings in the blinding rain. Her hands were clinched tightly to control the trembling. As several flashing police lights came into view, Jillian prepared herself for the scene above. She grew tenser as they reached the fifth level, their destination.

Jillian was left alone in the car while both officers walked over to the crime scene. Headlights were used as temporary lighting. She cringed as the coroner opened the door of the van and retrieved a gurney. Chilled by the morbid sight, she focused on her magenta heels while trying to block out the storm.

CHAPTER 2

"Detective Harrison Blake," the new arrival introduced himself to the patrolmen on scene. He displayed a gold detective's shield and assumed command of the investigation. He gathered all the necessary information from the patrolmen before heading over to examine the crime scene and body. The forensic guys were busy going through their routine. They took a moment to detail their initial findings to the detective. A seasoned detective with ten years of police experience, it is Harrison's dedication to law and order that has earned him the respect of the community as well as his fellow officers.

"Where's our witness?" he questioned the uniform officers on the scene.

One of the officers motioned toward the car at the end of the procession of police vehicles. "The lady's name is Jillian Newman."

"Thanks," Harrison said before heading toward the black and white. He wanted to interview this witness right away while the details were still fresh in her mind. Newman? He didn't know why, but the name seemed familiar. Then he placed it. Newman was that lady lawyer who represented the scum of the earth and blamed cops for the ills of the world. If he remembered correctly she had been married to Josh Williams. He didn't know which one to feel the sorriest for. Armed with this knowledge, he pulled the back door open and peered into the back seat.

Harrison was rooted in place as silken brown legs swung through the open door and lowered to the ground. His eyes helplessly trailed up their shapely brown length, before coming to rest at the hem of the woman's magenta silk dress. An expanse of brown flesh was exposed. Forcing himself to look away from the incredible pair of legs to his witness' face, Harrison was unprepared by the force of his immediate attraction.

Whiskey brown eyes in a soft round face returned his curious stare from behind a veil of sandy brown hair. A sassy fringe fell across her face and beckoned to be swept away. Her hair was long and hung gracefully down her back and across slender shoulders to finally rest temptingly at the swell of her full breasts. And Harrison fought valiantly to prevent himself from sweeping the locks away. He stepped back as she came to stand before him. Six feet, he guessed his witness to be about five-five, minus the two-inch heels.

Jillian silently watched the white detective growing more curious by the moment. Why was he staring at her? Did he suspect her of this crime because the victim was African-American? Defiant, she boldly returned his stare and soon discovered herself cataloging his attributes. He was tall and surprisingly handsome with a solid build. As best she could tell in the poor lighting, his complexion was more almond than red or pale and his dark hair fell in thick waves. Broad in the shoulders and narrow in the waist, he wore his clothes well. The black knit shirt stretched provocatively across the breadth of his chest should have been outlawed, and the form-fitting black jeans, banned permanently from public display. The leather holster slung across his mountainous shoulders held a deadly weapon. The sight alone of the man was menacing and intimidating; however, the weapon perched at his side left no doubt to his lethalness. Jillian chanced a glance into his dark brown eyes and knew immediately that she had made a drastic mistake. They had focused hotly onto her and challenged her as a woman. A little unsettled by their interest and stunned by the effect, she quickly looked away and caught sight of the black bagged body being placed in the rear of the coroner's van. Lightning crackled and eerily lit the macabre scene. She shivered.

"Ms. Newman, your name precedes you."

Jillian's brown eyes hardened with suspicion. "Is there a problem?" Her hand movement indicated that she was waiting for a name.

"I'm Detective Harrison Blake." He extended a hand in introduction.

Jillian nervously accepted the offered handshake. "Detective."

Harrison felt the slight tremor in her touch. "Are you up to this?"

Jillian heard the concern in his voice and couldn't help looking into his eyes. They had softened with worry. She forced a little smile. "Yes, I'm fine." She jumped from a clap of thunder and lightning. Recovering, she quickly removed her hand.

Harrison didn't believe her. She was as jumpy as a cat. But needing the information that only she could provide, and knowing that it was best to interview her now rather than later, he pressed on. "What time did you enter the garage?" He listened closely, while watching her sensual mouth.

"It was a little after eight o'clock, no later than eight fifteen," she responded noticing how his dark brows enhanced the intensity and beauty of his dark eyes. She folded her arms underneath her breasts and asked herself what the devil she was thinking ogling this white cop.

"How can you be so sure of the time?" Harrison wondered if her mouth tasted as good as it looked.

"I was late for dinner and checked the clock as I locked my office."

Harrison frowned, suddenly unhappy with the thought of some other man kissing those succulent lips tonight. "Well tell me all that you saw." Harrison listened closely as her sultry voice recalled the details of the evening. He scribbled down detailed notes as he listened. When she finally concluded speaking he was weak with an incredible compulsion to enfold her within his arms and convince her that the man she was due to meet was not worthy of her affection. What are you thinking?

Jillian missed the frown because she was too busy watching Harrison's hands. They were large and well maintained, and she foolishly wondered what they would feel like caressing her flesh. Uncomfortable with this newly discovered attraction she nervously ground her right heel into the pavement, oblivious to his dark eyes drawn to the sudden movement.

"Do you believe those men will come looking for me?" she asked a little shaky.

"They're probably long gone by now," he tried to reassure her, then wondered why he cared.

Harrison soon announced his questioning complete, then promptly cleared away sexual thoughts of the woman standing before him. He was white and she black and their paths would probably never cross again unless it was in court and he was testifying against one of her clients.

"Did you leave your car at the precinct?"

"Yes I did," Jillian answered. She was still trembling slightly from tonight's ordeal.

"That's good because I don't believe you're in any condition to be driving. Why don't you let me run you home." Harrison surprised himself by offering.

Jillian was surprised too and openly gaped at him. What was he up to? Her lawyer's mind became suspicious. Was this some police tactic to place her at ease in the hopes that she would incriminate herself? Well, Detective Blake was in for a rude awakening.

"I would appreciate the ride, but if you believe you're going to get me into your car and pry some confession out of me while pretending to be nice and concerned, you're wasting your time. I've told you everything that I know and just because the victim is black doesn't mean that I know him or that I did it."

Harrison cocked his head as he stared into her eyes. They shimmered oddly with anger. "I offered you a ride home, Ms. Newman, because I was concerned for your safety as well as the citizens of Birmingham because you are in no shape to drive. There was no ulterior motive. But since you obviously don't trust white cops, why don't I get one of the young black—or is it African-American—cops to take you home?" His dark eyes narrowed in resentment as his lips dripped the angry words. His slight southern accent gave way to his native east coast brogue.

Jillian instantly regretted her remark. The man was only trying to be nice and here she had gone and insulted him. She had to ask herself why? Was it because he was a cop or the fact that he was a white cop? Or was it because of the media images of white cops and black suspects? Shaking her head, she knew the truth. It was because she surprisingly found herself attracted to the man.

"I apologize, Dectective." She smiled feebly. "I would very much appreciate that ride home."

Harrison didn't respond right away. He instead stood there watching her. She was genuinely sorry for the outburst, but something else was going on inside that lovely head of hers. It was in her eyes for a fleeting moment. "Give me the directions and we're off," he finally said as pleasantly as possible.

"I live in the warehouse district."

"Sure no problem," he commented, then paused looking at her. "Are you in one of the newly converted warehouses on Morris Avenue?"

"Yes I am." She smiled.

"I've been itching to get a look at those." His face brightened into a full dimpled smile that transformed his appearance.

How the heck did I miss those dimples? "Well, you're welcome to look around," she extended an invitation, then quickly asked herself why she had done so.

Harrison wondered the same thing. It was obvious to him that the lady still was uncomfortable in his presence. Or maybe it was the effect of seeing a man lose his life that had her off balance. "Shall we go?" He ushered her away distancing himself with reserve professionalism.

Moments later Harrison stood in the doorway of Jillian's loft apartment. Artful lighting illuminated the spacious area. The gleaming hardwood floor echoed his steps as he followed her inside.

"This is beautiful," he said while taking in his surroundings. Earth tones were obviously the lady's favorite colors. Her sectional sofa was in a reddish-brown fabric, and the chairs in her dining room were a mixture of the same brown and beige. The curtains at the window were a rich buttercream and worked to soften the effect of the brown. He admired the way she had used the placement of furniture to define individual living spaces.

The galley-style kitchen was partially hidden behind a large china cabinet. And the row of bookcases to the right, he would guess, hid the sleeping area.

"I see you love to read as well." He pointed to the bookcases.

Jillian followed his line of vision and smiled guiltily. "Since I was a little girl." She tucked a strand of hair behind her ear, trying to hide her nervousness.

But Harrison saw the tremor and noticed the still overly bright eyes. She didn't need to be here alone tonight.

"Is there someone who could come over and spend the night with you? A boyfriend?" He had noticed she wasn't wearing a wedding band, so he assumed she hadn't remarried.

Jillian read the concern in his face and noticed that his eyes were trained on her fidgeting hands. "Don't have one. I'll be all right here alone." She placed her hands behind her back.

No man—that was good, but he didn't believe she would be all right and told her so. "You won't sleep at all tonight by yourself. And after the traumatic experience you've been through, you really need to rest."

Jillian knew he was right about the not sleeping. Although her body felt as though it would collapse at any moment, she just didn't see herself sleeping much tonight. Thinking of whom she could call, Jillian knew that it wouldn't be her parents. If she told them about what had happened tonight, they would fuss and never let her leave home again. There was always Faye...

"Oh my God, Faye!" Jillian shrieked.

Alarmed by Jillian's panic, Harrison clasped her hands. "Who's Faye? Was she in that garage tonight as well?" he asked thinking about the case.

"No. I'm sorry for the confusion," Jillian remarked, slyly removing her hands and tucking them away. "Faye is my sister and I was supposed to be at her place for dinner tonight. I know she's worried." Jillian walked over to her desk where the answering machine rested and noticed the blinking red light and the digital readout announcing that she had six calls.

With Harrison momentarily forgotten, she telephoned her sister.

"Faye, it's me. I'm sorry for worrying you, but you won't believe what happened tonight." Bringing her sister up to date, Jillian apologized profusely for not being more thoughtful.

"Are you all right?" Faye asked concerned for Jillian.

"Yes, I'm fine don't worry about me."

"Why don't you spend the night with us?" Faye offered, hating to think of Jillian spending the night alone after such a horrific experience.

"I'll be okay."

Harrison tapped Jillian lightly on the shoulder to draw her attention. "One moment Faye," she said into the receiver and covered the mouthpiece with her hand.

"I think you should stay with your sister. I'll drive you over," he offered, waiting for Jillian's response.

"Aren't you on duty?"

"Actually I was just getting off when the call came in on this case."

"If you're sure?"

"I am."

"Faye lives in Greystone."

"That's not a problem."

"Okay, I'll stay with you tonight," she told her sister. "No, there's no need for David to come. Detective Blake has offered to drive me over," she relayed, returning her attention to the white cop boldly returning her stare.

The ride over to Faye's was quiet. Harrison's mind was preoccupied with thoughts of the woman sitting beside him. What was it about her that tugged at him? Was it the big whiskey eyes overly bright with fear? Or the shaking hands that made him want to protect her? For the life of him, he couldn't get a handle on what was going on inside of him.

Jillian couldn't get the death out of her mind. She had had enough of death for one lifetime. As her mind traveled to another time, she silently began to cry. The tears, which she thought were no more, now came hot and free. Her shoulders shook as the pain once again resurged inside her chest.

A faint whimper pierced Harrison's musings. He glanced over at his companion and realized that she crying. He immediately pulled over to the side of the road.

"Hey, let it out," he crooned as he unfastened both their seatbelts and drew Jillian into his arms. He rubbed her back soothingly as her tears continued to flow. It seemed the more comfort he offered the more intense her pain. "You're safe, Jillian. I won't allow anyone to harm you," he heard himself say and knew that he meant every word.

Jillian heard him too, and for some foolish reason she wanted to believe him. She wiped her eyes with the heel of her hands and sat back in her seat. An apology slipped from her lips as she refastened her seatbelt and stared out the side window. She was a basket case and knew it. For too long now she had been trying to pretend that the past was behind her, but tonight had proved her wrong.

"I'm really sorry about that."

"Don't be." He watched her closely. She was crying about something other than tonight's case, that much he was sure. It was something big in the lady's life, but what? "Jillian, something else is going on here."

Whiskey eyes turned on him angrily. "What makes you believe something is going on? Isn't seeing a man's chest explode enough reason to fall apart? And who asked you to pry into my life anyway?" She stared heatedly at him because he was so damn perceptive.

"Look lady, I was only trying to help," Harrison replied just as heatedly.

"Well, thank you," Jillian was now yelling. "If I'd known a ride with you would include a probe into my personal life I would have turned it down," she ranted uncontrollably. "I tell you what, why don't I just get out right here." She reached back to unlock the car door. "And you can be..."

"Lock the damn door back." He pressed the lock button on the door panel. "If you want to be left alone, consider it done. Hell, I almost feel sorry for Williams." Harrison's voice rose in irritation.

"Just what do you think you know about Josh and me?" Her voice had reached a higher pitch.

"I have a damn good idea why he divorced you," he bellowed back.

Jillian reacted as if she had been slapped. The fire in her eyes was snuffed out, and the heat in her argument was gone. Tears welled up in her eyes but failed to fall as she stared at him numbly. Eventually she managed to say in a voice void of the earlier passion, "I doubt you do."

Harrison continued to stare at her. He didn't know what to say or how to react to this dramatic change, but he knew that he had hurt her terribly somehow. "Jillian, I didn't mean that," he apologized pathetically.

"No need to apologize, Detective Blake. You can't hurt me anymore than I've already hurt myself." Jillian effectively ended their conversation by looking out the passenger window.

Harrison pulled back out onto the road without anything further being said between them. The sooner he delivered Jillian Newman to her sister's, the sooner he could be rid of her and her bizarre behavior.

Jillian was now convinced that she had slipped over the edge into insanity. What else could have caused her to react so belligerently toward the man? It was all Josh's fault she told herself. If he hadn't come into her office, blaming her once more for their son's death, she would have probably had a better handle on her emotions. But as it was, she had just attacked a man for no real reason. She was a better person than that.

Fifteen minutes later, Harrison pulled into Faye's driveway and parked. He watched as Jillian reached into the backseat for her overnight bag. When she couldn't quite reach it, he retrieved it and exited the driver's door with it in hand.

Jillian watched him from her seat. What is he doing now? She soon had her answer when he came and opened her door. But he didn't relinquish the bag as she had thought he would do. He held on to it and motioned for her to walk ahead of him up the sidewalk.

Harrison knew that he was bugging the lady. Her brown eyes sparked with annoyance, but determined to say nothing to him, she had simply complied. She waited on the porch for him, no doubt preparing his send-off, but just as she was about to issue an obligatory thank you, Faye opened the door and called for them to come in.

Jillian walked passed her sister to stand in the middle of the living room. Harrison stopped just inside the doorway and observed both women. They were of equal height, but there the resemblance ended. Faye was willowy in a pale brown complexion with close-cropped hair. Her pretty face was slender and more refined than her sister's. She was regal in appearance and oozed class without trying.

Jillian on the other hand was sinfully curved in a honey-roasted complexion with a mop of thick auburn hair and exuding a smoldering sexual appeal. He realized that although they had spent the last three hours together, he wasn't sure he had seen the real Jillian Newman. He continued to observe her in silence. They were like oil and water. Knowing this, he cleared the thought away.

"Jillie, are you all right?" Faye was asking her sister.

"I'm fine now," Jillian answered, falling into her sister's embrace. Her eyes landed on Harrison still by the door holding her bag. She quickly untangled herself and made introductions.

"Faye Bernard, Detective Harrison Blake. Detective Blake, my sister, Faye."

Jillian advanced on him and attempted to remove her bag from his hand, but Harrison held on to it as he walked around her and extended his hand to Faye. Jillian craned her head back over her shoulder to glare at him. What is wrong with the man? Doesn't he know when it's time to leave?

"Ma'am," Harrison greeted Faye and clasped her hand. "Keep a close eye on your sister tonight. She experienced a horrible crime and sometimes the effect can sneak up on a person." He handed Faye the overnight bad.

"Thank you Detective Blake, I will." Faye glanced at him and then noticed that he watched Jillian. She suspected that he wanted a moment alone with her sister and promptly excused herself, taking the bag with her.

"Here's my card." Harrison held the item out to Jillian. "Call me if you think of anything further."

She accepted it and met his eyes. "Thank you and I will."

"Try to get some rest, Ms. Newman."

"You too, Detective." Jillian walked to the door and opened it. She watched as he headed down the walkway. When he was midway she called out, "Detective Blake."

Harrison didn't answer. He merely turned around and fastened those dark intense eyes of his on her.

"I'm sorry for my poor behavior. My anger was just the culmination of a bad day gone extremely wrong." Her apologetic eyes searched his for forgiveness. Seeing his jaw clenched tight and his eyes dark and brooding, Jillian thought him a hard man and that forgiveness wasn't in him.

At the moment, with the light from the house streaming through her silk dress and outlining every womanly curve on her body, Harrison could forgive Jillian anything. He felt the pressure in his crotch and knew that he had to leave in a hurry or embarrass them both.

"Apology accepted."

CHAPTER 3

"What was that about?" Faye asked her sister once she had closed and locked the front door.

Jillian didn't answer right away. She headed down the hallway to the guest bedroom and prayed Faye would drop it. She really didn't want to get into it with her about Josh again.

"Jillian, what were you apologizing to Detective Blake for?" Faye persisted.

Realizing that her sister wasn't going to let it go, Jillian reluctantly answered. "I apologized for being rude and taking my bad day out on him."

"And what brought on this bad day?"

"Hello, I just witnessed a man being murdered."

"I know, honey, I'm so sorry that you had to see such ugliness, but I know you and that wouldn't make you rude. And especially not to a police officer trying to help you." Faye's knowing eyes probed for the truth.

Jillian collapsed onto the bed knowing she would get no peace until she answered Faye's question. "If you must know, Josh came by the office today..."

"And reminded you of Travis' birthday, and how he blames you." Faye knew the routine. The man failed to acknowledge his role in the tragedy.

"Something like that." Jillian ruffled her hair. "And then, there was the murder coupled with the storm. It was too much, and before I knew it I was crying. Detective Blake pulled the car over and held me while I cried." She glanced at her sister who stood propped against the dresser.

"So what did you do and why?"

"When the tears subsided, Blake realized that I was crying because of something else beside the murder. He asked if I was in any trouble and I lost it." Jillian closed her eyes and shook her head. When she opened them, they held sadness. "He was too close to the truth and I unloaded on him. We got into a shouting match and things were said. He apologized when he realized his barb had drawn blood."

Pushing away from the dresser, Faye sat beside her sister. "What did he say?"

Jillian placed her folded hands between her legs as she glanced over at her sister. "He said he understood why Josh divorced me."

"Oh, honey." Faye wrapped an arm around Jillian. "He had no way of knowing."

"I know that. It just hurt, Faye."

"Well, this is all Josh's fault. I think I'll call him tomorrow and give him a piece of my mind."

"No, you won't." Jillian met her angry eyes. "He and I are finally able to be civil to each other and I don't want you stirring up trouble for me."

"Josh Williams was trouble from the moment you met him."

"It's over now." Jillian fell back on the bed staring up at the ceiling. "Josh has his life and I have mine."

The next morning, Jillian waved good-bye to her brother-in-law as he pulled away from the curb. She had caught a ride with him into the city to retrieve her vehicle from the precinct parking lot. She thought about Harrison and the kindness he had attempted to show her last night and her abhorrent behavior. On impulse, she headed for the precinct door to apologize again, but just as she reached it, she changed her mind. What would she say beyond I'm sorry? She had said that last night. She returned to the Lexus and pulled away from the precinct.

Harrison watched Jillian from across the street. She looked even better in the light of day. She was wearing a striking lemon yellow suit that appeared tailored to her seductive frame. He wondered if she had new information and was about to run across the street to ask, when she quickly returned to her vehicle and departed the parking lot.

He made a mental note to call her later at the office. Opening his car door, he headed inside the precinct. He poured himself a cup of precinct brew and went to his desk to review his case notes from last night. Jillian had provided them with two detailed descriptions of the shooters and the vehicle she believed they drove. It really shouldn't take long for a hit on the vehicle to surface.

"Morning, partner." Wade Martin took his seat exhausted. He ruffled his red close-cropped hair. His piercing blue eyes were red and showed signs of a sleepless night. "I heard we had a murder last night."

"Yes, we did." Harrison tossed him the folder. "An accountant in the Kelly Ingram Professional Building was shot around eight o'clock on the fifth floor of the parking garage. Suspects are two men, both black and well dressed."

"So we have a witness?" Martin glanced up from the papers.

"We most certainly do. And a very good one as well, but you aren't going to believe who it is." Harrison waited expectantly for Martin to start guessing.

"Man, I'm too tired after my date with Vickie to play twenty questions. Who is it?"

Harrison rolled his eyes disappointed. "You need to stick with one woman and preferably, one closer to your age. You can't keep up this pace much longer. The three five is a whole lot different than twenty-five."

"Speak for yourself." Martin threw a paper clip at Harrison. They both broke out into laughter. Martin, requiring a boost, went to the nearest coffee pot and filled a cup. After taking a long sip, he turned back to Harrison. "Okay, that's better. Now who is the witness?"

"Would you believe Jillian Newman?"

"You mean watchdog of the police and defender of the guilty." Martin held a real strong opinion of the woman.

"One and the same. Although the lady is a knockout in person."

Martin sobered and stared at Harrison. His buddy had said that last part with a little too much enthusiasm. "Don't be fooled by that pretty face and great body."

"So you have seen the lady in person?" Harrison was interested in hearing Martin's opinion of Jillian.

"Yeah, I've seen her up close and in person. When I worked narcotics three years ago, she represented a client who claimed that we planted drugs on him." Martin didn't look at his partner when he spoke.

The action wasn't lost on Harrison. He had been partnered with Martin for two years now and knew when the man was avoiding something. "Well, did you?"

Martin looked ill. "There were three of us, Glenn Sutton, Ben Hart and myself. I knew nothing about it man, I swear to you that I didn't. But, yeah Glenn dropped a bag in his vehicle."

"What a stupid thing to do. It's policing like that that gives us a bad reputation."

"I agree, but it wasn't like the guy was a saint. He had a string of small offenses and this bust would have sent him away for a long time," Martin explained.

"I take it the Newman woman got him off."

"Yes she did and even managed to get one of the guys to confess. She's something in court. However, she's made a lot of enemies on the force and Hart despises the woman for ruining his partner's career."

Harrison leaned back in his chair trying to figure out who the woman was. She was an enigma. On one hand she had been quite cooperative with the police investigation and then in the next moment she was verbally attacking him. But the hostility only came after his comment about her reason for crying so emotionally. He was sure there was another motive for the flood of tears than the murder. Determined to discover her secret, he headed to the police library.

Two hours later he had found what he was looking for. The car accident that had claimed her son's life had happened three years ago. The newspaper's account of the accident stated that Jillian had driven onto a washed-out road during a violent rainstorm and that her small vehicle had been swept into the rising water. Rescue workers managed to pull her free from the vehicle, but as they attempted to remove the child, the cable holding the car gave way. The vehicle was swept away into the churning water. The two-year-old had been found hours later still strapped into his car seat.

"Damn." Harrison couldn't imagine the pain and guilt she must be living with. He recalled her cryptic remark, now knowing what she was referring to. He found another article on the child's funeral. It contained a picture of Jillian and Josh. He studied the picture for several minutes. Though they had both lost a child and were at the funeral standing side by side, they appeared to be completely alone. Josh wasn't consoling his wife with a supportive arm and Jillian wasn't leaning on him for support. Running a hand through his hair, he pondered the reason why.

In an article dated two months later, he had his answer. The headline read, "Lawyer Blames Wife for Death of Son, Files for Divorce." Harrison slapped the side of the computer in anger. It wasn't bad enough that Jillian no doubt blamed herself for the death of her child, but her own husband had turned against her. He had never liked Josh Williams and now he knew why. The guy was a jackass. With his curiosity satisfied, Harrison unclipped his cell phone and headed out back to the parking lot. He had a telephone call to make and an apology to extend.

Jillian was recalling the horrible dream from last night. She had been back in the parking garage watching a man being murdered, but at the point of exiting the garage, her dream faded into rising water and a child crying. She shivered just thinking about it.

The intercom buzzed. Thankful for the reprieve, Jillian depressed the button and received a message from her secretary that Detective Blake was on line one. Her heart immediately began beating faster as an image of the handsome detective came to mind. Once more she cringed at her behavior last night. She blew out a calming breath before picking up the telephone.

"Good morning, Detective Blake," Jillian spoke in a professional tone.

"Good morning to you, Ms. Newman. I hope you managed to get some rest last night."

Jillian recalled the dream. "Not much, but I'm all right."

"It will get easier," Harrison assured her. "Ms. Newman..."

"Jillian, please."

Harrison paused for a heartbeat. "Jillian, then and please do call me Harrison."

Jillian smiled privately to herself at the invitation. "So Harrison, you were about to ask?"

He laughed seductively. "Actually I was about to apologize for the uncalled for remark last night."

Jillian laughed then. "Oh, you had cause, Harrison, so there is no need to apologize."

"If you say so," he conceded. "Now to my other reason for calling. Have you remembered any more from last night? Like did you see any other witnesses in the garage? Hear part of their conversation?"

"Nothing. I'm really sorry I'm not much help."

"Are you kidding? The descriptions you provided of the perps and their vehicle last night were superb. It won't take us long to pick these guys up." Harrison was quite confident.

"I sure hope so. I hate to think of them running free in the city."

"Just be very careful for the next several days until we catch these guys. I don't believe they will come looking for you or anything, but just be vigilant. I would hate for anything to happen to you. I really mean that."

Jillian smiled to herself, touched by his concern. "I promise and thanks for the shoulder last night."

There was a long awkward pause. "I'm available anytime for conversation or a good cry." He listened as Jillian laughed. "Perhaps we could do coffee sometime?"

"I'd like that."

"You have my card if you should need me."

"Yes, I do and thanks." Jillian returned the phone to its cradle as there was a knock at her door.

Dale Morgan opened the door and stuck his head in. Jillian rose from her chair to meet him at the door. Private investigator extraordinaire, Dale had the ability to obtain the most obscure piece of information about a person. Jillian had used his services for a year now and was quite pleased with his thoroughness and discretion.

"Come on in and have a seat."

"Thanks."

"I was surprised to hear from you so soon. So what do you have for me?"

"Just what you wanted to know." He passed her a folder and waited while she read through the pages. When she finally resurfaced from the various documents that he had assembled, Dale knew that she wasn't prepared for what he had found.

"What is the guy into?" Jillian asked.

"You name it, Jillian, and he's right in the thick of things. Listen, I don't know how much of this information you're planning on using, but let me warn you—the man plays for keeps."

"I hear you, Dale." She slapped the folder against her leg while she thought out loud. "I now understand why my client is concerned. This Compton guy is bad news."

"You're absolutely right, so please be careful." Dale placed a hand on Jillian's shoulder as he stood. "This is big money we're dealing with here. Mr. Compton won't tolerate anyone interfering with his business. Lawyers included." He gave her a meaningful look.

"Don't worry about me. I'm not stupid."

"I know that, but if Compton discovers you have that information, and that I gave it to you, he'll come after both of us. I just want you safe." His piercing hazel eyes expressed his seriousness.

"How did you come by these documents?" Jillian eyed him suspiciously.

"All you need to know is that no laws were broken," Dale replied, walking out of the office without another word.

Jillian sat there wishing that she hadn't asked. This Compton guy was the wrong man to mess with. Deciding that she didn't want to leave this file in her cabinets, she placed it in her briefcase to deposit later in her safety deposit box at the bank. The sooner that file was tucked away for safekeeping, the sooner she could relax.

Harrison hung up the telephone from speaking with Jillian, when he spotted DA Williams enter the squad room. The two men eyed each other with contempt. Josh headed into the captain's office while Harrison tried to figure out what Jillian Newman saw in the man.

"Blake and Martin, in my office," the captain called from his office doorway.

"On the way, Captain," the men chorused. Harrison looked over at Martin and whispered. "I wonder what the DA wants now?"

The last time District Attorney Williams had stopped by the precinct making demands, he had threatened Harrison with the removal of his badge. However, the production of a suspect with airtight evidence had reversed his decision, and garnered DA Williams' a conviction.

"I'm sure we'll find out. Come on."

The two men entered the office and shot DA Williams curious glances. Martin sat on the battered sofa while Harrison rested on the credenza. When they were both seated, the captain nodded giving Williams the floor.

Josh Williams loved being the center of attention. He got a high from being in control and loved sticking it to Harrison Blake whenever he could. The man annoyed him with his arrogance and blatant disrespect for procedures. The cowboy tactics may have worked on the East Coast, but in Birmingham, they operated by the book.

"Detectives, I want to know what you are doing to solve the murder of Willie Melvin, the accountant? I have his influential clients calling my office demanding an arrest. Blake, I'm told you reported to the crime scene." Josh turned hard eyes on Harrison.

"Yes, I did, and we're doing what we always do—question our witness and chase down leads."

"We have a witness?" Josh asked surprised. "Good, may I have the name?"

Harrison sprang from the credenza. "Why? So you can call a press conference and blab her name?"

"Her?" Josh looked at Harrison with a critical eye. "A little protective aren't you? Is the lady one of your castoffs?" He smiled with superiority.

"No, yours," Harrison shot back. "Our witness is Jillian Newman, your ex-wife."

Josh's eyes bulged and Harrison got a perverse sense of pleasure from seeing his shock. "That can't be. I read that the murder took place around eight. Jillian was leaving the office at five. She was having dinner with her sister's family."

So Josh had seen Jillian earlier in the day. Harrison mulled that bit of new information over. He wondered what the reason was for the visit, but then Josh supplied the answer.

"I know what I'm talking about. I went to see Jillian because it would have been our son's birthday had he lived."

More like you went to rub it in on Jillian that she was responsible for your child's death. No wonder the woman tore into me. "Evidently you don't know as much as you think you do about Ms. Newman, Josh, because the lady was in the parking garage. She witnessed two shooters both black. We got detailed descriptions of both and the vehicle they were driving. It shouldn't take us long to find the car, then them. Now, do you really want to hold that press conference?"

If it were possible, Josh's eyes hardened and narrowed even more. It was obvious to all that he didn't appreciate Harrison having more knowledge of his ex-wife than he. "Of course not," he finally said. Turning back to the captain who had remained quiet during the exchange, he demanded, "I want to be kept abreast of this case. Since Jillian is involved I have a personal stake."

Harrison didn't like the way Josh seemed to still think of Jillian as his. "What personal stake? The lady isn't married to you any more."

"Blake," the captain warned.

"It's perfectly all right. Detective Blake is correct. But as the district attorney of this city, I'm making it personal. Now you, Detective, just do your job and keep me informed." Josh grabbed his briefcase and departed the office with great theatrics.

"Man, were you deliberately trying to piss him off?" Martin spoke for the first time.

With a broad smile that answered the question, Harrison followed Josh and walked out the office, but Martin wasn't finished. He followed Harrison back to their area of the room and sat down on the corner of his partner's desk. "Why were you so protective of Josh's ex-wife?"

Harrison turned his dark eyes onto Martin. What exactly was he asking him? "I'm protecting my witness, Martin."

"You've protected witnesses before, but not with so much passion," Martin taunted.

Harrison pushed Martin off his desk. "Sit your butt on your own desk," he ordered, then reached for the file on his desk. "If you must know, I get a kick out of aggravating the DA."

Martin accepted the answer but felt there was more to it. "So where do we begin?" he asked Harrison as they got down to discussing the case.

"First, we find out who Willie Melvin was."

"We know he's an accountant."

"Correction, was an accountant, Martin. The man is dead and believe me there is a reason out there just waiting to be discovered."

"So you're thinking one of his clients did him in?"

"It's a possibility, because how many street thugs do you know who come dressed in their Sunday best to commit murder?"

"I see your point." Martin thought for a moment then asked. "Did Ms. Newman know the accountant?"

"No, she didn't."

"Did you ask her whether she has seen him with questionable characters before? I mean they did share a building."

Harrison could have kicked himself. He was a better cop than this. Why hadn't he asked that fundamental question? A little voice inside his head whispered. You were too busy checking out the DA's ex-wife.

When Harrison didn't respond, Martin stared at him. "You mean to tell me you didn't ask? Harrison, what the devil is going on with you?"

"Nothing man," he lied. "The question simply slipped my mind."

"More like you had something or someone on your mind," Martin commented as he headed out of the squad room.

Harrison realized that Martin wasn't far from the truth. He had been too preoccupied with Jillian Newman's long shapely legs to think of the proper questions to ask. And as his mind replayed last night, Harrison couldn't forget the image of her silhouetted in the doorway and the desire he had to take her in his arms. Steeling himself for the upcoming task, he followed Martin.

"Ms. Newman, two detectives are here to see you."

"Thank you. Send them in please."

Jillian rose from her chair to greet the two detectives. She knew one of them had to be Harrison and for some peculiar reason her stomach fluttered with excitement. She opened the door as they were preparing to turn the knob.

"Come on in, detectives." She greeted them warmly but with a little reserve. She had to keep a handle on this attraction.

"Thank you for seeing us." Harrison allowed Martin to take the lead and remained silent. He stood off to the side of Martin and Jillian. While she was focused on his partner, he was free to admire her beauty undetected.

"Detective Martin, isn't it?" Jillian extended a hand. "I couldn't have won that case without you," she stated gratefully.

Harrison glanced over at Martin now realizing that he was the cop who had confessed. His admiration for his friend and fellow officer grew by leaps and bounds.

"Ma'am, I have a few questions about the night of the murder." Martin kept the conversation on course.

"Go right ahead and ask." Jillian couldn't resist glancing at Harrison. He hadn't spoken a word to her and she wondered why.

"Ma'am, had you ever met the deceased before?"

Returning her attention to Martin, Jillian responded. "No. I have seen him in the building, but we were never formally introduced."

"Have you ever seen him with shady characters? Possibly clients that didn't fit the description of his normal clientele."

"No, I'm sorry, but then the men I described were dressed in business suits."

Martin looked at Jillian for a moment or two longer before concluding that the trip over had been a waste of time. "Thank you for seeing us, Ms. Newman."

"No problem, Detective Martin. I want these guys caught as well." Her attention slid from Martin to Harrison who was still quiet. He too was looking, but for the life of her, Jillian couldn't read his expression.

"Are you coming, Blake?" Martin asked from the open doorway. Neither Harrison nor Jillian had realized that Martin had moved.

"Sure, partner." Harrison glanced back at Martin. "Ms. Newman," he replied with a wink and left the office.

Jillian stood there in front of her desk for several minutes after the men left her office with a silly schoolgirl smile on her face. She didn't know why, but Harrison Blake was fast becoming of interest.

A quarter till five two days later, Jillian turned off the lights and secured her office door. She joined her secretary and the other building occupants in the great end of day exodus. Every since the murder, she had made it a habit to leave on time and in the company of others. The elevator opened to her parking level below and she exited with five other people. She was pleasantly surprised to see Harrison waiting for her. He was leaning on a dark sedan parked next to her vehicle. As she approached their eyes connected. That feeling from the other day resurfaced and she didn't dare question it.

Harrison watched as Jillian advanced toward him. She wore a bright coral linen pantsuit that highlighted the red pigments in her brown skin tone. Her hair was loosely curled and blowing carefree in the gusty breeze whipping through the garage. Her smile bright and wide in welcome caused his heart to give a little flutter. By far she was the best looking woman he had ever laid eyes on and in that moment he could no longer deny the desire she inspired in him.

"Hi," Jillian whispered as she came to stand in front of him.

Harrison looked down at her upturned face and desperately wanted to taste her smiling lips. "I'm glad to see you came out with a crowd," he commented.

Jillian watched his eyes knowing that something else was on his mind besides the crowd she walked out with. "I've learned my lesson."

He nodded. His eyes roamed her face in an attempt to commit every minute feature to memory. "I know I suggested coffee, but I was hungry and was wondering if..."

"I'd love to," Jillian cut him off. She smiled when he exhaled in relief.

"I was so afraid you would say no." His brown eyes showed his happiness.

Jillian held her briefcase with both hands in front of her as she stared into his eyes. A warm smile lit her face. "Why would I turn down a dinner invitation with you?"

Harrison shrugged his mountainous shoulders like a schoolboy without an answer. "I'm simply glad that you didn't. So, do you like Italian?"

Jillian's smile grew wider. "I love Italian," she drooled. "A Touch of Italy is the best."

This time it was Harrison who smiled. "Since I agree with you, I take it it's A Touch of Italy."

Jillian nodded. "Most definitely."

"Well how do you want to do this? We each take our own cars or one of us rides with the other?" He would allow her to make the decision.

Jillian shivered. "Why don't I follow you over, that way we won't have to return to this garage after hours."

Harrison suddenly realized his mistake. He reached out touching Jillian's cheek. "I'm sorry, I forgot. That was really stupid of me to suggest coming back here so late."

Jillian could feel the heat from his hand against her cheek. It was comforting and felt so right. She found herself visually measuring the distance from his mouth to hers and realized that she was hoping for him to kiss her.

That very thought was riding Harrison hard, but fearing frightening Jillian away by being so aggressive, he suppressed the urge. "I'll follow you over," he said instead and removed his hand.

Jillian exited Highway 280 at the Summit and turned into the hilltop restaurant parking lot. She waited and watched as Harrison pulled in beside her. When he was parked, she exited her vehicle and together they walked into the restaurant. Jillian was very aware of Harrison's hand pressed lightly against her back as they entered. She was also aware of the inquisitive glances in their direction. Curious, she took a peek at Harrison and wondered if he was aware of the interested glances.

"That bright suit you're wearing sure is drawing a lot of attention," he whispered against her ear.

Jillian's eyes widened. Then she saw the humor dancing in his eyes and laughed. "It's the suit, is it?"

"Has to be," he stated before joining her in laughter.

Just then Harrison was greeted warmly by a twenty-something hostess. They exchanged pecks on the cheeks in an old-world fashion. As the woman continued to speak, Jillian picked up on a slight Italian accent. She couldn't help wondering if it was real or manufactured for the job. But when Harrison requested a table for two and the woman's eyes landed on her, Jillian knew the woman's unhappiness was quite real. Silently she followed the woman to a rather private table for two overlooking the city below. She removed her jacket before accepting the chair Harrison pulled out for her.

Harrison only had eyes for Jillian and when she removed her jacket to reveal a lace blouse with ties, he thought he would drool all over himself. The blouse was quite feminine. The crisscross ribbon ties accentuated her breasts and made him ache to release them.

"I don't think your friend appreciated your bringing me here," Jillian commented, completely unaware of his thoughts.

"What?"

"The hostess?" Jillian stared at him, now aware that he hadn't been listening. "You weren't listening to me, were you?" She eyed him curiously.

Harrison gave her a dimpled smile. "I'm sorry, my mind was elsewhere."

Jillian didn't appreciate being ignored. She glanced in the direction of the hostess. "Is that where your mind was?"

Harrison quickly sobered as he followed her glance. "She's a kid. I like women." His eyes bored into Jillian with so much heat until she was forced to look away or be singed.

Their meals were ordered and subsequently served. The food was delicious as always and the wine perfect for the meal. Harrison had ordered with the skill of a sommelier, causing Jillian to question who he really was. They talked about the usual subjects for a first date with just enough laughs mixed in to keep it light.

"So Jillian," Harrison remarked as he replaced his coffee, "I know you like Italian food, and that you're smart, but what I don't know is, what do you do for pleasure?"

Jillian took another sip of her coffee before answering. "My case load doesn't allow for a great deal of free time, but when I can catch a moment, I enjoy reading."

"That's right I do remember the bookcases. What do you read?"

A shy smile broke out across her face as she looked at him under-eyed. "Romance," she whispered.

Harrison looked surprised then broke out laughing. "I don't believe it," he teased.

"What's wrong with romance? Do you know how many people, men included, read romances?"

"I'm afraid I don't know any of those men," he laughed with his eyes as well as his voice.

Jillian rolled her eyes at him, then laughed herself. This wasn't the first time she had been teased about her choice of reading material. "You know you really should read one. There are wonderful writers out there that you're missing because of some preconceived notion about romance novels."

"Perhaps, but I think I'll pass."

"So Mr. Man, what do you read?"

"Science fiction."

"Oh yeah, like that junk is real," Jillian teased him back.

Harrison enjoyed her laugh and the way her eyes sparkled with humor. "I guess romance is just like the science fiction books I enjoy. They are both about escaping reality for a moment."

"Exactly. So what do you do for pleasure, besides reading?"

"I enjoy horseback riding."

"Really?" she responded.

Harrison cocked a brow. "You sound surprised?"

Jillian smiled over at him. "I had you pegged for a motorcycle rider, not a horse."

"Can't stand the things. They're dangerous."

"I agree." Jillian laughed once more as a new image of Harrison Blake was taking shape.

After a change in subject, coffee and a shared dessert, Harrison finally signaled for the check.

In the parking lot he assisted Jillian into her vehicle. He stood in the open doorway taking in her beauty. "Thank you for joining me." His eyes were dark and moody.

Jillian rested against her seat returning his moody stare. The attraction between them was strong and undeniable. "Thanks for the invitation."

"Maybe we could do it again?" He didn't give Jillian a chance to respond. Instead he moved in close and lowered his lips to hers in a kiss that was tender and sweet and over entirely too quickly. "Drive carefully." He stepped back closing her door, then got in his own vehicle and followed her out to the traffic light. One went right and one went left, but each carried away a sense of hope.

CHAPTER 4

A week later, Jillian's life was finally returning back to normal. The nightmares of the shooting had begun to subside. She had read in the *Birmingham News,* that there were still no new leads in the accountant's murder case, and that Detectives Blake and Martin were working vigorously to solve the murder. She still couldn't get over how handsome Harrison Blake was or her unexplained attraction to the man. But he hadn't called since dinner and so she filed this attraction in the back of her mind.

Fifteen minutes later, Josh Williams strolled into her office with her secretary trailing behind him. "I'm sorry, Ms. Newman. I tried to stop him."

Jillian stared pointedly at Josh, wondering about the sudden visit. "That's all right. I can handle Mr. Williams." She waited for her secretary to close the door. "What can I do for you?"

Josh noticed a change in Jillian. Maybe it was the hair brushed straight, or maybe the summery coral dress she wore. But something was definitely different. "What were you doing in that parking garage last week?"

"How do you know about that?" Jillian was concerned about her identity becoming public knowledge.

"I'm the DA, Jillian, I have to know about a witness if I'm going to be prosecuting a case." His expression indicated that he didn't appreciate being questioned.

"So the police simply gave you my name?"

"No. I had to ask that arrogant, smart-mouth Harrison Blake." His face hinted at his dislike for the man.

Jillian didn't know why but she took great pleasure in knowing that Harrison obviously annoyed her ex-husband, and evidently could handle himself when cross-examined by the great Josh Williams. "Yes, I was there."

"But why?" he bellowed, pounding the desk. "You told me that you were leaving the office at five for dinner at Faye's."

"I know what I said, Josh," Jillian's voice rose as well. "And don't come in here questioning me like some criminal or your wife, because I am neither," she fired back.

Josh was around the desk before Jillian could react. He grabbed her by the arm dragging her to within inches of his scowling face. They stood in front of the window facing off.

"I know who you are, Jillian." He stared into her angry eyes. "You're the woman who killed my son and are now trying to get yourself killed. That accountant worked for a notorious ex-crime boss named Antonio DeMarco." He shook her a bit while making his point. "You had no business being in a downtown parking garage that late at night. Men like DeMarco don't leave witnesses."

Jillian had never appreciated being manhandled. She snatched her arm away. "Your concern for my safety surprises me. I would think you would be happy if this man had me murdered. You've made it no secret that you wish it were me laid out in the cemetery rather than Travis."

Josh sobered. At times he did feel that way, but to hear it verbalized and to know that Jillian was aware of how he felt made him ashamed. "Jillian, I was hurt and angry."

Jillian just looked at him. Who the devil did he think he was talking to? "Josh, you behave as though I didn't give birth to Travis. He was a part of my body, not yours, so don't speak to me about being hurt and angry. I live with both, plus a ton of guilt for taking my child back out into that storm. If I could change things I would in a heartbeat and take his place in the cemetery. But don't you dare," her voice rose an octave as she pointed a finger at him, "pretend to be concerned about me. When I needed you the most, you were nowhere to be found, and then you divorced me. So save your concerned ex-husband routine for the public, because I know you don't care about me." Jillian's chest rose and fell with each word. She walked across the room, giving him her back.

Josh stood in front of the window looking out for several minutes. Every word Jillian had hurled at him was the truth. But at the time, he hadn't been thinking clearly. He had been too full of himself and his growing popularity in the city to care about his wife and her emotions. He pinched the bridge of his nose as he turned around to face her. She had always been a sexy woman, but age had matured her body, and she more comfortable with it, drew men's attention like bees to honey. Yet, she chose to be alone and he knew that it was because of him and the pain he had inflicted.

"Jillie."

"Don't call me that." She glared at him. "You lost the right the day I came home and found you in our bed with another woman."

"Jillian, enough," Josh's voice dripped with regret. "Come here please." He beckoned for her to join him by the windowed wall. "Please."

Jillian slowly walked across the room. She folded her arms across her body defensively and stood before him.

"Who do you think had them executed?" Harrison gestured with his chin in the direction of the two men inside the burned vehicle. They each had a bullet to the head.

"Whoever hired them to do the job," Martin responded. He reached in his pocket and proceeded to light a cigarette. "He has hired a professional to clean house."

"I know, Martin, and Jillian is bound to be on that list," Harrison verbalized what they both were thinking. "Let forensics wrap up here and we'll pick up Jillian."

Just at that moment the radio in their unmarked car screeched to life.

The glass window exploded under automatic gunfire. Josh and Jillian were showered with glass as they fell to the floor. Bullets tore through the office piercing the walls and decorative artwork. Wood from the desk splintered and flew through the air. The sofa moved under the force of the bullets piercing it. The telephone was rendered useless as it toppled off the desk shattering into pieces.

Jillian frantically screamed as glass sliced across her forehead. She crawled to the front of the desk, low to the ground, as Josh led them through the now opened door into the secretary's area. One of the gunman's bullets had shattered the lock on the dividing door and forced it open. When they reached the safety of the hallway, Jillian collapsed with fear. Her legs curled up under her as she sat shaking on the floor. The bullets continued to rip through the office and then all suddenly went quiet.

Martin turned the corner with sirens wailing. He had broken every rule governing police response on the books. Their twenty-minute ride across town had taken ten by the time he pulled to a screeching halt outside of Jillian's office.

Harrison was out of the car before it came to a complete stop. He didn't wait for Martin as he ran to the building entrance flashing his badge to the uniform police just arriving. He ran for the elevator and cursed its slowness to arrive. When it did, he punched the number sixteen and patted his booted foot anxiously as it made its climb. Its ascent was so slow, that he seriously thought about getting off and taking the stairs. He was half-crazed with worry by the time it reached Jillian's floor. His thoughts kept going back to the night they had shared dinner and how he had told her that he would call. He hadn't. He had been concerned with the strong attraction and the knowledge that a relationship with Jillian would be difficult. Society not withstanding, his own personal baggage would be a challenge that he wasn't quite sure of being ready to tackle. And to have Jillian in his life, he would definitely have to deal with a few issues. The door began to open and he slipped through the meager crack. He forced his way through the milling crowd of onlookers as he entered the hallway. His eyes searched frantically for Jillian as he called her named like a madman.

"I'm...here, Harrison."

He was relieved to hear her voice and completely oblivious to the curious stares as he burst into the opening and finally spotted Jillian sitting on the floor. Josh was beside her holding a handkerchief to her head. Only then did he realize that her dress was covered in blood. He went down onto his knees beside them as officers rushed passed him to check out the office.

"Was she hit? How bad is it?" he asked Josh in rapid-fire succession. Then without thinking he took Jillian's hand in his and hung on to it.

Josh took in the scene not believing his eyes. Jillian and a white cop. No, correction, Harrison Blake of all cops had the hots for his ex-wife. That explained his concern for her safety the other day in the office. "Flying glass struck her across the forehead and gashed her pretty good. She'll probably require stitches."

Jillian turned wide frightened eyes in Harrison's direction. Tears streamed down her face as she drew strength from his touch. "They tried to kill me," she whispered, still in shock.

"But they didn't. You're alive and I'm going to make sure that you remain that way." He placed Jillian's hand over the handkerchief and scooped her up in his arms and carried her into the waiting area. Martin had managed to clear the hallway and the crime scene area for the forensic team that would identify the caliber and type of weapon used. Josh Williams stood beside Martin, nicked and blood splattered like Jillian.

"Where are those damn paramedics?" Harrison barked, taking in the complete destruction of the office.

On cue they appeared carrying a stretcher and equipment. They quickly went to work cleaning up Jillian's wounds. The tiny nicks from flying glass were flushed and left to heal on their own. But the gash across her head would require stitches.

Josh was administered to as well, but didn't have any major injuries. While the paramedics attended to Jillian, Harrison went to speak with Josh. "You were with Jillian when this happened?"

"Yes. We were standing in front of the window when it exploded." He looked at Harrison curiously. "You've got a thing for my ex-wife," he stated, already knowing the answer. He had never seen Harrison come so undone as he was at the moment. Jillian had gotten through the arrogance to find his heart. Josh didn't like the idea of the two of them together.

"That has nothing to do with what's going on," Harrison replied. "I need to know what the hell happened here. Did you see anything? The sniper? His location?" Harrison was firing one question after another.

Martin stepped in. Harrison was in no shape at the moment to conduct a successful interview. His mind and eyes were focused on Jillian. "I've got it. You go take care of Jillian."

Harrison propped his hands on his male hips looking helplessly at his friend. "Thanks man. That call took years off my life."

"I thought my driving did that," Martin teased trying to lighten the mood.

Harrison did manage a weak smile. He patted Martin on the back before glancing at Josh. "Why were you with Jillian?" He saw Josh's uneasiness and knew instantly that the sorry, no-good, jackass had harassed her again about their son. "Get out of my sight and stop browbeating Jillian about the death of your child."

Josh took offense. "What do you know about it, Blake?"

"I know that Jillian doesn't need this right now."

Glancing at her fragile state, Josh knew that he was right. He would back off for now. But Blake and he had a matter to settle later. "Can I go?"

Josh was instructed to ride downtown with one of the uniformed officers and give a written statement. Martin walked over the crime scene with the forensic guys while Harrison rode to the hospital with Jillian. He wasn't leaving her side until he knew that she was safe.

At the hospital, Harrison was met by Faye and her parents. He didn't know how or who had told them Jillian would be arriving. But as Jillian was whisked away into a trauma room, he was cornered by Faye. "What happened, Detective Blake?"

Harrison quickly brought her up to speed on the case and the shooting. He assured her that Jillian would be all right and that the injury was minor, but required stitches.

"How did you hear about the shooting?" he asked Faye.

"The trauma doctor." Faye pointed to the room where Jillian was. "Is my husband. He received the call from the paramedics about a possible gunshot victim. When he heard the address and that the name of the victim was Jillian, he called us."

"I see." Harrison nodded as he glanced back at the trauma room. "I'm glad you all are here for Jillian. She's in pretty bad shape, mentally."

"I can't believe this happened."

"Know that it won't be happening again, Mrs. Bernard. I'll make sure Jillian is safe."

Faye didn't doubt him. For some reason and she speculated on the most conceivable, Detective Blake was taking a murder attempt on Jillian's life personally. Her sister would be safe with him.

"Would I be correct if I said there was something more between you and my sister than this case?" Faye asked Harrison point-blank.

His dark expressive eyes swung to her face. In it he saw not disapproval, but a friend to lean on. "You would."

Faye's smile brightened. It was about time Jillian got back out there and found herself a man. And what a man she had found.

Harrison interviewed Jillian immediately after she was placed into a private room. She had been curled on her side with the covers drawn up to her chin. Her head was bandaged and wrapped with gauze. But it was her eyes that drew him to her side. They held fear and a sad expression. She had blinked when he entered the room. A tear tracked down her cheek. A small hand had come from under the covers and extended in his direction.

Harrison had crossed the room to the bed in two long strides. He enclosed Jillian's hand, and then dragged the lone chair in the room to the side of the bed with his foot. He sat down not releasing her. Neither spoke verbally, but their eyes said so much. Eventually Harrison got down to questioning Jillian. He asked for a recount of what had happened in her office. Much of what she said was identical to Josh, although she stated that they were arguing rather than discussing as Josh had tried to lead him to believe. Jillian snuggled further down into the bed, her eyes growing tired, but refusing to give in to the sleep her body demanded. Harrison began stroking her hair gently while encouraging her to sleep.

"I promise I'll be right here when you awake."

Jillian had looked at him from under heavy lids and smiled faintly before her eyes closed finally in sleep.

Martin tapped on the door a few minutes later and stuck his head in. He immediately noticed that Harrison held Jillian's hand in sleep. He looked at his partner knowingly. The man was a goner and didn't even realize it.

"How's she doing?" he asked inching closer to Harrison.

"She'll be all right after a good night's sleep. The cut required liquid stitches, but other than that she's all right." He finally glanced at Martin.

"The captain is asking for you."

"I'm not leaving her."

"I understand. That's why I brought an officer to post outside her door," Martin went on to explain.

Harrison glared at his friend as though he thought the man didn't understand English. "I said I'm not leaving her, Martin. Some hired gun out there tried to kill her and I'm not giving him another chance. Besides, I promised Jillian that I would be here when she woke up."

"What's really going on here, Harrison?" Martin asked. His blue eyes searched his friend's face for the truth.

He didn't bother pretending that he didn't understand the question. Finally releasing Jillian's hand he led Martin over to the window of the room, and looked out through the blinds. "I don't know, Martin, and that's the truth. But that lady has lost so much in life, that I don't plan on her losing anything else."

"Are you talking about her divorce from Williams?" Martin asked taking a peek at Jillian. He was a little uncomfortable having this conversation with her lying in the bed.

"That and the death of her child."

"She lost a kid?" Martin was shockingly surprised. "That's rough, man."

"What's rough is when you need your spouse the most, they publicly divorce and blame you for your child's death." Harrison stared at his friend eye to eye.

"I always knew the guy was a jerk."

"Now you know just how big." Harrison slapped Martin on the back. He made his way back to the chair beside Jillian's bed. "Tell the captain that I'll be bringing Jillian in as soon as the hospital releases her."

"Okay. The safe house should be ready for you both. I assume you will be guarding the lady." Martin smiled.

Harrison returned the smile. At the moment he felt that it was too soon to begin examining his feelings for the lovely Ms. Newman, but knew that he didn't trust her life with anyone other than himself. "You assume correctly."

"While you're protecting our witness, I'll be working the street trying to locate the professional and the deep pockets paying him." Martin headed to the door, then turned back around. "Do you think it's possible that Jillian saw something in that garage and just doesn't realize it?"

"I've been thinking about that and I believe it's a good possibility. Which means that until she remembers what she saw in that garage, her life is in danger."

"Between the two of us, we'll get this guy before he gets to Jillian."

Harrison rose from the chair to embrace Martin brotherly. "Thanks man."

Jillian tossed and turned in bed as images of the window shattering replayed in her mind. A small whimper escaped her lips as she fought to escape the nightmare. Covers were flung back as she tried to run from the spray of bullets.

"I'm here, Jillian," Harrison whispered softly near her ear. "You're safe. Go back to sleep." He stroked her hair until she was once again settled. He repositioned the covers over her and leaned back in his chair watching the door. His gun was lying across his lap. If anyone came through that door to harm Jillian, he intended for them to be hauled out, feet first.

Jillian awoke an hour before sunrise to find Harrison right where she last saw him. He sat in the chair, still holding her hand and watching her. His beautiful brown eyes were weary from a lack of sleep.

"Morning," Jillian croaked and cleared her throat. It was a little raw from screaming yesterday.

Harrison leaned in closer. Dark morning stubble cast a shadow on his face. His eyes though red and a little bleary, still managed to be intense. "Good morning. How are you feeling?" He kept his voice low as one would with someone with a hangover.

"My head hurts a little, but other than that I guess I'm okay." She managed a weak smile. "Well as okay as a person can be with someone trying to kill them."

Harrison eased out the chair to sit on the side of the bed. He was careful not to jar Jillian's head. With her hand still secure in his, he said, "They won't succeed. The captain has arranged for you to be placed in protective custody until we can unravel this mystery."

Jillian raised slightly on her elbow bringing her face within inches of his. She studied his face liking the bold masculinity of it—the flared nostrils, wide sensual mouth, and the stubborn determined chin. "Will you be with me?"

"Every step of the way." His eyes strayed to her lips before looking away. This is no good, Harrison. You can't protect the woman if your mind is on her delectable body. After a private counseling session, he soon got his mind back on track and began conducting himself like a cop. "You must have seen something or someone in that parking garage the night of the shooting for there to have been an attempt on your life."

"But I didn't," she stated adamantly. "I'm not holding anything from you, I swear. Just the two men I described."

"Don't get excited. I believe you. But if you didn't see anything, then someone saw you and believes that you in turn saw him, and it wasn't one of the two men you described. We found their bodies just before we got the call about you."

Jillian fell back against the pillow exhausted. This couldn't be happening to her she thought. "What am I to do?" She looked pleadingly at Harrison.

"For starters you should stop stressing. As soon as the doctor releases you, we're headed down to headquarters until arrangements can be made for you to move to the safe house."

CHAPTER 5

Jillian was released from the hospital around six a.m. She had been escorted under heavy police protection out through the morgue entrance. At the loading dock a paneled van was waiting to whisk her away. Martin and Harrison were with her every step of the way. At the precinct she had been driven around to the back entrance. The area had been searched thoroughly. Once again as they exited the vehicle, Martin and Harrison flanked her.

She was led down an empty corridor with several doors leading to it. Near the end of the hallway, Harrison had tapped on a door and waited for it to be opened. There she was escorted into a small office of eight people. On the door across the room, it read Detectives in stenciled block lettering. Jillian suddenly realized that her arrival was even being kept secret to the masses working at the precinct. It was a terrible reminder of just how dramatically her life had changed.

Harrison led Jillian over to a worn wooden bench just outside the captain's office. He had offered coffee, but then warned her of the lethalness of squad room brew. She had ignored the warning and accepted the offer. But sitting on the bench observing the activity around her, she had wished that it were much stronger. Her nerves were raw and the incessant ringing of the telephones was driving her crazy, as well as not knowing what the captain, Martin, and Harrison were discussing. She would have preferred to be included in their discussion; after all it was her life that was in a delicate balance. And then there was the hateful sneer thrown her way by Detective Hart. It was obvious that he still blamed her for his partner's downfall.

After what appeared to be hours of sitting around and numerous phone calls, the men finally emerged from the office. Martin walked to a desk and sat down. Jillian surmised that it was his and that the vacant desk across from it was Harrison's. Shortly, Harrison came and sat beside her. She could see that he was dead on his feet. He had been up all night sitting with her at the hospital and had been by her side all morning long.

"How are you doing out here?" he asked a little weary as he stretched out his arms along the back of the bench. His dark head casually turned in her direction.

"I would feel better if I knew what the three of you were discussing. It is my life and I think I have a right to know what's going on around me." She searched his face for understanding, but saw caution. "What is it?"

Harrison rubbed her shoulder soothingly. He didn't want Jillian getting upset and doing more harm to her already abused system. "It's best that you don't know where we're taking you. That way when you call your family before our departure, we don't have to worry about you revealing our location. And secondly, we use the safe houses all the time. It's not good practice to have people out there who know where they are."

Jillian nodded. "Makes sense. I don't know why I didn't realize that." She looked apologetic.

"I know how difficult it is to place complete trust in strangers especially when your life is at stake."

"I'm glad you understand, although we aren't strangers. You've seen me at my best and worst." Their eyes connected.

"Yes I have and you're right, we aren't strangers." His brown eyes crinkled as he smiled showing dimples. The intensity of them as they searched her face held greater meaning.

Jillian wondered about it. Was that his way of saying that there was indeed more between them than mere friendship? Her brow furrowed.

"Jillian, what's wrong?" Harrison asked seeing the expression on her face.

"What's wrong? Everything." Especially the way we met and the feelings you stir inside of me. "So what happens next?"

Harrison didn't buy her answer although it was quite legitimate. "In an hour the car will arrive for us. It's specially equipped with dark tinted windows, bulletproof glass, and reinforced doors. But what makes it really special is that in the trunk will be your bags that your sister packed for you." He was rewarded by a big smile.

"Oh, Harrison, thank you." She reached out touching his leg in an expression of gratitude. But what she received was the knowledge that the man was solidly built and that the feel of him, although quick under her hand, was an erotic experience. She withdrew her hand and placed it in her lap. Her eyes refused to meet his because she knew that he watched her closely. "When can I call my family?" she asked needing distance.

Harrison sprang from the bench as though shot. The sight and sensation of Jillian's delicate hand on his thigh was like a dream come true. After having her in his arms the day of the shooting and feeling the curves of her body trustingly resting against him, his mind had dreamed of a time when she would touch him. In the daydream, her pretty brown hands were on his chest, caressing his abs, and down lower to the junction of his thighs. Her small hands had held him, and what they had done, had left him weak with desire.

But this wasn't a dream. The blood surging in his body was making a beeline to his crotch and he couldn't let that happen. He took Jillian over to his desk to use the phone as a distraction. He quickly excused himself and headed to the restroom. On the way out he passed Martin, who with one look at him knew his problem.

"Are you sure you should be secluded with this woman?" His blue eyes twinkled with humor. "I mean a man of your age, thirty-five isn't it, should really take it easy. Find a woman closer to his own age and speed. That woman over there is five years younger and well, I would hate to think of the abuse she could do to your aging body."

"Go to hell, Martin," Harrison growled out on his way to the restroom.

"It looks like you're already there buddy."

Martin's raunchy laughter followed him down the hallway. At the restroom door, he threw it open with more force than necessary, just barely missing one of the other detectives.

"Sorry," he said to the stunned man. He went to the sink and turned on the cold water full blast. Cupping his hands, he splashed his face several times, trying to lower his body temperature and wash away images of his dream. He dried his face with several paper towels. He stood in front of the mirror while doing so. His thoughts turned to Jillian, as they always seemed to do lately. He wondered what she saw when she looked at. Did she see a white cop? White man? Or simply a man? He knew which he preferred. He had never dated a black woman before. Not because he didn't find black women attractive. Oh, he had looked plenty and admired the diversity in the race. And yet he had never asked a black woman out, or found his mind preoccupied by a black woman. But Jillian Newman had changed all that. His attraction to her had been instant. Her reputation as a tough criminal lawyer and sometimes watchdog of the police force hadn't mattered. He had still been captivated by her stunning good looks and incredible whiskey-brown eyes.

Their heated argument in the car hadn't dampened his attraction. In actuality, her passion had intrigued him even more. She wasn't intimidated by his size, or the fact that he was male and a cop, like a lot of women were. He liked that. She was extremely intelligent and successful. But in the end she hadn't been too full of herself to apologize for poor behavior. A woman like that could keep a man interested for life.

The thought made him think of Josh. He knew that it had been Josh who initiated the divorce. Was it possible Jillian was still in love with the man? *What do I care if she's in love with Josh?* Harrison didn't give himself a chance to answer the question. He tossed his paper towels and exited the restroom. On the way back he told himself he should really place a little distance between himself and the lovely Ms. Newman. He had a job to perform and thoughts of Jillian would only hamper his ability to do it properly. Besides what did he really know about this woman, other than what he had read in the newspapers? Maybe there was a reason for Josh's anger and rush to divorce her. At the threshold of the detectives' room, he mentally took a step back from Jillian.

She glanced up at his return and sensed something different about him. She smiled as he approached, but didn't feel the usual warmth she received from his presence. Maybe she was mistaken. He was probably just exhausted. What could possibly have happened in a span of minutes?

"Thank you for allowing me to call my family. Of course they're concerned, but I assured them that the best detective on the force would be watching out for me." She smiled timidly up at him, searching his eyes for that bright light that was usually there when it was just the two of them. She didn't find it.

"We're all working together to protect you, Ms. Newman." He sat down in Martin's vacant seat and began placing phone calls. He had effectively shut her out.

Jillian sat back in her chair confused. What was going on with him? She hadn't imagined the dinner or the kiss they shared later. Nor had she imagined his sitting beside her all night. So what had happened to change his behavior toward her? While she sat pondering the question, her attention was suddenly drawn to his telephone conversation. He was speaking to someone named Patty. Her heart took a nosedive as she realized he was talking to a woman. She had assumed from his little speech the other night that he wasn't seeing anyone. But as she thought about it, all he had said was that he didn't date kids, but women. Well from the sound of things, this Patty was definitely a woman. Jillian shook her head wondering how she could have misread the seductive smiles, smoldering gazes, gentle caresses, and that kiss. Obviously she had because Harrison sat not five feet away talking to another woman affectionately over the telephone. For some reason she had gotten the impression that he was a one-woman man, but obviously her observation was incorrect. Jillian suddenly felt abandoned and completely alone. Someone wanted her dead and there was no one to turn to for comfort.

"I know sweetheart. I'm sorry I'm going to miss your birthday, but I promise to make it up to you when I get back." He listened for a while then responded. "I'm going to hold you to that." He laughed. "I love you," he said then hung up the phone. The captain signaled for him to join him in his office.

"I'll be right back," he said to Jillian without looking at her. If he had he would have seen the hurt and confusion in her eyes.

So he was in love, Jillian thought to herself as she watched him enter the captain's office. God I'm an idiot. How could I think that white cop was interested in me? Dinner the other night was no doubt a part of his investigation. Ply me with drink and food and see what else I reveal. Reconciled with the truth of their relationship, Jillian got her head out of the clouds and began focusing on staying alive. All she required of Detective Blake was for him to do his job and protect her.

Harrison returned shortly with Martin and several other detectives in tow. "We're ready to move," he addressed Jillian.

She rose from the chair indicating her readiness. With her daydreams tuck away, she faced Harrison like the case she obviously was to him. "I'm ready, Detective."

It was something in the way she said detective that made Harrison really look at her. She wouldn't meet his eyes so that he could get a read on her emotions, but he knew without having to ask, that Jillian had picked up on the change in him. It had to be done he convinced himself. There was no other way for him to stay focused on this case if he allowed his attraction for Jillian to dominate his thoughts. It was for the best.

"This way," Harrison said in a commanding voice.

Martin glanced at his friend wondering what was going on. His demeanor toward Jillian was more professional and impersonal. This couldn't be the same man he ran into earlier with a hard-on for the lady. Taking a look at Jillian, he noticed she too was acting peculiar. Her big brown eyes hadn't glanced at Blake once. He followed his partner and Jillian out to the waiting vehicle realizing that he had obviously missed something.

Harrison assisted Jillian in the black sports utility vehicle with blacked-out windows. He slid beside her. Martin sat directly behind her, while another officer drove and one rode shotgun. Before the vehicle pulled away from the curb, Harrison produced an eye mask.

Jillian shot Harrison a warning glare. "Don't even think about it. I'm not going to be led blindly somewhere by complete strangers."

That hurt. Although they really didn't know the personal things about each other, he had felt that they had somehow connected on an emotional level, and that she considered him a friend. She had all but said so earlier. He had lost his mind trying to get to her yesterday on hearing of the shooting and sat with her all night in the hospital holding her hand, and now he was a stranger. He was angry now. "Ms. Newman, we are here to protect you. Someone has already tried to murder you and if you aren't taken to the safe house they will succeed." His eyes were locked with hers. "But we aren't going to jeopardize the location of our safe house for some suspicious, cop-hating lawyer," he growled out catching Jillian and Martin by surprise. "Now, you can either place this mask on, or I let you out on the corner and see how long you last. It's your decision."

The tears welled up in Jillian's eyes so quickly that she didn't have a chance to fight them back. Was this the same man who had sat with her in the hospital all night? It couldn't be because that Harrison had been kind and gentle with her fragile emotions. This man beside her now was cold and obviously didn't think too highly of her. Knowing that all eyes were on her and not wanting any of them to see her tears, Jillian snatched the mask from Harrison and placed it on her face. She sat forward and didn't utter another word.

Harrison saw the tears in Jillian's eyes when she grabbed the mask. He knew that his words had hurt her, but she had hurt him and now they were even. But why did he feel so lousy?

Martin slapped Harrison on the shoulder to get his attention. When he did, he mouthed, "What the hell was that about?" to which Harrison merely shook his head and faced forward. Martin sat back with a new understanding. His partner was trying to fight his growing affection for the lady by deliberately pushing her away. Martin wanted to laugh because he knew it wouldn't work. Harrison wasn't like him, chasing a different woman every week. When Harrison met a woman that interested him, she was the only woman in his life. His emotions didn't turn off and on so easily. Martin often wondered why his friend had never married because he was definitely the marrying kind. On further consideration, perhaps he knew the answer to that question.

With mask in place, Jillian rode in complete darkness and despair. The ally she believed she had was no more. Why had he been nice to her before? Had he been ordered to befriend her in the hopes that she would reveal something more about the case? She suddenly realized that his behavior towards her hadn't changed until he was forced to be separated from Patty. He must really love her, she thought as they approached a busy intersection.

They had been riding for about forty-five minutes she guessed. From the sound of things, they were probably near a busy shopping area. The car was stopped at a red light. As it pulled off, the driver suddenly slammed on the brakes sending everyone forward. Unable to see, and only held by the seatbelt,

Jillian stuck her arms out blindly to brace herself, but a solid arm across the chest held her in place. She didn't need to see to know that the arm belonged to Harrison. The driver apologized as he cursed at a driver who ran the red light. They were moving again.

Harrison withdrew his arm from Jillian's soft breasts feeling as though he had been stung. His armed burned with the warmth from her body. This was going to be harder than he imagined. He wondered if he could talk Martin into trading places with him, but knew that it wouldn't be fair to Jillian or Martin. Repeatedly he told himself that he could do it. He could protect Jillian without getting distracted by his attraction.

Jillian was concentrating hard on the noises around her. They had turned left about twenty minutes from the busy intersection. The sun was on the left side of her face, so she guessed they were heading south. They rode for about another hour. She was starting to lose track of time.

They were leaving the city. It was too quiet now with only an occasional sound of a passing vehicle. What was that? Jillian listened closely as the sound came again. This time she recognized the sound as that of a small engine airplane. As she listened closer, she could hear more, so that could only mean that they were close to a small airfield. About ten minutes away, they left the paved rode and were now on a graveled surface. They rode for several more minutes rounding a U-shaped curve before coming to a stop. Jillian listened as the doors were automatically unlocked. She waited for instructions. She sensed when Harrison left her side and grew concerned. Her heart was racing with fear. "What's going on?" she couldn't help asking.

"They're just checking out the cabin and surrounding grounds," Martin responded from behind her.

"I thought I was being left alone," she responded with nervous laughter.

"We're not going to let anything happen to you, Jillian, I promise," Martin said, reaching out touching her shoulder.

It was the first time that he had called her by her first name. It was a nice touch considering she didn't recognize Harrison any more. "Thank you, Detective Martin."

"My friends call me Martin."

"Is that an invitation?" Jillian tilted her head in his direction as she asked.

Martin smiled to himself. He was beginning to see what attracted Harrison beyond the obvious to Jillian. "It most certainly is."

"Martin, it is." Jillian smiled for the first time since their trip began.

Harrison discovered them both wearing silly smiles on their faces when he returned to the vehicle. He glanced first at Jillian, then at Martin. He glared at Martin wondering what was going on.

Martin didn't bother to explain. He would allow his partner to stew in his own mess for a while. He left the vehicle without a word.

Jillian's head dipped in Harrison's direction. She was surprised at how well she knew his scent. But he wasn't saying anything and that made her nervous. She tore off the mask not caring if he got angry with her or not. She couldn't stand being in the dark while activity went on around her.

"Why didn't you say something? What are you trying to do, scare me to death?" Her eyes were wild with fear and a little hurt.

Jillian's eyes had taken on that blazing whiskey color that he remembered from their first meeting. She was the most beautiful woman that he had ever met. The bandage around her head didn't distract from her great looks. And his body wouldn't allow him to ignore the effect she had on him. His heart rate changed when she was around. His brain went to mush when those eyes watched him, and her voice, a blend of accents, caused his body temperature to rise. He was a mess around this woman and yet, there was no other place he wanted to be. But if he was to be effective at keeping her healthy and alive, he had to keep his mind on business.

"Of course I wasn't trying to scare you," he bit off the words due to frustration. "Come on let's get you inside." He stood back as Jillian stepped from the vehicle. He tried to assist her, but she pulled away from his touch.

"I'm quite capable of getting out of a vehicle, Detective." Jillian shot him a withering look. "You were assigned to protect me and I don't expect any more from you than that." She walked off in the direction of the beautiful log cabin home.

Harrison followed behind her. The jeans hugging her sweet pleasing rump reminded him of how difficult this assignment was going to be.

Jillian approached the structure in awe. The cabin was a two-story structure with gables and a chimney on the left end of the house. The roof and trimming were in dark green. There was a large front porch with rocking chairs that she would love to sit in, but doubted that she would be permitted to do so. The front door was rustic in style with black iron fixtures and quite sturdy she noted as she pushed it open.

The floor plan was spacious and open. From the door she looked into the living room to the right and further back into the dining room. An L-shaped staircase was directly in front with the kitchen probably behind it. There was a large den to the left. The downstairs area was open clear to the upper level, with a railed balcony that looked into the areas down below. The rooms were all along the back side of the house. A skylight was placed in the center of the roof and beamed natural light into the cabin. It was magnificent and just the place a man like Harrison would feel right at home in.

"There are two bedrooms upstairs and one downstairs," Harrison said from behind her. "We'll be using the two upstairs."

Jillian nodded, then headed up. She caught sight of Martin watching them. She offered him a timid smile as she made her way upstairs.

"You take the room at the end of the hall," Harrison directed.

Jillian turned her head slightly to glare at him. She didn't appreciate being ordered about, but with no other choice, she did as ordered. The room was large and spacious with two windows. It was decorated in a pale blue. The checked comforter and draperies matched. The oak furnishings were basic, but clean—dresser, hutch, nightstands, and bed. There was a comfy chair in front of the television and a private bath directly behind it. Jillian noticed that the open closet contained her luggage and briefcase.

She turned back to face Harrison. "It's nice. More than I expected for a safe house."

"It was confiscated from a drug lord."

"Well that explains it." She continued to examine the room. "Thank you, it's nice."

Harrison didn't quite know what to say or how to behave around her anymore, now that he had put his idea into motion. "We want you comfortable," he finally said. "I'm next door if you need me."

Jillian was hung up on the we again. The man was making it painfully clear that she was a police matter and nothing more to him. "Tell your captain that I thank him for the protection." She raised her chin as she met his curious brown eyes. They were trying to read her, but as one of the best lawyers in town, she was quite schooled at masking her emotions and Harrison found no answers.

CHAPTER 6

By the time Jillian returned downstairs everyone was gone. She found Harrison in the den cleaning one weapon while another was holstered at his side. He looked up as she entered but didn't say anything and neither did she. Her eyes admired his strong masculine features masked in concentration. His dark hair gleamed in the sunlight coming through the window behind him and tempted her fingers to run through the thickness. However, unable and unwelcome to fulfill that desire, she balled her hands into fists as she stepped into the room.

The den was large and cozy with a definite homey feel to it. The brown leather furniture was oversized and made for relaxation. The stone fireplace drew her attention and would no doubt be spectacular all ablaze in the wintertime. She sat in front of it quietly. The sound of Harrison fitting the gun back together caught her attention. She admired the skill and ease with which he reassembled the weapon. When it was complete, he squeezed the trigger to make sure that it fired properly. As she watched him manipulate the weapon, she noticed that his hands were a darker almond brown than the evening they had shared dinner, and that the veins in his hands appeared more prominent because of the darker color. His arms were darker as well and roped with muscle. Glancing to his face, she realized a little too late that Harrison sat watching her. She glanced away immediately.

But not before Harrison saw the interest and longing in her eyes. He had wondered what she was thinking. Did she crave his touch as much as he did hers? They both needed a distraction. Picking up his weapon and ammunition, Harrison advanced on Jillian.

"How do you feel?"

"Much better, thank you."

"Good because we have work to do. Do you know how to handle a gun?"

Jillian's head snapped back as she looked at him foolishly. "Where would I learn how to use a weapon?"

"I thought your husband might have taught you for protection," Harrison spit out the words then wished that he could take them back. He hadn't deliberately meant to hurt her, but saw by the look in her eyes that he had.

Jillian scowled. Maybe Harrison's momentary attraction to her had been designed to agitate Josh. "That's right, you do know that the great Josh Williams is my ex-husband." She smiled sadly to herself feeling used. "But what you don't know is that he would rather shoot me than teach me how to protect myself." Jillian got up from the fireplace and walked across the room. She fingered the books on the bookcase.

"Jillian, I didn't mean to hurt you." Harrison placed the gun and ammo on the table then walked up behind her.

She didn't turn around as she spoke. "As I told you before, Detective, you can't hurt me any more than I've hurt myself."

He moved closer until there was no space between them. He wrapped his arms around Jillian to prevent her from moving. For the first time, he realized that she had removed the gauze that had been wrapped around her head. Only the taped bandage remained. "His death wasn't your fault," he whispered softly against her ear. His chin caressed her hair as he spoke. "It was an accident and nothing more."

Jillian tried to pull free, but Harrison wouldn't let her go. His arms were like steel bands around her.

"Well I know you didn't get that version from Josh, so who told you?"

"No one told me."

"No one told you?" Jillian stopped speaking as she realized what Harrison was saying. "You checked me out." He released her as she began to struggle violently against him. Her eyes shot daggers at him. "How dare you pry into my personal life? I'm the witness, not the criminal."

"I know who you are, Jillian..."

"Am I Jillian or Ms. Newman, Detective?" she cut him off. "You can't seem to keep it straight," she hissed.

"Right now you're a pain in the butt," Harrison responded just as heatedly. "We don't have time for the temper tantrum. Someone wants you dead and you had better learn how to defend yourself." He grabbed her by the wrist, not too gently and pulled her behind him. He stopped long enough to grab the gun and ammunition with his free hand.

"I can walk," Jillian shouted to the back of his head.

Harrison ignored her and kept heading to the back of the house. They entered the kitchen and went straight out the back door. Harrison finally released her when they were outside and Jillian faced him.

"We'll talk about why I pried into your background another time. As for right now, you are going to learn how to load and fire a weapon."

"I don't like guns," Jillian said while folding her arms.

Harrison's left brow hiked with annoyance as he stared at Jillian. She was really trying his patience. He was fighting to remain in control of his rational thoughts and give her the training she needed to stay alive. But the more that passionate temper of hers rose and her stubbornness set in, the more Harrison wanted to kiss her into submission. And she would submit, he would make damn sure of it.

Jillian saw the smoldering passion in his dark eyes as they watched her. They were now on her mouth and the look in them was hungry and indecisive. The muscles in his jaws flexed as his eyes slowly left her mouth to meet her eyes. The look was scorching and Jillian grew angry. This man couldn't play with her emotions and get away with it. She wanted answers for his fickle behavior and now.

"Why did you give me the cold shoulder earlier?"

"Jillian, now is not the time for this conversation." Harrison tried to walk around her, but Jillian wasn't having it. She blocked his path and folded her arms waiting. "Because you muddled my brain."

Jillian's eyes narrowed. She was sure Harrison thought he had explained himself with those cryptic words, but she was still confused. "Are you pushing me away because you believe my past will reflect badly on you?"

Harrison shook his head. "No. I'm the last person to be concerned about what people think."

Jillian thought about his answer. "So, are you in love with that woman Patty you called this morning?" Her heart beat rapidly while she waited for his answer.

"No," Harrison answered disgusted. "Patty is a child. She's Martin's niece and I was invited to her birthday party."

"Oh!" Jillian chimed relieved and ecstatic.

"You thought Patty was a woman? My woman, and you were jealous, weren't you?" Harrison turned the tables on her. He watched Jillian fidget and thought it cute and girlish. Jillian turned to go into the house, but Harrison caught her by the hand and forced her around to face him. "You started this, so answer the question."

Jillian rolled her eyes annoyed. She was supposed to be the one asking the questions. As a lawyer she knew never to ask a question that she didn't know the answer to, so why had she forgotten? "I wouldn't call

it jealousy. More like a little curious." She used her thumb and index finger to demonstrate.

"Jillian Newman, I never took you for a liar," Harrison challenged her.

"All right, I was jealous. Are you satisfied now?" She raised her chin in defiance.

"Not close, beautiful, hence my problem."

"I don't understand. If it's not my past, no other woman, and you're attracted to me." Jillian paused and looked at him questioningly. "You are attracted to me?"

Harrison released a frustrated laugh. He stood akimbo, wondering how the devil he was going to survive being confined in close quarters with Jillian. Her nearness made it impossible for him to think clearly. "Oh, most definitely."

"So what's the problem and why were you pushing me away and yelling at me?"

Harrison didn't answer right away. Instead he reached out clasping Jillian around the neck and drew her against him. He kissed her head affectionately, before tipping her face up toward his. "It's my responsibility to protect you from whoever out there wants you dead. I can't do my job properly if my mind is filled with thoughts of you. Earlier in the house when I had you trapped against the bookcase, I wasn't thinking about protecting you as much as I was thinking about getting you out of your clothes."

Jillian's eyebrows shot up as she raised her head.

"Hey you wanted to know so I'm telling you like it is." He smiled as he saw understanding dawn in her eyes. "You aren't simply another case to me. A case doesn't do this." He placed her hand over his bulging crotch.

Jillian's eyes sought and held his. She could see the humor dancing in them and smiled. "May I have my hand back?"

Harrison's eyes were smoldering as he broke out into a full dimpled smile. "Sure you can."

With her hand free, Jillian tugged a strand of hair behind her ear. Anything to give herself a chance to recover from the proof of Harrison's attraction. "So what you're saying is that I'm a distraction and for the benefit of my safety and your career, we need to place our attraction on the back burner until this case is solved."

"You've got it."

"Okay, then, but first..." Jillian leaned forward and pressed her lips to his in a lingering kiss, then eased away with passion blazing in her eyes. But a moment too late, she realized that she was playing with fire as Harrison's brown eyes darkened and his hand whipped out hauling her into his hard frame. His lips came down hard on hers and pried her lips apart. The tip of his tongue slid through the opening going deep. He learned the shape and taste of her mouth. At first she had been timid, but the more he taunted her and encouraged her to join in, the more she relaxed and returned the kiss.

They stood in the open yard lost in each other. The sound of their passion rivaled the singing of the birds. When his hips thrust forward into Jillian, Harrison tore his mouth away stunned by his actions and his complete carelessness. He cursed loud and long, breaking the passionate moment.

"Damn it, Jillian, you make me forget everything and everybody." He pushed away from her. "Look, this is wrong and we shouldn't be doing it. Now go!" He pointed to the house.

"I'll go inside like you asked and give us both a chance to cool down. But in an hour, I expect my first firearm lesson. Do we have a deal?"

"Deal." Harrison watched as Jillian returned inside. He sat down on the back porch suddenly exhausted. He wove his fingers together while his head fell forward and his eyes closed briefly. Taking a deep breath he looked out over the backyard. He licked his dry lips and tasted Jillian. What was he going to do? Her very nearness was a distraction that neither of them could afford. But there was no way he could forget the feel of her pressed against him.

How could he be so completely taken by a woman after knowing her for such a brief period of time? He was never a believer in love at first sight, and he didn't dare call what he was feeling for Jillian love, but it was mighty close and just as powerful. The timing for them was all wrong. However, now that she knew his predicament, maybe things would be easier.

Jillian sure didn't think so. Now that she knew for sure that their attraction was a mutual thing, she wanted to act upon it. Yet, Harrison had made a valid point. Her life was in danger and this attraction of theirs could prove to be a deadly distraction. But Lord help her she was physically attracted to the man. She wondered how they had looked together. The image of a Hershey's Hug popped into her mind. Brown and white blended deliciously together. They had kissed with passion and wild abandonment. The feel of his body against hers had been wonderful. It had been two long years since she had felt the need and warmth of a man. She moaned softly to herself as she recalled the little thrust Harrison had performed. It had left nothing to the imagination and increased her appetite for him even more. But he was right; they really should put this thing between them to rest until the case was solved and she out of danger. Okay, intellectually I understand, but what the devil am I to do with my awakened hormones?

An hour later and in better control, Jillian found Harrison sitting on the steps of the back porch. "I'm ready for my lesson if you're still interested."

Harrison glanced back at her. He could tell that she was resigned to their situation and determined to make the most of it. All right this can work. "Of course I'm interested." He rose to stand in front of her. "I heard you say earlier that you didn't like guns," He smiled when she made a comical face. "I'll let you in on a little secret," he whispered conspiratorially. "I don't like them either."

"But you're a cop?" Jillian looked confused.

"Yes, I'm a cop, but I don't like guns. I respect them and have learned how to properly use them, but I'll never like the damage they can cause in the wrong hands."

Jillian nodded as she listened. "I can respect that." She smiled and pointed to his holstered gun. "So what's first?"

"You'll be using this one." He removed another gun from the bend of his back. It was a smaller caliber than the one he currently wore holstered, but just as deadly looking. He explained the difference between an automatic and semiautomatic weapon. He pointed out the safety lever and instructed her to use it at all times when the weapon wasn't being fired. She was taught how to load and unload the gun. Place a round in the chamber and clear it for safety purposes. Eventually he felt she was ready for a little practice. A berm of soil was position at the end of the property for target practice. There was a stash of aluminum cans in a barrel. He sat four cans up and walked back to take up positioned behind her.

"Relax," he whispered against her ear. "You're in control of this weapon. Remember that at all times. Now get a firm grip." He corrected and adjusted her hand position. "Now focus on the front sight. You don't jerk the trigger; pull slowly. It's going to recoil, but don't fight it." When he felt she was ready, Harrison stepped away and allowed her to fire on her own. "You're in control."

Jillian glanced over her shoulder at him with doubtful eyes. She took a deep breath and did as instructed. When she had her target in sight, she slowly pulled the trigger and missed. She screamed when the gun recoiled. "Oh, my God! I don't know if I can do this."

"You can. Look, you know how it feels now. Line it up and try it again."

"You're enjoying this, aren't you?" Her big brown eyes dared him to lie.

Harrison's eyes expressed the humor his face tried to hide. "Maybe a little," he eventually said with a dimpled smile.

"Remember I have a gun," she teased.

"Yeah, but you can't hit anything," he replied laughing.

Jillian stuck out her tongue. Then turning back around, she sighted and concentrated on her target. She fired and hit her target dead center. "I did it," she screamed and faced Harrison with a smile on her face. She held her weapon pointed toward the ground.

Harrison was just as proud of Jillian as she was of herself. "Just had to make a liar out of me, didn't you?" His smile was broad.

"You betcha." She laughed deeply, trying to ignore how adorable he looked.

"Laugh all you want, but can you do it again?"

For the next hour Jillian trained with the weapon. By late afternoon she was hitting more targets than she was missing. Her smile was testament to her success. Harrison's smile was due to his ability to concentrate on something other than Jillian. They returned to the cabin and secured all doors.

Jillian inspected the refrigerator as her stomach grumbled. "I'll see what I can whip up in here for dinner."

"Before you do, let me show you how the alarm system works." He waited for her to close the refrigerator then led the way to the stairs. The wooden panel under the stairs was actually a doorway. Pushing lightly, it popped open. Harrison pushed it back into place and stepped aside for Jillian to follow. He flipped the light switch to the right. Numerous screens displayed various angles of the house. Cameras out in the surrounding trees swept the grounds and the back and front of the property. A portion of the gravel road they had traveled on was monitored as well. He instructed her on how to activate the distress alarm that was monitored back at the precinct.

"There is also a monitoring system in the bedroom where I'll be staying. The upstairs bedroom gives me a clear view of the areas below. With any luck, we'll see trouble coming before it finds us."

Jillian nodded and continued to listen as he explained all the features of the room. There were so many knobs and gadgets, that she felt as though she was in a James Bond movie. Patiently, Harrison took his time and explained each one. He informed her that there was a back-up generator to maintain security in case of a local power outage. She appreciated his attention to detail and his making her an active player in her own protection.

"Come here." Harrison moved off to the side of the narrow room. He hit a button and waited as a door in the floor opened up. "This passageway leads outside, just beyond the trees. It'll give us a head start in case we're ambushed."

"Do you think that's possible? I thought this place was supposed to be safe?" Her eyes conveyed her concern.

Harrison reached out touching her cheek. "No place is totally safe, Jillian, but there is no reason to worry about that now. Who knows, Martin could be arresting the people responsible right now."

"Don't try to humor me, Harrison. I prefer it when you're straight with me." She looked up at him. "So once we're outside, then what?"

"Can you run?"

"All day with the right incentive," she quipped. "Seriously, I run an eight-minute mile."

Harrison whistled impressed. "Great. We shouldn't have any problem putting distance between ourselves and would-be attackers if they're on foot.

The woods are too dense to accommodate any type of vehicle so I believe we'll have a fighting chance." He turned and pressed the button to lower the door.

Jillian reached out to touch his arm. She wanted him to know how grateful she was to him for helping her, but remembering his remarks from earlier she withdrew her hand. This wasn't the same as his teaching her how to hold a gun. What she was feeling at the moment had more to do with caring about him as a man.

Harrison turned around just in time to see Jillian withdraw her hand. "What is it? You were going to ask me something?" He searched her eyes, which were avoiding his at the moment.

"No," Jillian responded, touching her forehead. "I just wanted to say thank you for being here with me. I promise not to be any more trouble." She started to walk away.

"Does your head hurt?" he asked coming up behind her. He turned her around to check her bandage. There was no fresh sign of blood, so he assumed the stitches were okay. "I didn't hurt you out back earlier, did I?"

At the mention of their earlier escapades, Jillian blushed with embarrassment. "No you didn't," she answered and rushed out the small room. She returned to the galley-style kitchen and began assembling vegetables. In the freezer she found a frozen bag of chicken strips. She quickly separated a few and returned the others to the freezer. It was several minutes before she realized that Harrison was watching her. There was a strange expression on his face.

"How long have you been there?" She was suddenly uncomfortable. For a man who wanted to cool things between them, he sure had a way of looking at her.

"A couple of minutes," Harrison lied. He had actually been watching Jillian the whole time from the privacy of the surveillance room. It had started innocently with his checking the grounds, but then one of the cameras had switched to the inside of the house and Jillian in the kitchen. He had watched her move around comfortably. It was obvious that she was used to cooking and taking care of a family. She cleaned as she went along. He thought of his mother's complaints about today's women. Her soft southern voice would say, "They don't take care of their men the way women of my day did. They're too busy to cook and clean. You don't want a woman like that, Harry. A woman too lazy to cook is probably too lazy to give you babies as well."

He and his siblings would laugh and glance at each other. However, standing in the kitchen watching Jillian prepare their meal, Harrison knew instinctively that she hadn't been one of those women. She was a modern working woman with a career of her own, but family and home still came first with her. His eyes traveled down her shapely body. He suddenly thought of children and wondered if Jillian wanted any more.

"I owe you an apology."

Jillian's eyes narrowed with curiosity. "For what?"

He walked further into the room and took a seat on the counter. His legs dangled over the edge. "For prying into your background."

Jillian's eyes suddenly misted as she recalled his words. "Why did you do it?" Her voice was soft with emotion. "Did you believe you would find something to link me with the accountant's death?"

"Not at all. I believed your account of the events." He dropped his eyes to the hardwood floor.

Jillian walked until she stood in front of him. "Look me in the eyes and tell me why you pried."

Harrison met her demanding eyes. He owed her the truth and gave it to her. "Your crying spell in the car was too emotional for someone you didn't know. Even witnessing a murder wouldn't trigger deep gut-wrenching sobs like you cried. Only something personal and painful could have that effect and my curiosity got the better of me. I wanted to know what made the fearless Jillian Newman weep like a baby."

Jillian backed up to the opposite counter for support. She recalled that night and the chain effect it had had on her. The heavy rain and lightning had brought the scene of the accident back to life.

"So you know. Now what?" She raised her chin stubbornly.

"So now I would like to hear the truth about that night from you. You've pointed out the fact that Josh holds some animosity towards you because of the accident. I think there's more to his bitterness than what you did. Knowing Josh as well as I do, I would bet he had a hand in your being out in that storm. Am I right?"

Jillian glanced off for a moment before facing him. She tried composing herself, but the emotions wouldn't be swept away this time. Before she knew it, she was in Harrison's arms crying like a baby again.

CHAPTER 7

They sat at opposite ends on the sofa in the den. Their plates were empty and their stomachs were full. They sipped on the homemade lemonade Jillian had prepared with the meal. Her chicken stir-fry was excellent, and Harrison had complimented her efforts profusely. It was now time for Jillian to answer his questions. She had promised that she would after they ate. The extra time had given her a chance to gather her emotions and for some strange reason, she wanted to tell Harrison about that night.

"It had been raining heavily all that week. By Friday, the ground couldn't absorb any more. Josh had insisted that we move into this new development in a wooded area. The homes were large and befitting a newly elected district attorney." She made a "who really cares?" expression. "Anyway, the streets were beginning to flood and since it was Friday, I left work early. I went by the daycare center and picked up Travis." Her voice faltered.

Harrison took both plates and sat them on the coffee table. With them out of the way he grabbed Jillian's hands while she spoke.

"I raised the garage door and noticed Josh was already home. I pulled in beside him and took Travis into the house. Josh wasn't downstairs, so we went upstairs." She looked directly at him. "I heard noises, not really voices."

"That jerk was in bed with another woman," Harrison all but shouted. "I'll be damn." He got up from the sofa and began stalking around the room. "That's what's eating at him, Jillian. Not the fact that you were driving, but that he and some woman drove you out of your own home and back into that storm."

"I guess?" She shook her head doubtfully, then picked up her story. "When I saw them, I must have made a sound because he looked right at me, then called my name. I still held Travis. I wasn't thinking clearly. I was too hurt to stay in that house, so I grabbed my keys and ran back to the car. I didn't even strap Travis in until I was at the end of the block. I remember thinking I had to get to Faye. She would tell me what to do. I don't remember the water appearing to be that high when I approached that road, but evidently it was. My car began to float and next thing I knew we were being swept away. After some time, I don't know how long, we came to a stop. I could see rescue workers stopped on the side of the road. A cable was thrown out and hooked onto the car. Then a fireman came out and got me. I remember pleading for him to take Travis first, but he just shouted for me to come on. He said they would get my baby."

Tears ran freely down her face. She didn't try to wipe them away this time. With a tear-streaked face she looked at Harrison who sat on the edge of the table facing her now. His dark expressive eyes conveyed his sorrow at her lost.

"The cable snapped and Travis was swept away in the raging water. We held his funeral three days later. It was all a blur to me, but what I do remember is the cold shoulder I received from Josh. There was no concern for me or my feelings, just his own, and how much he couldn't stand the sight of me. At the funeral we stood side by side, but each of us was very much alone in our grief and pain. The next thing I know, Josh had filed for divorce and evidently spoken to the papers about me, the accident, and the divorce. I was made to look like an irresponsible woman who endangered her child's life needlessly." The tears had stopped. "If it hadn't been for my parents and that spitfire of a sister of mine, I don't think I would have survived. But each day they made me get up and go on with my life."

Harrison raised her chin to face him. "I'm very glad that they did. Otherwise, I wouldn't have had the opportunity to meet you."

"Thanks," Jillian whispered and looked away.

"You're now afraid of thunderstorms," Harrison stated.

Jillian's eyes swung back to him. She smiled and nodded. "Very much. When its thundering and lightning, I can't sleep, think, or breathe comfortably. Images of that night and my baby being swept away haunt my thoughts."

"Have you tried counseling?"

"For a short time, but I stopped. I didn't feel it was helping."

"Did you give it a chance?" His dark eyes studied her knowingly.

Jillian glanced away, unable to stand the look in his eyes. "I guess I didn't really give it a chance," she finally commented. Her lips curled up at the corners.

Harrison chuckled. "Why doesn't that surprise me?"

Jillian laughed with him, then turned the tables on him. "So tell me about yourself, Harrison. I can tell by your poor southern accent that you weren't born and raised here."

He laughed, then glanced away and rose from the table. He didn't trust himself to look into her eyes and not be able to tell the complete truth. "To think I thought I had mastered the accent," he said over his shoulder, staring out the window.

"Sorry to burst your bubble. So where were you born?"

"Jersey."

Jillian frowned when he offered no more. It was clear to her that Harrison wasn't comfortable talking about himself. Perhaps in time he would feel secure enough with her to share. "Hey look, if you don't want talk about yourself, I completely understand." She unfolded from the sofa and headed upstairs.

Harrison misunderstood and swore under his breath as he went after her. "Jillian, wait."

She turned to face him as he tried to explain. She silenced him with a finger to the lips. "When you're ready to tell me who you are, I'll be available to listen." She smiled down at him. "Goodnight and thank you for everything." She took to the stairs again.

Not quite ready for bed, she decided to unpack her bags. As she sorted through her luggage it was obvious that Faye had thought of everything. Makeup, hair products, toiletries, and curling irons were all there. The clothing she had selected was sensible and comfortable like the footwear. She unzipped a small compartment with a square imprint. She wasn't sure what it could be, but when she stuck her hand in and removed the object, she couldn't believe her eyes. In her hand was a full box of condoms. What in the devil was on Faye's mind? she asked herself as she stared at the box. Didn't her sister realize that she was in witness protection, and not on vacation? However, Faye was quite perceptive. There was a possibility that she had seen through her and Harrison's hostility and picked up on the attraction between them. She quickly threw the box in the nightstand drawer and continued with her unpacking. By the time she finished, she was completely wiped out. The day had proven quite eventful. After a quick shower, she slid into a pair of boxers and a T-shirt, then slipped under the covers. She fell asleep the moment her head hit the pillow.

Downstairs, Harrison prowled around the house for several more hours. His mind was filled with images from throughout the day with Jillian. At the hospital she had been brave and courageous. Her determination and competitive spirit had shown through with the shooting lesson. He had seen her sensitive, feminine side while she talked about the accident and her son. And in the kitchen he had been bowled over by her domestic abilities. But what had him on edge and determined to fight, was her strong sexual appeal and her passion. What the devil had Josh been thinking when he went out searching for another woman? Jillian was all any man could need or possibly hope for. He plopped on the sofa. His head was tilted back against the softness of the cushion. He must have sat that way for hours thinking of Jillian, because when he finally moved to go upstairs, his neck was stiff. He tried to rub the kink out on his way up to bed.

Harrison walked past his room to listen at Jillian's door. He could just make out her even breathing. He backtracked and entered his own room where he removed his holstered weapon. He stripped down to the skin, then retrieved his gun off the dresser where it was placed and walked into the bathroom. Harrison took a quick shower because he wasn't comfortable being under the water too long. He needed to be able to hear the alarm in case of intruders and Jillian in case she needed him.

He lay across the bed dressed in a comfortable pair of nylon gym pants. His chest and feet were left bare and the covers folded back. He wasn't here to get a good night's sleep; he was here to protect the woman next door. A woman who was fast becoming the most important person in his life. With his gun lying across his chest, he settled down for a night of catnapping.

Back in the city Jillian and Harrison were the topic of conversation.

"Care for a drink?" He offered his guest brandy.

"Sure, why not? Is the prey all settled in?"

"Just like I told you."

"So when is the hit?"

"Not for a couple of days."

"Days, she could remember something by then."

"Who's doing this, me or you?"

"All right." The guest took another swallow. "So what's the plan?"

"The plan is to let them settle into a routine."

"But what if she remembers?"

"From what I've observed, remembering what happened in that garage is the furthest thing from her mind."

"What are you talking about?"

"I'm talking about Blake and the lady being too preoccupied with each other to see our people coming until it's too late."

"So the man of steel has a weakness for his charge."

"Major, and it's that weakness which is going to be their downfall."

"Sounds like everything is in order."

"I told you I would take care of it."

"And you have."

"How about another drink?"

The sun had been up for hours by the time Jillian made it down to the kitchen. She had slept like a rock to her surprise, but was now in dire need of a cup of coffee. Harrison could be heard banging around in the kitchen. She smiled wondering what he was getting into. An image of him at the stove with spoon in one hand and gun in the other flashed across her mind. She laughed as she entered the kitchen, then fell immediately silent as she saw the fresh stack of pancakes and bacon on the counter.

"Good morning," she greeted him, crossing the threshold. The aroma of coffee beckoned her. Jillian followed her nose to the coffeemaker on the counter and quickly poured herself a cup. She added a splash of milk and a teaspoon of sugar. Satisfied, she finally took her first sip and smiled with pleasure.

"You're a caffeine junkie," Harrison said watching her.

Jillian hiked a perfectly arched brow at him as she took another long sip. She turned around to lean against the cabinet, facing him. "Guilty as charged," she replied with a smile.

The sun was streaming in through the window blinds over the sink and cast Jillian in a warm golden glow. Her hair was pulled back into a looped ponytail and secured in place by a decorative barrette. The style allowed for a clear view of her face. Her beautiful eyes appeared to be glowing in the sunlight and Harrison could have looked at her all day. But he was cooking and so returned his attention to the stove. He flipped a pancake out onto the top of the stack, which sat on the counter with a platter of bacon. He carried both over to the table. Turning around he noticed Jillian watching him.

"What's on your mind?" he asked facing her. His eyes helplessly slid down the length of her body. She was dressed in white denim shorts and a collared red, white, and blue halter shirt, which she wore tucked inside her shorts. A red leather belt to match her near-nothing sandals was secured around her waist. Her gorgeous brown legs were blemish free and looked freshly shaven. Fire-red toenails winked at him from the sandals. Damn, I've got to get out of here.

That smoldering look he gave her nearly wiped the thought clean out of her mind. "I was...ah...thinking that I never would have pegged you for a man who cooks," she finally managed to say over the lump in her throat.

Harrison ran a hand through his dark hair. "I'm sure there are a great many things about me that would pique your interest."

Jillian's brows rose at the dubious statement while also noticing the hand movement. She suddenly realized that Harrison did that when he was uncomfortable. She pushed away from the cabinet to join him at the table. Tipping up her chin, she remarked, "Care to share?" She selected a slice of bacon while she waited and took a bite. The oils glossed her lips and drew Harrison's immediate attention.

"Not now. Why don't you eat while I go check the monitors?" He rushed from the room not giving Jillian a chance to say anything further.

She stared after him bewildered. Alone and with nothing to do, she eventually took a seat and began filling one of the plates on the table. She bowed her head and said grace. Her first bite of pancake was delicious. It was soft and fluffy just the way she liked. It soon became quite apparent that Harrison wasn't planning on sharing breakfast with her. She was a little disappointed to be eating alone. When she finished eating, Jillian rinsed her dishes and placed them in the dishwasher. She was about to place the remaining food in the oven when Harrison returned to the kitchen. He had changed into a well-worn pair of jeans and an Alabama T-shirt, which had seen better days. The wash-worn fabric hugged and caressed his broad chest like a second skin. The ever-present gun was secured in the shoulder holster. Navy athletic shoes were on his feet.

Jillian thought he looked good enough to eat. He was causal, yet possessed just the right amount of lethalness to make her heart skip a beat. Just looking at him one would think he was a bad boy, not the gentle, kind man she had gotten to know. But remembering their conversation from yesterday, and seeing the strain on Harrison's handsome face, Jillian followed his lead and headed out of the kitchen. She stopped in the doorway to compliment his meal.

"Breakfast was delicious. Thank you."

"You're welcome, and thanks for the compliment." Harrison watched her leave. He released a sigh of relief. Watching and allowing her to leave had been the most difficult thing that he had done in a long time. He wasn't sure how long he could resist the pull of her soft brown skin, or her fresh berry scent.

He finally sat down at the table to eat. While alone, he recalled the image of Jillian's lips all glossy from the bacon. Lord, how he had wanted to lick her lips clean. "Stop it, Blake," he scolded himself out loud. "Keep your mind on your job and off Jillian." Right. That should be easy.

Harrison located Jillian in the den after cleaning up the kitchen. She was curled up on the sofa reading a book. She hadn't heard him enter and so he stood there watching her. No one would believe the beauty curled on the sofa was a dynamic attorney with a track record to prove it. She was such a contradiction.

On the one hand she was gorgeous and so very feminine and on the other hand, she was fierce in the courtroom and critical of the police. Now looking at her curled on the sofa, all he could think about was joining her.

Jillian picked that moment to raise her head and glance in his direction. Her eyes held questions that he wasn't in a position to answer or act upon. She swung her feet to the floor and rose from the sofa.

"I'll go upstairs to read if you want to watch the television." She moved to step around him in the doorway.

Harrison reached out grabbing her on impulse. He removed the book from her hand and looked at the cover. It was a romance. "I don't recall seeing any of these on the shelf."

"You didn't. Faye included a couple in my luggage." She reached for her book, but Harrison held it out of reach.

He opened it to the place where she was reading and began to read out loud. "Xavier's hands were everywhere all at once. He wanted to bury himself so deep inside Nicole at the moment until he hurt with need." Harrison cursed and closed the book with force. "Here, take this thing. I don't need any more ideas."

Jillian accepted the book with a smile.

He looked down into her laughing eyes. "You don't have to leave if you don't want to." His voice had lost the commanding tone he usually spoke in.

Jillian searched his eyes for a moment and saw the uncertainty in them. The passage from her book had reminded him of what he was trying to ignore. She shook her head. "I think it's best if I do. You're barely hanging on as it is. If and when we make love, I don't want you to regret it, so I'm going upstairs to give you your space."

Harrison's eyes softened as he listened to her brave words, knowing that she was in as much discomfort as he. But she was right. If something happened to her because he got careless, he would never forgive himself. He stroked her cheek and nodded.

"Dinner will be served at five," Jillian called back on her way upstairs.

Harrison collapsed on the sofa and clicked on the television. Soap opera after soap opera had beautiful couples making love. He swore from the bitter irony. At the last one, Harrison paused. Brown and white limbs were tangled together in the sheets. Harrison had never given thought to how he and Jillian would look making love together, but watching the couple on the screen, he now knew they would be beautiful. He swore once more and clicked off the television.

CHAPTER 8

Jillian and Harrison fell into a routine over the next several weeks. He prepared breakfast while Jillian saw to dinner. Lunch was a kind of every man for himself. They ate more alone than they did with each other. And once the meal was over, they always went their separate ways. Jillian was usually upstairs with a book while Harrison entertained himself with the satellite television.

This particular evening, Jillian had cleaned the kitchen and was headed back upstairs when Harrison called her name.

"Yes." She turned back around and entered the den where he sat.

"Stay down here with me. Unless you would prefer to go back upstairs." He watched her with hopeful eyes.

Was he kidding? she thought to herself. She hated being cooped upstairs in that room alone. She was a people person and all the time spent alone was about to drive her crazy. "If you're sure you don't mind?"

Harrison's face broke into a warm welcoming smile. "I'm sure."

Jillian returned the smile and sat on the floor with her back propped against the sofa.

"You feel like a game of Scrabble?" Harrison asked, drawing a peculiar look from Jillian.

She glanced over her left shoulder staring at him. "Why the sudden change? I thought being around me was a distraction? Or are you immune to me now?" She deliberately gave him a scorching look.

Harrison winced and shook his head. "Do you want to play or not?"

"Sure, why not?" Jillian cleared the coffee table of newspapers and magazines while Harrison retrieved the game from the bookcase.

Soon they were engrossed in the game challenging each other with their intelligence. As one played a word unknown to the other, they laughed and challenged the other for proof. It was Jillian's turn, and she held an a, i, f, and m. She racked her brain while studying the board for a way to use all her letters and to win the game. Finally she saw it and quickly placed her letters. Off the a in cornucopia, she placed her m above it, followed by the f, i, and a. "Mafia," she said proudly while showing him her empty tray. She counted up her points and waved her arms victoriously.

Harrison glanced at the board, then Jillian. His eyes searched her joyous face wondering if there was some hidden meaning. Did she know about DeMarco? "That's an odd word to use."

"Oh, come on, Harrison. Surely you're not a sore loser?" She laughed over at him.

"Not at all," he replied satisfied that there was no hidden agenda in her choice of words. He continued to watch her celebrate as she returned the game to the shelf.

"Why do you represent criminals?" he asked out the blue, catching them both by surprise, then suddenly realized that he really wanted to hear her answer.

Jillian's back stiffened as she leveled him with a stare. "What the devil is going on here? I play the word mafia and what, you believe I'm a mob lawyer?" Her hands were planted firmly on her hips as her voice rose with her temper.

"That's not why I asked." Harrison tried to explain.

"Then what exactly am I being accused of?" She waved a hand annoyed. "I have never nor would I ever have anything to do with someone connected to organized crime." She returned to the sofa and stood glaring down at him still sitting on the floor. "Does this have anything to do with my case?"

"No Jillian, not at all." Harrison felt as though he had been kicked in the gut. "I asked the question based on something Martin said to me."

Jillian's eyes narrowed in anger. "Oh, I see. First of all, Detective, I don't represent criminals. I defend people who have been accused." She raised her brows making her point.

"Martin told me that the guy was innocent and what the cops had done, but he also said that the guy was a scumbag with a list of crimes."

"That scumbag was a 16-year-old kid trying to make money to help his mother and siblings. Sure he took the wrong course of action, but I felt he was worthy of a chance." She finally sat on the sofa. "A friend of mine does mentoring and he was introduced to Kyle. They began spending time together and he discovered that Kyle was an A and B student despite his troubles with the law. He saw potential. Kyle expressed an interest in being a lawyer, so he approached me about allowing him to work in my office. I agreed and he soon became a valued employee. But we had a contract. I would pay for his college if he stayed out of trouble."

"You're amazing," Harrison said relocating to the tabletop across from her. He rested his arms on his thighs while listening.

"No I'm not. I'm just trying to help. I make a good living and my son was gone, so I thought helping another child succeed was a good idea." She fought against the tears she suddenly felt. "Kyle never really sold drugs. He made deliveries, and on that night the police accused him of making a pickup in the brick-yard."

"And you didn't believe that he did it?"

"I knew that he hadn't, Harrison. He had been with me in the office and there was no way possible for Kyle to have done what he was accused of. I couldn't allow them to lock away a promising young man when he was just turning his life around, and especially when I knew he was innocent."

"It's dirty policing which turns the community against us and makes our job difficult."

"I know and understand that. I respect the law and those who serve. But I will not stand by when the law is abused by the very ones selected to uphold and protect it." She pounded her right fist into her thigh, making her point. Her brown eyes were bright and filled with determination. And Harrison knew in that moment that he could no longer run from his feelings. He reached out taking her fist in his hand and opened it. He wove their fingers together, then brought her hand to his lips and kissed it.

"You are an incredible woman," Harrison said while loving her with his eyes. The wound on her head was healed and only a thin scar remained. He leaned in with the intention of kissing her.

"Hey, I thought we agreed to play it cool. Your muddle head and all." Jillian's whiskey-brown eyes teased him as she taunted him with his own words.

"Forget what I said. Come here," he said, wrapping an arm around her. He pulled Jillian to the edge of her seat and leaned forward kissing her. He transferred one leg then the other around his waist and pulled Jillian onto his lap so that she straddled him. Then he focused completely on kissing her.

Jillian wrapped her arms around Harrison's neck and matched him stroke for stroke with her tongue. She applied just the right pressure to increase the pleasure. Harrison tore his mouth away. He nipped her bottom lip, then licked the pain away, before fusing their mouths together again. Jillian combed her fingers through the silkiness of his hair while their mouths made love and Harrison's hands cupped her bottom. She sighed with pleasure deep in the back of her throat as they finally came up for air and stared into each other's eyes. Her hands caressed the length of his muscled back.

"Who the devil taught you to kiss like that?" Harrison asked Jillian, tilting her head back. He was breathing heavily. His fingers were buried in the thickness of her hair massaging her scalp.

Jillian's eyes were heavy with desire as she smiled seductively into Harrison's own intoxicated eyes. "I could ask you the same thing." She arched a dark brow at him.

He gave her a dimpled smile. "Candice Murray, my brother's girlfriend." He laughed when Jillian pinched him.

"Your brother's girlfriend? How could you?" She laughed.

"She was eighteen, beautiful, and eager to teach me." His dark eyes danced with mischief.

"No doubt she was blond and blue-eyed." Jillian rolled her eyes annoyed.

Harrison watched Jillian closely. "As a matter of fact she was. But the woman who has my attention now is a beautiful black woman with whiskey-brown eyes, and an incredible talent for kissing." He pecked her lips.

Jillian smiled and questioned her next words. "Are you as comfortable with us as you appear?"

"Yes, but that's not to say that I wasn't surprised by my attraction to you. Or that I didn't question why I was attracted to you and not some other black woman."

Jillian nodded as she pondered his words. "I experienced some of those same feelings. I was, however, a little unsettled by the fact that I was attracted to a cop."

"You mean white cop, don't you?"

She smiled and shook her head no. "Of course the thought entered my mind, but I was reared in a military family and lived around all types of people. My friends and I were our own rainbow coalition."

"So you're saying that your parents didn't necessarily expect you to marry a black man?"

"No," Jillian answered with confidence. "Now, they were probably relieved that I did, but it wasn't expected." Jillian caressed his handsome face tenderly. "My mother always told us that she didn't care who we married as long as the man was good to us." Jillian shrugged a shoulder and removed her hand from his face. "Faye married a fine black man like our father, and I married Josh."

"Everyone makes mistakes every now and then. The key to success is not to repeat the same mistake." He smiled at her.

"You know, I had real doubts about Josh and me. But the man can be so persuasive and can talk circles around you until you believe his every word." Jillian closed her eyes remembering all the promises he had made her.

"Sounds like Josh was a born politician," Harrison added.

"He is and he's in the past, so let's not talk about him."

"Fine by me," Harrison said, pulling her closer. "Look, I've tried to stay away from you in an attempt to keep my mind focused on protecting you."

"Didn't work, did it?" Jillian stated smugly. "You thought of me more."

"You too?" Harrison asked with a foolish smile plastered on his face.

"Yes."

"Well, we might as well spend our time together. We just have to be more vigilant and have some self-control. We're adults and can conduct ourselves as such."

"I agree."

"Good." Harrison brought her to her feet as he stood. "I need to go check the wooded area around the cabin. I haven't done that today and should check it out. While I'm outside, I want you to take this and go into the monitoring room." He handed her the gun from practice. "You know what to do if there's trouble."

He kissed her briefly and was out the door. Jillian heard him lock the door a short time later. She did as instructed and went into the camera room to watch and wait.

Harrison checked the grounds around the cabin first and seeing no signs of intruders he ventured further into the tree-lined area. He moved slowly and with caution. Dusk was falling and he didn't want to disturb any signs of someone being there by being impatient.

As he came to the property in back of the house, he made sure that all the blinds were secure and no one could see into the house. All the lights were on, making it impossible to know where they were at any given time. Satisfied that all was in order, he wove his way back around to the front door and stepped on something just prior to leaving the trees. He squatted down and searched the ground. An ink pen was inches from his left foot. He retrieved it and examined it. In the waning light he could see that it was a city pen with Birmingham, the Magic City printed on it.

All the city agencies had them. Judging from its slightly discolored condition, he assumed one of the guys must have dropped it while searching the property the day they brought Jillian to the cabin. He wondered how he had missed it on his previous searches of the grounds, but considering the size of the area, it was always possible. He stuck it in his pocket and headed back into the house. Jillian greeted him at the door and waited until he activated the alarm system.

"Is everything all right out there?"

"Fine. It's just you and me." He kissed her deeply. "Come on let's check out a movie."

"Come on in."

"I was glad to hear from you. How are things at the cabin?"

"That's not why I called you." He rose from his desk chair.

"It's not? Then what could be so important?"

"These." He held up several documents.

"That was quick."

"I keep telling you that I'm well connected."

"I believe you."

"Good, now sign."

"Can I borrow a pen?"

"Sure, I have one..." He searched his breast pocket. "I must have left it somewhere." He opened a desk drawer and produced a pen. "Here."

"There you go." The documents and pen were returned. "How's our other little business?"

"Going as expected. It won't be much longer, I assure you."

"I sure hope not."

"Stop worrying."

"How can I? If she remembers everything could be ruined."

"Don't start borrowing trouble."

"You're right. I'll see you later."

"I'll keep you posted on developments."

"So what did you think of the movie?" Harrison asked Jillian as it went off. He glanced down to his leg where her head rested and discovered her asleep. The image caused a warm surge inside of him. He bent and kissed her sleeping head lightly, then sat back savoring the moment. It could be this way every day for them, he thought. But there were some major hurdles for them to overcome before they could start planning a future together.

He sat there for several minutes just thinking about the possibilities. Several years ago he had come close to marriage, but drive and ambition had ruined the relationship. He stroked Jillian's head wondering about her own ambition. Had her career replaced the love of her husband and child and was she willing to try again. It had been three years, and yet, when he met her, she had told him there was no man in her life. Was it by choice or simply a dry spell?"

His lack of a significant other had been by choice. He hadn't found a woman worth fighting for and he knew unquestionably that he would have to fight to keep her. But Jillian was worth a fight and so he geared up mentally for the battle, because she would undoubtedly put up one heck of a fight before surrendering. Harrison had to smile at his own cockiness, but he was sure Jillian's feeling for him were as strong as his for her. He just wished this case were solved so that they were free to openly explore their relationship without looking over their shoulders.

Exhausted himself and tired of daydreaming, Harrison scooped Jillian up into his arms and carried her upstairs to bed. The feel of her once again in his arms was comforting and so very right. In the bedroom, he managed to pull the covers back, then gently placed Jillian on the bed. He removed her sandals but didn't dare remove anything else. He covered her with the sheet and exited the room.

Downstairs he checked the monitors. All appeared quiet so he returned to the den where he planned on sleeping tonight. Something about that pen from earlier bugged him. He picked up the telephone to check in with Martin.

"This better be good," Martin's angry voice greeted him.

"I take it I'm interrupting something?" Harrison asked through his laughter. It was obvious from the purring voice in the background that Martin had company.

"Yes, you are," he growled out. "Is everything all right there?" he suddenly grew serious.

"Fine, man. Just a little concerned I guess, but I'll talk to you tomorrow."

"Don't hang up," Martin called out.

Harrison heard him tell his company that he would only be a moment.

"What are you concerned about?" Martin asked returning to the telephone.

"It's probably nothing but I found an ink pen in the woods to the rear of the house today."

"What type? Was there anything written on it?"

"It's a city pen. You know, Birmingham, the Magic City."

"One of the guys could have dropped it while checking out the grounds the day we brought Jillian to the cabin," Martin said offering an explanation.

"Yeah, that was my thinking as well."

"I think you called for another reason," Martin changed the subject. "You two getting along all right?"

"Better than all right, but we can't do a thing about it right now."

"Sounds like someone needs a little bit." Martin's raunchy laughter filled his ear.

"Watch your mouth, buddy," Harrison warned.

Martin sobered upon realizing that Harrison wasn't laughing. "It sounds like you're serious about this woman."

"I am. And before you say it, I know I have a lot to tell her and I will, but just not right now."

Martin didn't like it and proceeded to tell Harrison so. "There's no better time than while the two of you are alone. Hell, she can't go anywhere."

"Perhaps not, but she would probably do something foolish to get herself hurt. I can't risk that."

"But you're taking a mighty big chance on losing her by not being honest."

"I'm not going to lose her."

"You keep telling yourself that, but if Jillian discovers the truth on her own, you won't stand a chance of winning her back." Martin shook his head troubled. He could see the writing on the wall, but couldn't seem to make Harrison see it. And it wasn't like Harrison to be deceitful. The only thing he could conclude was that the woman was indeed extremely important to his friend and that Harrison knew she would walk when the truth was revealed.

"Any new developments?" Harrison changed the subject.

"Just one, but you don't want to hear it."

"Let me be the judge of that."

"All right, the accountant worked for Antonio."

Harrison swore loud and long. "Does the evidence point back to him?"

"Not that I can tell. I just thought you might want to know. The computer guys were able to access a password-protected file containing client list and accounting records. I contacted his bank and obtained aprintout of the last six months transactions on the account. From my initial check, it appears our guy was busy stealing from his clients."

"Which makes all of them suspects," Harrison added.

"Right." Martin responded. "Hey, I'll fax the file to you in the morning. Maybe you and Jillian can make some sense of it."

"Sounds good and thanks for the advice and information. Tell your friend I'm sorry for interrupting."

"Hey, I needed the chance to recuperate." The two men laughed before disconnecting.

CHAPTER 9

Early the next morning just as promised, Martin faxed the file on the accountant to Harrison. He sat in the camera room reading it in private. There were four complete pages of clients, which also made them possible suspects. But the name Antonio DeMarco stood out. The case just seemed to keep getting worse, Harrison thought as he closed the file. He tossed it in a drawer before leaving the room.

Jillian was coming down the stairs when he walked out. He waited for her at the base of the stairs. She wore a summery cotton dress in blue and no shoes. Her hair was worn straight, and small gold hoops dangled from her ears. She looked incredible and Harrison had the strongest urge to haul her upstairs to the nearest bed and make love to her until neither of them could move.

Jillian saw the heat in his eyes as she descended the stairs. She immediately made up her mind to greet him cheerfully, but would bypass on the morning kiss she had originally planned. The flexing jaw muscles warned of his internal struggle and she wouldn't be accused of enticing him.

He stood at the bottom of the stairs wearing loose fitted workout pants and a mesh tank top that exposed his hairy chest. His hair was still damp from his morning shower and his morning beard dark. The gun was also present.

"Good morning," she said perky and bright. "Thanks for tucking me in last night."

Harrison didn't respond right away. He just continued to look at her. His nostrils flared. "You appear to have a lot of energy this morning."

"I slept well last night."

"I'm glad one of us did."

Jillian hiked a brow. "You didn't sleep well?"

"Not at all. I spent the night thinking about you," he said as he grabbed her around the waist and spun her, taking a seat on the third step. He pushed Jillian's dress up and forced her to straddle him on the step. He kissed her hard and thorough while he crushed her breast against his exposed chest. She felt and smelled so good that he thought he would lose his mind with want. He ended the kiss and sat back looking at her. She was as turned on as he was.

Jillian bit her lower lip while returning his heated stare. When she could stand the heat no longer, she made idle conversation. "I've never met anyone named Harrison before." She smiled when he raised a brow. He was so handsome and devastatingly male that the womanly need in her surged with force. "The only Harrison I know is Harrison Ford from *Raiders of the Lost Ark.*" She stroked his lips with a thumb.

Harrison's eyes darkened as a purely sexual smile slid across his face. "I may not be Harrison Ford, beautiful, but I am looking for a little treasure myself," he said slipping his hand past the elastic in her panties and finding his target.

"Oh my!" Jillian jerked at the contact of his fingers against her. Her head fell back and her eyes closed helplessly. She held on to his shoulders as Harrison manipulated the sensitive flesh between her thighs and whispered in her ear.

"That's it, sweetie, relax and enjoy it," he crooned.

There was nothing else for Jillian to do. She was too weak from the building sensation to even think about moving, which she wasn't, especially while Harrison played her like a fine instrument. Round and round, in and out, his finger went until Jillian began to tremble in his lap. She took a deep breath and moaned with pleasure.

"You're almost there, sweetie," he continued to whisper as his tempo increased.

Jillian convulsed, then released a scream that came from deep within. She fell damp and limp against him trying to catch her breath.

Harrison removed his hand and kissed her sweetly on the lips. He continued to hold her while she recuperated. He whispered in her ear, "When we make love it's going to be magical."

"It already was," she whispered back still under the haze of his touch. Their hearts were beating fast and as one. Jillian sighed again as she buried her nose into the side of his neck and inhaled Harrison's natural male scent. She wanted them to stay like that forever. "You smell good," she groaned against him.

Harrison smiled lazily to himself as he continued to hold her. This was what he wanted. A life with Jillian, making love and having babies. The thought was crystal clear and so perfect. He kissed the side of her face and cuddled her closer.

The telephone rang, interrupting the moment. Jillian moaned and forced herself up. She leaned against the stair railing and watched Harrison go to the telephone. She glanced down at her dress and saw that it was completely wrinkled from their little escapade. As he greeted their caller, Jillian returned to her room for another shower and a change.

"Hello." Harrison watched the sway of Jillian's hips as she climbed the stairs wishing that he could follow her and continue what he had started. She had been so responsive to his touch and uninhibited. They were going to be great together.

"I'm headed up to the house," Martin notified Harrison.

"I'll be looking for you." Harrison clicked off the phone and ran to his own bathroom. He was back downstairs just in the nick of time, as Martin pulled up. He opened the door and waved his partner and friend inside.

"Is something wrong?" Harrison asked Martin the moment he entered.

"Not with me, but you sounded on the edge last night." He glanced past Harrison to Jillian coming down the stairs. "I see your problem," he whispered so only Harrison could hear. Jillian was a knockout in a fitted white eyelet peasant shirt that stopped just above her navel. Denim shorts with cargo style pockets hugged her hips and showcased her legs. She wore canvas tie-ups on her feet. As he turned his attention onto his friend and saw the raw hunger in his eyes, he knew that he had been the one to interrupt this time.

"Martin, how are you?" Jillian greeted him with a warm smile.

"I'm doing well. I wanted to check on you both and see if you needed anything."

"Only my first cup of coffee."

"You're a caffeine junkie too?" he asked following her back to the kitchen.

Jillian laughed as she quickly assembled the coffeemaker. "Where have I heard that phrase before?"

"Can you believe, a cop who only drinks one cup of coffee a day?"

Jillian laughed and glanced back at Harrison. "Some people find other ways of boosting their energy levels."

Harrison fought to keep a straight face. He knew Martin was gawking at him. Eventually he gave in and met his knowing blue eyes. He mouthed. "Nothing happened." Then broke out into a wide grin.

With his back to Jillian, Martin mouthed a return message. "Liar."

Both men broke into laughter and drew Jillian's attention. "What am I missing here?" she asked.

"Apparently nothing," Martin quipped, low enough for only Harrison to here.

"Is that coffee ready?" Harrison rushed to fill the void.

"Almost and breakfast is my treat this morning." She smiled meaningfully into his eyes.

Fully aware of Martin observing them, Harrison thought to change the mood in the room. "I received your fax this morning. It makes for some pretty interesting reading."

"I thought so too," Martin replied. "Thank you," he said to Jillian as she placed two mugs of coffee on the table. "Jillian," he called halting her retreat. "Have you remembered anything else from that night?"

Jillian glanced briefly at Harrison then back at Martin. "No. Nothing." She returned to the stove and quickly got breakfast underway. Harrison and Martin discussed possible leads while she listened. It appeared the accountant was associated with several known criminals and anyone of them could want her dead. She placed the food on the table and joined the men.

Harrison noticed her pinched features when she sat down and knew something was bothering her. Concerned for Jillian, he covered her hand. "What's worrying you?"

She smiled at his intuitiveness and raised her eyes to his. "Trying to find the person who wants me dead could take forever. Is it possible for you to narrow down the field?" She glanced at Martin for an answer.

"Actually I did that and came up with only four major suspects from his list of clients."

"Is it possible for you to provide photographs of these men so that I can see if anyone stands out?"

"That's a good idea," Harrison concurred with her suggestion.

"Sure, not a problem. I can bring them out tomorrow and you can have a look."

With a plan decided they concentrated on the meal and what was happening back in the city. Jillian enjoyed watching and listening to Harrison and Martin razz each other. It was obvious to her that they were very close. It suddenly occurred to her that she knew nothing of Harrison's private life. They had spent so much of their time talking about the case and her life, but every time she asked a personal question of Harrison, he dodged answering.

She sipped her coffee and glanced at him over the rim of her mug. He caught the look and winked at her. The coffee suddenly lost its taste as she grew concerned. He was so open and unguarded with Martin. They shared private personal moments and Jillian realized that he had never done that with her. She needed space.

"I'm going to go to my stood suddenly drawing both men's attention.

"Are you feeling all right?" Harrison asked concerned. "You seem a little quiet."

Jillian forced a smile as she pushed in her chair. "I'm feeling well, but I know you both have work to discuss and I'm hindering it, so I'll see you both later." She turned to Martin. "Will you be joining us for dinner?"

"Sure he will," Harrison answered for him. "We have a lot to discuss and he can't miss one of your fine meals."

"Seems like I'm staying."

"Great." She smiled. To Harrison she said, "And thanks for the compliment." She left the men alone in the kitchen.

Martin had left two hours ago. He had just called back to thank Jillian for dinner and to tell her that he had the photographs she requested. They made plans for lunchtime tomorrow. She and Harrison were finally in the process of cleaning up the kitchen. Dinner had gone extremely well. Martin and Harrison had both eaten ravenously while paying Jillian compliment after compliment. The conversation during dinner had been of general topics. There had been plenty of laughs, mostly at Martin's expense. Jillian really liked him and told Harrison so while he helped her with the dishes.

"He's so different from what I thought. But then I guess we met under unusual circumstances."

Harrison stacked while she washed. "He feels the same way about you." He walked to stand behind her. His arms wrapped around her waist. "He knows what's going on between us."

"How do you feel about that?" She turned in his arms so that she could see his eyes. They were so telling. Jillian didn't believe Harrison knew how easy it was for her to read him now. And yet she knew nothing about him that wasn't related to the case. Her fear, she admitted while locked in her room earlier, was that Harrison was playing a role to seek information. However, when she looked into his eyes like now all she could see was honest emotion.

"What kind of question is that?" He looked at her strangely. "I thought it was inevitable that our friends would find out about us," he stated a little agitated and released her. "Unless you have no plans of continuing our relationship once this case is solved?" His eyes were near black with anger.

Having her faith in him confirmed, Jillian's eyes misted as she moved closer to Harrison and placed his arms back around her waist. "I want you, my very own Harrison, by my side always. I want you to meet my friends and get to know my family." She kissed him with all the passion she was feeling.

Harrison returned her passionate kiss, trying to drink her in whole and ignore his conscience telling him to be honest with her. He pushed her back against the sink. His hands pulled the stretchy shirt and bra straps down to expose the swells of her breasts. He dipped his head and rained kisses on them. The more his conscience nagged him, the more his passion escalated. He returned to her mouth, flicking his tongue in the corners while his hands tangled in her hair. And when the words nearly chocked him to be spoken, he kissed her like there was no tomorrow. His tongue found and mated with hers, hot and aggressive, the way that he enjoyed making love. He kicked her legs apart and rubbed his body against the notch of her thighs. He watched her desire-laden eyes turn that enchanting whiskey-brown just before the cabin went completely black.

"What happened?" Jillian asked anxiously.

"Get down and stay quiet," he ordered back in control. He cursed and removed his weapon from his holster while waiting for their eyes to adjust to the sudden darkness. He had gotten careless and now Jillian's life was in danger. He led her out into the hallway, working himself back towards the staircase; he needed that file. "Here," he said and raised his right pant leg and removed the smaller gun from a leg holster. He wrapped her hands around it. "You're in control," he reminded her.

Jillian clutched the gun and removed the safety as instructed. She commanded her hands to stop shaking. With her back against the wall, she watched the front door while Harrison entered the camera room. "See anything?"

"No and that's what's bothering me." He switched the cameras to different angles, but nothing moved in view of the cameras. The motion sensors never activated the outside lights. He knew this wasn't a power outage because the generator would have kicked on immediately. Someone was out there and they would soon be inside. He grabbed a black backpack that someone had left behind and opened the drawer where he had stashed the faxed information. He tossed it inside along with his cell phone, then removed the extra ammunition that was kept stored in the room. He zipped the pack as he exited and hoisted it onto his back.

When he left the room Jillian was nowhere in sight. He quickly searched in the den for her but found it empty. A noise upstairs caught his attention. He ran to the top of the stairs and was met by Jillian coming down. "What in the hell where you doing up there?" he whispered angrily.

"I had to get something," she said, patting the folded papers in her pocket.

Harrison grabbed her by the arm and dragged her back down the stairs. "Stick close to me," he ordered.

"Are we going out through the tunnel?" Jillian whispered and watched Harrison, not liking the expression on his face.

"No."

Jillian stared at him confused. "Why not? I thought you said we could escape that way?" her voice trembled with fear.

Harrison looked down into Jillian's frightened expression and drew her into his arms. "Whoever is outside knows about that tunnel and the security system on the property. If we go out that tunnel, there is sure to be someone there waiting for us."

"That makes no sense. That would mean..." Her eyes grew large as she realized what he had avoided saying outright. "Dear God," she exclaimed and nearly collapsed in his arms.

"Don't you dare fall apart on me," Harrison scolded and gave her a good hard shake. "I know it looks bad, but they haven't gotten us yet and I don't plan on them doing so. So take a deep breath and ..."

The glass windows exploded as automatic gunfire tore through the house. Pictures fell off the walls, lamps shattered, and mirrors cracked. Harrison instructed Jillian to stay close as they low-crawled into the den. They huddled behind the sofa while he explained the plan.

"They'll be watching all the major exits and the tunnel for us, but we're going out this way." He pointed to the window on the opposite wall of the doorway. "That window is completely hidden from the outside by the overgrown shrubbery. I was intentionally looking for it the other night and almost missed it. I had hoped it wouldn't be needed as an escape, but I'm glad I found it."

Jillian nodded in understanding, too scared to say anything. She felt as though she was outside of herself watching this nightmare unfold. "So when do we go?"

"In a moment, when they're reloading. But we have to make it quick because they'll be making a push into the house."

"Oh, God!"

"Come on, sweetie, pull it together." He rubbed her back.

Jillian shook her head and indicated that she was okay with a wave of her hand. "Let's just do it."

"That's my girl." Harrison managed a quick smile. "When I open the window you go first and stay close to the house until I'm out. It's a short run to the woods. I'm counting on them being out back near the tunnel's exit."

Jillian touched his cheek and managed a smile. "I'm counting on that too."

"Let's go." Harrison crawled to the window as the gunfire slowed. Jillian followed and crouched against the wall. She prayed silently as Harrison unlocked and tried to raise the window. "Damn," he cursed.

"What's wrong?" Jillian asked anxious.

"The window has been painted shut. I'm going to have to break the seal of the paint." He holstered his gun and removed a leatherman. With the knife, he proceeded to slice at the paint seal. Halfway through the process the front door burst open and a black-clothed figure stepped through. He spotted and aimed at Harrison who was reaching for his own weapon. A single gunshot rang out. The man's eyes connected with his before falling lifeless to the ground. Harrison glanced down at his own weapon, not yet fired, then turned in the direction of Jillian. She sat with her back pressed up against the wall with her recently fired gun clutched in her hand. Her eyes were overly bright and focused on the body on the floor.

"Let's go," he yelled throwing the window open. He couldn't give her time to think about what she had done. Grabbing her by the arm, he took her weapon and pushed her through the window then followed. He closed the window back then led the way to their crossing point. Parting the foliage, he didn't see anyone and decided to chance it. "Don't stop running until you're in the trees, then we'll pick a direction."

Harrison went first plowing through the bush. Jillian took off right behind him expecting to hear gunfire, but as she made it to the forest and pulled up alongside Harrison, she realized that they had made it. Harrison motioned for her to be quiet and to remain put. He then slipped off into the darkness.

Jillian sat crouched on the forest floor straining to see Harrison. She heard gunfire coming from the cabin and knew that it was being ripped apart. Soon the sound of overturned furniture drifted to where she crouched. Her heart was pounding so hard in her chest that she was afraid of having a heart attack. It seemed liked she waited for hours for his return, but she knew it was only minutes. She suddenly realized that her legs were trembling. Taking a seat on the ground, she rubbed them and tried to release her fear. Keep trying, Jillie.

Harrison quietly came into view. His gun was holstered and Jillian assumed the one that she had used was as well. He motioned for Jillian to remain low and to follow him deeper into the wooded area. After about five minutes he rose and broke out into a full run. He checked occasionally over his shoulder to make sure Jillian was with him. They kept a steady yet fast pace as they placed distance between the cabin and themselves, oblivious to the slicing leaves and prickly underbrush. It seemed like they ran for hours before Harrison finally whispered that they were stopping.

He chose a cluster of thick foliage for them to rest in. Neither possessed a flashlight and so they prayed there were no dangerous critters around. What light the moon provided was minimal, but appreciated. Harrison crouched low and drew Jillian down beside him. "How are you doing? Can you make it a little further?" he asked concerned. His own breathing was rapid but slowing.

"I'm doing fine," she huffed in answer to his question. "Are we headed to that airfield we passed on the way up here?" she asked.

Harrison gaped at her in wonder. "You were listening for clues to your relocation," he stated with admiration.

"I was forced to use my other senses."

"Well, you're right. We're headed to the Shelby County Airport. It's about another mile that way." He pointed into the distance.

"Why the airport? Who are we going to call for help?" She looked panicked.

Harrison reached out and drew her into his arms. He kissed her lovingly as he realized what he had to do. But for Jillian's protection, he was willing to lose her. He pulled out his cell phone from the backpack. Jillian immediately sat up surprised.

"I didn't know you had a cell phone? Why didn't you use it back at the cabin?"

"Cell phones are too easily traced, but we don't have a choice right now. We need help and I'm getting it from the only place I know." He quickly punched in a number and waited. "It's me. I need help and like fast." He listened. "I need pickup for two from the Shelby County Airport. It has to be before dawn. I'll call to confirm pickup." He listened a little more, then disconnected.

"You called the Feds, didn't you?" Jillian asked with relief. "I don't know why I didn't think of that."

Harrison smiled and nodded at her, then closed his eyes. God what a mess!

Pretty soon they were back on their feet and running in the direction of the airport. They had to find somewhere safe to wait out the night. He wanted to be in position in case their unexpected visitors remembered the airport and came searching for them there. He wasn't banking on recognizing anyone, but there was always hope. Maybe they could overhear a conversation and garner information.

The airport was just up ahead when Harrison stopped running. He fell to his knees just inside the tree line. Jillian was beside him. Movement around the parked airplanes drew their attention. Four men in black could be seen checking out the area. They carried deadly assault weapons. After an hour of searching and discovering nothing, the appointed leader ordered them to pull back.

"Don't get your hopes up that they're leaving, because they're not. They'll wait to see if we emerge," Harrison whispered.

"What are we going to do? How are the Feds going to get us out with them watching?"

Harrison motioned for her to follow him down further to an overgrown area. "We'll spend the night here." He checked his nightglo watch for the time and saw that it was a little after midnight. "Why don't you lie down and try to get some sleep?" He removed the backpack and placed it on the ground. "Use this for a pillow."

Jillian stared at him knowing that he was avoiding answering her question. She didn't like being in the dark where her life was concerned. "Answer my questions, Harrison."

"All right, but stretch out and rest." He propped his back against a tree and positioned the backpack against his legs. He motioned for Jillian to lie down. When she did, he stroked her hair and answered her questions. "We stay put until the coast is clear. If those guys are still there in the morning, they will probably be killed."

Jillian shivered as his words brought back the memory of what she had done back at the cabin. She turned so that she could glance up at Harrison. There were tears in her eyes.

"I killed a man tonight." Her voice was low and filled with disbelief.

Harrison bent over and kissed her head. "I know, sweetie, but it was him or me and I'm glad you chose me." He tried to lighten the moment, but knew that taking a life was something that always remained with you. "Get some sleep."

CHAPTER 10

Harrison placed another phone call before waking Jillian. He gave the person on the other end of the telephone specific instructions. Satisfied that all would be in order for their arrival, he shook Jillian awake a little before five in the morning. Their guests had finally given up and driven away as the airport began to come alive with activity. He had placed a call to confirm pickup and now they waited. As Jillian slowly came awake, he stood watching her. She was beautiful and he didn't simply mean physically. Her heart was good and generous and her mind sharp and intelligent. Her whiskey-brown eyes intrigued him and were now watching him.

"Are they gone?" Jillian whispered and stretched. She noticed the fatigue in Harrison face and knew that he had guarded over her all night. She felt guilty for sleeping and leaving him awake. She rose gently working out the stiffness.

"Yes they are." He opened his arms to receive her. He cherished the feel of her in his arms. She was alive and well, and he intended to make sure that she stayed that way. "Our ride should be here any moment."

Jillian pulled back to look at him. "Where are they going to take us?" she asked caressing his face. There were bags under his tired eyes and deep creases around his mouth. "Why didn't you wake me? I could have kept watch while you slept."

"I got you in this mess by being careless. I didn't intend for them to get a second chance."

Jillian cupped Harrison's handsome face between her hands loving everything about him. Her heart was filled with so much love for him that she thought it would burst. "You saved my life last night. When I wanted to fall apart you wouldn't let me." She allowed her eyes to convey what she was feeling. "You guided me to safety and watched over me all night, and now you've arranged for the Feds to rescue us. I know how jurisdictional you guys can be."

"This is about something more important to me than any case. What I've done here is about you and me. Please remember that despite whatever else may happen that I care for you."

Tears spilled from Jillian's eyes as she kissed him. "I care for you too."

He crushed her against him praying for time to stand still. He wanted and needed more time for them. He needed to be so deep inside Jillian's heart, that no matter what, her faith in him would be unshakable. But it wasn't to be. The sound of an approaching airplane drew his attention. Harrison ran to the edge of the trees and recognized the plane immediately as their ride. Relieved, that he and Jillian were still alive, yet doubtful about the future, he returned to her. "That's our ride."

Harrison waited in the trees until the plane stopped and the door opened. Two armed men in dark suits with assault weapons emerged and stood guard at the base of the steps. Only then did he and Jillian show themselves. The men immediately ran in their direction offering protection.

Harrison urged Jillian up the stairs while he talked privately with both men. He was informed of their destination, then led onboard as well. He saw Jillian's relief when he came to sit beside her. She reached out taking his hand in hers.

"Thank you for delivering me to safety." She leaned over kissing him.

"Fasten your seatbelt. We'll be taking off soon." Harrison caught the curious stares of their rescuers. Ignoring them, he finally relaxed and was soon asleep.

Jillian watched Harrison while he slept. She was thankful that he was finally getting some much-deserved sleep. As she looked at him, she noticed the numerous cuts and abrasions on his body from the foliage. Red welts from insect bites dotted his flesh. His face was smudged with dirt and blood, his clothes ripped and torn, not to mention filthy.

Jillian quickly checked her own appearance and realized she was just as dirty. The cute little white shirt she had put on yesterday morning would never be white again. And her shorts were just as battered as his. The cuts and abrasions on her arms were only now stinging. The insect bites covering her arms and legs were too numerous to count or care about. They were alive and that was all that mattered.

She settled back into the supple leather of the seat and took in her surroundings. This was her first time on a private jet and she intended to enjoy it. The plane seated six. There was a large movie screen up front. A stocked bar was positioned to the left of it with a restroom in the very rear. The opulence of the cabin was beyond her imagination. She couldn't believe the Feds owned something so extravagant, but considering the various types of jobs they performed, she concluded that it was probably used in undercover operations.

She sensed they were turning and looked out her window. They were following a coastline, but to where they were headed she didn't know. She sat back in her seat and caught one of the agents watching her. Glancing down at herself, she knew that she must be a fright. He smiled shyly and approached her.

"You will find everything that you need in the restroom to freshen up."

Jillian smiled with appreciation. "Thank you," she replied and anxiously unfastened her seatbelt. She entered the restroom and locked the door. In the bright light of the mirror she saw just how awful she really looked. Taking a washcloth out of the decorative basket on the sink, she turned on the hot water. There were several different scented soaps in the basket as well. She sniffed them all until she found one with a light clean fragrance.

She eventually emerged from the restroom feeling human again. Her hair had been brushed back into order and her body cleaned, but unfortunately she couldn't do anything about her clothing. Returning to her seat, she smiled her gratitude to the agent. Harrison was awake when she returned. He took her hand and assisted her back to her seat. She refastened her seatbelt.

"What are you doing awake? You need to rest," she whispered so only he could hear.

"I sensed your absence and woke up." He raised her hand to his lips. "I see you made good use of the restroom."

"I did what I could but it still isn't pretty. I wish I could burn these clothes." She made a face.

Harrison leaned over and kissed her tenderly. He pulled back and looked deeply into her eyes. "You'll always be beautiful to me."

"Thank you," Jillian replied kissing him.

Harrison rose to use the facilities, but turned back. "And about clothing, everything you require will be made available when we reach our destination."

"Which is?" She searched his face.

Harrison didn't see any harm in telling her where they were headed now. "The Caribbean."

The plane prepared to touch down on a private island in the Caribbean. The turquoise water surrounding it shimmered in the bright sunlight as they came in for the landing. Palm trees and ferns blew in the breeze below. White sandy beach stretched as far as the eye could see. Off in the distance sat a beautiful French Caribbean-style home with smaller bungalows and a pier. The plane finally came to a stop near several waiting jeeps.

As the door to the plane was opened and the stairs lowered, one of the men on board signaled for Harrison. He nodded and turned to Jillian. "Let me go see what these guys have planned. I'll be back for you in a moment."

"All right," she replied. But the moment Harrison and the men exited the plane, Jillian was out of her seat and at the window. She watched as Harrison shook hands with one of the men and then was embraced. Their smiles and pats on the back indicated that they were well acquainted. She wondered about that for a moment. Harrison never mentioned having worked with the Feds before, but knew the number from memory. As she thought further, she acknowledged that Harrison hadn't mentioned a great deal about himself to her. That niggling doubt was returning. She quickly jumped back into her seat as Harrison headed for the plane.

"They're ready for us, sweetie." Harrison reached out a hand to Jillian. He looked at her long and hard. Something wasn't right. Her features were pinched and her hand he noticed was trembling. "What's the matter? Are you not feeling well?" He placed the back of his hand against her forehead.

Jillian swatted his hand away. "I'm fine, just exhausted," she lied and discreetly removed her hand or so she thought.

Harrison didn't comment on her actions or pursue the truth with questions. There were more pressing matters at the moment. Like trying to keep his two separate worlds from colliding. He followed her off the plane and to the appointed jeep where he set behind the wheel. They were soon underway to the house.

Jillian rode in silence taking in the beauty of the island while Harrison zipped along. It was obvious to her that he had been to the island before. Blooming oleanders lined the narrow road they traveled. Their sweet floral fragrance perfumed the air. The sky was cloud free and the bluest she could ever remember seeing. But the late August sun was hot, sweltering hot, despite the breeze provided by the moving jeep. She glanced at Harrison wondering if she knew the man at all, then frowned because intellectually, she already knew the answer. Her heart, however, recognized him as the man who protected her with his life and saw her to safety. He was also the man who held her while she cried over the death of her son and the man who stirred the flames of desire inside of her.

Covering his hand with her own, Jillian held on to her faith in him and prayed that she wasn't being foolish.

Harrison glanced down at their hands. He looked at Jillian and saw all the unanswered questions in her eyes, but also the willingness to trust him. He grasped her hand and brought it to his lips. The time had come to lay his cards on the table. Jillian would either stay by his side or leave as he feared. Either way it had to be done. So he decided that after they were showered, clothed, and fed, he would speak to her. He prayed it wouldn't be the last meal they would share. Just then the villa came into view and he unconsciously squeezed Jillian's hand.

She glanced at him curiously. He was staring so oddly at the villa as though it held some great secret that he didn't want exposed. Her own fears escalated because somewhere in the back of her mind, she knew it held the secret of Harrison Blake.

The jeep stopped and Harrison climbed out then walked around to Jillian's side and reached for her. He led her to the front door and walked in as though he owned the place. The décor was stylish and casual. Rattan furniture decorated the main living area. Plants abounded throughout. The tile floor was in a rich, warm terracotta. The back side of the house was virtually a wall of glass overlooking the ocean.

Harrison didn't lead her out back, but instead turned right down the hallway. He pointed out the kitchen on the left. It too had a view of the water. On the right was a well-stocked library. Further down the hall was a large bathroom. And to the rear, four suites: two on the opposite sides of the hallway. The ones to the left had a view of the ocean and the others the manicured front lawn and gardens.

"You'll find everything you need in here," Harrison said as he led Jillian into the last room on the left. "I thought you would like the view of the ocean."

Jillian didn't comment and so he turned and faced her. "We need to talk," she said, searching his eyes.

Harrison nodded. "I agree but after a bath and some food." He opened the closet. Clothes with price tags still hanging from them filled the space. And rows of shoes lined the floor. "I hope I guessed your size correctly. A ten in clothing and a seven in shoes?" he asked.

Jillian was too stunned and frightened to respond verbally. She merely shook her head and accepted the kiss Harrison gave her.

"I'll meet you on the patio for lunch," he said and was gone. He closed the door to Jillian's room behind him and leaned against it for strength. It wasn't going to be pretty. Eventually pushing off he entered his suite. Going into the bathroom, he found everything as he had left it. He stripped away his grungy clothing and deposited the items into the trashcan. Finally standing in the marbled shower he turned on the water and enjoyed the feel of being cleansed.

Tears streaked Jillian's face. She was scared and knew that the man she cared for was indeed a stranger. The price tags of the clothes lining the closet must have totaled into the thousands alone. No cop or federal agency could afford to spend that kind of money on a witness. Something bigger, much bigger was going on here and she had nowhere to turn. With a heavy heart she dragged herself into the bathroom and thought she had died and gone to heaven. The bathroom was as big as her bedroom back home. Mirrors wrapped around two-thirds of the room. A double sink vanity stretched the complete length of one wall with an abundance of cabinets and drawers beneath it. A wicker basket contained an assortment of soaps, oils, and lotions. The fixtures were gold and the floor tiles white with blue and gold flecks. A double shower stall in white marble sat just inside the door. Further down the largest marble bathtub she had ever seen called her name. For the moment her fears and doubts could wait. Green vines grew around the base of the tub and candles in little gold holders lined it. Jacuzzi jets waited to be turned on. A window high above viewing offered bright sunlight as well as the skylight above.

Jillian stripped and washed her hair quickly in the shower. She promptly wrapped it with a towel afterwards, then proceeded to turn on the water in the bathtub. She selected a sea-breeze scented bath milk and added it to the water. Soon the whole bathroom was filled with the relaxing fragrance. Turning off the water, she slipped into the tub and sighed with pleasure. She had taken a towel and rolled it to use as a pillow. Now stretched out she allowed the water to soothe the aches and pains in her body. The cuts on her legs and arms stung initially, but the soothing water was slowing taking that away. With her eyes closed she replayed the last couple of days in her mind. One moment she and Harrison had been frolicking on the stairs, and the next they were running for their lives. She had killed a man. The thought caused her to cover her face with her hands as she cried. In between sobs, she prayed that the Lord would forgive her. Eventually the tears subsided and she began to scrub away the two-day grime.

Jillian tried to decide what to wear. She was back in front of the closet after towel drying her hair and creaming her body. The clothes were all beautiful and designed for island living. A sarong floral skirt and matching tube top caught her attention. It had an island flavor that she liked and would definitely be cool in. She quickly dressed but opted for no shoes. After having her feet closed in running shoes for several hours, she wanted nothing on her feet.

She left the suite in search of Harrison. The door to his suite was open so she guessed he was somewhere in the house. As she rounded the corner of the living and dinning room area, she saw him. He stood on the patio dressed in white linen pants and no shirt. His feet were bare as well. His hair was still wet from his shower and slicked back off his face. He turned in profile looking down the beach. Jillian seized the moment as an opportunity to observe him. His profile, though masculine, was softened by his eyes. She realized that they were his best feature. They were expressive and vibrant and now staring at her.

Harrison's stomach fluttered with anxiety. Jillian was examining him with a critical eye and it unnerved him. He watched as she walked through the open door of the patio. Her beauty took his breath away as she moved in his direction. The ensemble she had chosen to wear made her look very ethnic and apart of the island's history. Her hair was a mass of shining auburn ringlets. The gentle sway of her hips caused an ache in his groin and her bare feet invoked images of their escapades on the stairs. Damn, I can't lose her.

Jillian stood before him uncertain. She fought the urge to walk into his arms even though she knew he would welcome her.

"Lunch is served." Harrison waved to a table with covered dishes. He grabbed Jillian's hand taking her over. He couldn't ignore the resistance in her grip as she was led. She was going to put up one hell of a fight. He pulled out a chair for her, then took his own. Shrimp salad, bread, fruit, cheese, and juice awaited them. Harrison watched pleased as Jillian began eating. He guessed her stomach overruled her many questions. He too began to eat.

When the meal was devoured and they were stuffed, there was nothing left to occupy their attention from the pending discussion. But Harrison wasn't ready to get into it. He wanted to savor her love for a moment or two longer. He rose from his chair and asked for her hand. Jillian complied without argument to his delight.

"Let's walk on the beach."

Jillian pulled away and stared at him. "Let's talk."

"After our walk. I promise you that I'll tell you everything."

Jillian chewed on her lip a moment, then nodded her consent. She placed her hands behind her back when Harrison reached for her hand. They left the patio in silence and headed down toward the beach. There they walked side by side as Harrison assured her that she was safe on the island. "It's privately owned and secured. No one knows that we're here, so we should be quite safe."

"Forgive me if I don't believe everything that you say," Jillian shot back. She snapped her fingers and continued. "But then you don't say much do you?" She walked off ahead of him down the beach. It was beautiful and a paradise that she would love to share and explore with Harrison, but she no longer knew him. Everything that she thought she knew was crumbling into a heap of nothing.

Harrison caught up to Jillian and stopped her from walking away. "If you believe nothing else I have ever told you, believe that I care about you." His eyes were open and honest and he prayed Jillian could see that.

When she didn't pull away from him, he took it as a good sign. He cupped her face between his hands and kissed her. At first the kiss was a tender expression of his love, then it switched to passion and desperation. He ravaged her mouth with his own, kissing her deep and with purpose. His tongue mated with hers until he had heightened her passion. He lowered Jillian to the ground and spread out atop her. "You're in my heart."

Jillian lay staring up at him. She so desperately wanted and needed to believe him. Sandwiching his face with her hands, she forced him to meet her eyes. "If that's true, then tell me what's going on. Tell me who you are and where we are." She raised up returning the kiss with one of her own. "All I'm asking for is honesty. I can handle anything as long as you are honest with me."

"Oh, sweetie, if only it were that simple." He stroked her face lovingly.

"It is Harrison, just tell me," she pleaded.

Harrison wanted to believe her. Perhaps it was that simple. As he stared into her pleading eyes, he began to weaken. It was his only chance to save their relationship. Then his name was called and reality came crashing in on him. Jillian stilled and glanced up at Harrison. He was looking back in the direction of the house. His face was drawn and resigned. Jillian tried to crane her neck in the direction that he looked, but couldn't because of the way she was laying. Harrison sighed and rolled off. He sat facing the water with his head hanging down.

Jillian scrambled to her feet and shook the sand from her hair. She turned to see a tall man walking in their direction. She glanced back at Harrison noticing that he hadn't moved. The man was now upon them. He was dressed similar to Harrison except that he wore a linen tunic that made his olive complexion appear even darker. His eyes were a rich brown and piercing. Dark thick hair only showed a sprinkling of gray at the temples. He was handsome and oddly familiar. He extended his hand in introduction and smiled. Deep dimples framed his mouth as he spoke and Jillian knew instantly who he was.

"You're Harrison's father," she exclaimed excited.

He glanced down at his son and smiled. "Yes. Antonio DeMarco."

CHAPTER 11

Jillian snatched her hand back as though burned. She looked from one man to the other as Harrison rose and stood beside his father. Tears blinded her eyes as she realized she had been used and led to the slaughter. Her heart raced with the knowledge that she was trapped and there was no one to help her. But she had to try to escape. She wouldn't make it easy for them to get rid of her. Without a sound she took off running down the beach trying to make it to the grove of trees on the rise. Maybe she could lose them in there. Her feet dug into the sand trying desperately to place distance between herself and Harrison, who was pursuing. The trees were in sight and her hopes had escalated when she was pulled down from behind. She fell hard, having the breath knocked out of her and was roughly turned over and pinned.

Harrison glared down at her. "You never have to run from me, Jillian. I love you," he shouted in desperation.

"You liar, let go of me." Jillian struggled, freeing an arm. She took a swing at him and missed when he moved out of reach. But the next swing connected with the side of Harrison's face.

He grabbed the swinging arm and forced it down beside her. "Stop fighting me. I don't want to hurt you," he shouted trying to get her attention.

"No, you want me dead," she screamed.

"I love you, Jillian," Harrison reiterated. "I love you so much that I would give my life before I allow any harm to come to you."

"Stop lying," Jillian screamed and twisted, trying to get free. "You played with me like a mouse in a cage, knowing that you would feed me to that snake later."

"Jillian, think about what you're saying. I was with you when those bullets tore through the cabin. I could have been killed just like you. My father didn't do this. He's trying to help us."

Jillian heard what she wanted to hear. She was too angry to be rational. "Help you maybe, but he wants me dead. I know Melvin worked for your father. Who do you believe killed him, Harrison, if not your father?"

"Yes, he worked for Pop, but their business was legitimate."

Jillian rolled her eyes in frustration as she tried to throw him off again. "Stop lying to yourself. Josh told me that the police suspected Antonio DeMarco of ordering Melvin's murder."

Harrison cursed. He released Jillian's arms to bury his fingers into her mop of hair. Tugging the strands, he forced her to look at him as he spoke the next words. "Josh told you about my father to get back at me. I pissed him off in the captain's office and he dropped my father's name to you the first chance he got. He expected you to run to the media and demand my father's arrest, subsequently focusing a light on me as well."

"Are you saying that your father isn't a suspect?" She shoved against his chest.

"My father will always be a suspect, Jillian. You know how the law is. He's a member of a crime family. It doesn't matter that he's no longer in the business, he will always be under suspicion."

Jillian mulled this over. "How did Josh discover your connection?"

"Simple," Harrison said releasing her altogether. She was talking to him and not screaming so he saw it as a good sign. He sat facing the water with his knees raised and his arms resting atop them. "When I applied for the police force I had to consent to a background check. You have to disclose any criminal activity in your past and your family's." He looked over at Jillian who was now sitting beside him. "I told the truth on my application."

Jillian shook her head trying to process all of this. The man she had fallen in love with was the son of a notorious crime figure. "What possessed you to become a cop?"

Harrison smiled and looked out over the water. "Guilt. I remember in grade school that I thought my Pop worked in an office somewhere. He would be dressed in fine suits and discuss business over the phone. Then when I was in high school, I started hearing rumors and following the articles printed in the newspapers. But I still couldn't believe or maybe I didn't want to believe that my father was the man everyone was whispering about. My Pop wasn't evil or brutal like the newspapers reported. The man I knew was soft-spoken, kind, and good to my mother and us kids. Pop was always at our school functions and sporting events." Harrison paused to look at her and was pleased to see that the fear was gone. He never wanted Jillian to be afraid of him. "Then one day I could stand the whispers no more. I walked into his home office and boldly asked him if the rumors were true."

Jillian touch his arms drawing his attention. "What did he say?"

Harrison covered her hand with his and was pleased when she didn't pull away. He looked her in the eyes as he spoke. "Pop asked me if he had been a good father, to which I replied yes. Next, he asked if I went without, and I replied no. He asked me if I had ever seen him do anything criminal and again I replied no. Then he looked at me and asked to be judged based on his actions." Harrison rubbed her hand and looked back out over the water. "And that's what I did."

"You couldn't stop loving him despite what you knew." She was looking at him. "So you became a cop to make up in a way for the wrongs your father committed."

"If you say so." He looked over at her and smiled.

Jillian returned the smile then leaned against him. Only time would tell if she was being a fool, but at the moment she believed him.

"So where does Blake come from?"

Harrison smiled and kissed her head. "It's my mother's maiden name. We all use it."

"How many is we?"

"Two boys and two girls. I'm the third oldest."

"So where is home?" She rested her chin against his arm as she looked at him.

"That's a little difficult to say. I was born and raised in New Jersey, just outside of Trenton. But my parents currently reside in Florida. This place has been a vacation spot for years." He caressed her head with his.

"Why join the Birmingham Police Department? It's so obscure when you think of all the other police forces."

"I joined for that reason and the fact that Birmingham is my mother's home. When I came to town, my grandparents were still living and so I got to spend time with them."

Jillian sat up and faced him. "Your mother is from Birmingham? Well, how in the devil did a southern girl end up married to an East Coast crime figure?"

Harrison laughed at Jillian's obvious surprise. "They met in college like most couples."

"Did she know what your father did for a living?"

"I never asked her, but there was no doubt in my mind that she knew. They are very close and I can't see him marrying her without giving her the choice of walking away."

Jillian didn't think about her next words, she simply let them free. "Their love was built on mutual trust." She looked at him meaningfully. "Why didn't you trust me with the truth? You claim to love me. Couldn't you have given me the chance to decide if our love was worth staying for?"

Harrison suddenly stood and walked to the water's edge. The incoming tide surged over his feet then back out. He wasn't looking at Jillian when he began talking. "I dated a girl in college. We were in love and both talking about marriage. But she was a political science major with aspirations to enter politics one day and I felt obligated to tell her about my family. I really didn't think it would matter. Of course, her plans would have to change, but we were in love and I thought she would choose me. I purchased an engagement ring and took her out to a nice restaurant for dinner. Later I proposed, but before she answered I told her about my family."

"She chose her career over you," Jillian finished the story. She came up behind him and encircled his waist. Her head rested against his strong back. "And you were afraid that if you told me the truth, I would leave too."

He rubbed her arms. "Yes. I knew I had to tell you, but I wanted to be so deeply imbedded inside your heart that the truth wouldn't matter."

Jillian smiled against his back at the thought. "For starters, Harrison, I'm not a girl. And secondly, you are deeply imbedded inside my heart. I love you. Lastly, as long as I know you aren't involved in illegal activity, I don't care who your father is. But I'm trusting you when you tell me he's legit."

"I give you my word that he is."

"What about the armed guards?"

Harrison turned in her arms to face her. "He's made enemies over the years. The guards are strictly for his protection. My siblings and I have never had anything to do with his business nor have we been touched by it, but when I called him needing help, Pop didn't hesitate to come to our rescue."

"I'm grateful for that." Jillian smiled up at him.

"So, you love me?" Harrison asked wrapping his arms around her. His eyes were soft and expressive.

"Most definitely." Jillian kissed him. She wrapped her arms around his neck and held him close. "All I ask is that you be honest with me."

"You have my word."

The remainder of the afternoon was spent with Harrison opening up and sharing his life with Jillian. They spoke of childhood memories and desires for the future. Kisses were shared and loving touches exchanged. Eventually they made their way back to the villa. On returning, a note from Antonio was discovered on the dining room table. It contained an apology for upsetting Jillian and disrupting Harrison's life once again. He ended by saying that he would return in a couple of days to make a formal apology. Harrison continued to stare at the note long after they both had read it. He was quiet and thoughtful.

"Where will he spend the night, if this is the family estate?" Jillian asked.

"There's a bed and breakfast on the neighboring island. Pop won't have any trouble getting boarding. Despite what people think of him in the states, he is highly respected down here."

"He loves you."

"I know."

"And I love you." She leaned in kissing him.

"That, I'll never get tired of hearing."

Jillian chewed her lower lip as she eased from his arms and walked across the room. She turned back facing him. Her face held a comical expression. "Speaking of hearing. You don't think your father heard me call him a snake, do you?"

Harrison looked at Jillian and burst out into laughter as he joined her across the room. He reached for her but she dodged him.

"Don't laugh at me." Jillian punched him in the arm.

Harrison laughed even harder. "Oh, sweetie, the whole eastern seaboard heard." His eyes held tears.

"What am I going to do?" She walked up to him and buried her head in his chest.

Harrison continued to laugh. He eventually managed to pull himself together. When he did, he kissed Jillian's bowed head. "He's going to love you as much as I do." His voice, a blend of east and south, held so much emotion that Jillian raised her head to look at him.

"I hope that you're right, but what if your parents are opposed to us? Will that affect our relationship?"

Harrison looked at Jillian closely and realized that she had gone from being playful to serious. He took her in his arms and held her close. "I'm a 35-year-old man, Jillian. No one tells me who to love." Then he set her back from him so that he could look into her face. "And what about you? How will you react if your parents aren't pleased about us?"

"I told you, my parents didn't place limitations on us."

"That's not an answer."

Jillian huffed and glared at him. "The only person that can destroy my love for you is you, Harrison. You laid your life on the line for me at the cabin and got me out of that house when I wanted to fall apart. You risked losing me in an effort to save me, and the thing I love most about you, is the fact that you held me when the pain of my son's death got to be too much, even though I was a stranger." Her eyes held all the love and emotions that she expressed.

"Ah, sweetie." Harrison pulled Jillian back into his protective arms. "I'll be your shelter through any storm, be it natural or man-made."

"You have been. From the moment this case began up to now, and that's why it was so easy to fall in love with you."

Harrison's heart swelled with pride and love. Her words made speaking impossible as he fought to keep his emotions in check. But no one had ever made him feel more special or loved than Jillian.

After a light meal the couple sat on the patio enjoying the beauty of the twilight hour. A gentle breeze carried the fragrance of island flowers. Jillian was lying in Harrison's arms on the chaise wishing that her life could be as perfect as the moment, but she knew that wasn't possible. Someone out there wanted her dead and Travis would never be in her arms again.

Harrison sensed her distress. When he leaned forward to get a glimpse of her face, there were tears in her eyes. He held her a little tighter and whispered that he loved her. He left her to her private thoughts and simply held her.

Eventually the events of the last two days began to take their toll. Jillian and Harrison both grew weary and called an end to the evening. Harrison secured the villa, then led Jillian down the hallway to their respective rooms. They shared a kiss then parted. Harrison leaned against his closed door fighting thoughts of Jillian sleeping alone in the bed across the hall. The pressure in his crotch grew heavy with the need to crawl in beside her. He forced himself away from the door and entered the bathroom where he took a much-needed cold shower. Stepping out of the shower, he grabbed a towel and dried off quickly, then returned to the bedroom where he crawled in between the cool crisp sheets. It didn't take long before he was sound asleep.

Jillian lounged briefly in the tub across the hall. The peach scent of the bubble bath perfumed the room and helped to mellow her mood. She replayed all that had happened to her over the last several months, not recognizing her life. One moment in time had changed the course of her ordinary life. Now here she was being protected and loved by the son of a known crime figure. She rose from the tub and reached for her towel, then proceeded to dry off and step out. She stood before the mirror while moisturizing her body. As her hands traveled over her stomach, she examined the two tiny marks, evidence of her carrying a child. She covered her flat abdomen with her hand and wondered if it would ever hold life again. Suddenly she felt empty inside and depressed. Quickly dressing in a sheer white, island gauze gown, which was the closest thing to being nude, Jillian returned to the bedroom and eased into bed. The exhaustion poured from her body as she gave in to sleep.

CHAPTER 12

Around midnight a stormed moved in. The wind picked up as lightning flashed and thunder rumbled overhead. The rain came down in sheets and beat against the windowpanes. A storm shutter somewhere in the house thumped in the wind. Jillian was instantly awake as a clap of thunder shook the house. She sat up in bed as blinding lightning lit the room. The trees outside her window could be seen swaying in the turbulent wind, first in one direction then in another. Her pulse increased as the storm intensified and grew louder by the moment. She covered her ears with her hands to block out the sound, but it didn't work. The sound of the raging storm still could be heard. She jumped out of bed and flipped on the light switch hoping to lessen the effects of the lightning, but when she did, nothing happened. Desperate for lighting, she entered the bathroom and lit one of the candles from around the tub.

Something woke him up. Harrison opened his eyes and glanced out the window. Lightning flashed and the rain poured down. His thoughts instantly went to Jillian as he realized a storm had set in. He rolled over with the intention of going to her when the room was illuminated by a flash of lightning, and there just inside the doorway stood Jillian. She held a candle in her trembling hands. Her eyes were fixed on the window and the storm outside. Harrison's eyes were fixed on her beautiful body visible through the sheer gauze gown. When a clap of thunder rocked the house again, Jillian whimpered and drew his attention once more.

Her eyes were wild with fear as she looked at him. "I...couldn't... sleep," she forced out the words while keeping an eye on the window. She jumped as lightning flashed again.

Harrison's heart went out to her. He hated to see her like this and knew that the storm brought back memories of that tragic night. "Come here, sweetie." He held back the covers for her to climb in.

Jillian didn't hesitate. She practically ran across the room and deposited the candle on the nightstand, before sliding into bed beside him. She backed in and slid into his waiting arms. Pressing against the length of his body, Jillian suddenly realized that Harrison was nude, but the thought was quickly forgotten as the storm intensified and something slammed against the window. "What was that?" she cried, pressing closer.

"Calm down," Harrison crooned while stroking her hair. He tightened his arms around her and caressed her cheek with his own. "Something hit the window, but its okay. We're safe in here."

"I hate storms," Jillian cried.

"I know, sweetie." Harrison kissed her cheek.

Jillian turned in his arms to rest her head against his chest. He was warm and solid, the perfect shelter from the storm. "The memories are stronger on nights like these," she wept.

"Then it's time to make new memories." Harrison kissed her cheek and grabbed the hem of her gown, slowly raising it over her hips, then up her torso and over her head. He tossed the flimsy garment to the floor and gave her his undivided attention. A flash of lightning illuminated Jillian's gloriously nude body. He wrapped a hand around her neck and back and gently eased her body down beside him. His eyes searched hers for any doubt or resistance to what was about to happen, but found none. The whiskey-brown of her eyes held passion and quiet anticipation. A clap of thunder broke the moment, as Jillian's eyes strained to the window, but Harrison soon got it back when he lowered his mouth to hers. He pressed gently against her soft lips, then trailed kisses along her jaw up to her diamond-studded lobes. His hands grasped dark ringlets of hair as his mouth returned to hers.

Jillian met his kiss with equal fervor. Their tongues twined and dueled while the storm raged outside. Her hands caressed his back while his mouth performed love acts yet to come. The performance escalated her passion and caused Jillian to arch into him. She drew his practiced tongue into her mouth for a performance of her own. Stroke after stroke, she teased him.

Harrison sighed with sheer pleasure and allowed Jillian to have her way. He was completely content to kiss her all night. That mouth of hers was as talented as his and together they stoked the fires of passion. He rolled onto his back carrying Jillian with him. While their mouths feasted, his hands learned the feel and shape of her body. The palms of his large hands skimmed the flesh of her soft, smooth back, and the round firm cheeks of her pleasing rump. He squeezed gently as his teeth nipped her lower lip.

Jillian gasped and wiggled in his hands. She then returned the love bite and proceeded to sink her teeth into the flesh behind an ear, the column of his neck, and lower to claim a male nipple between her teeth. Her tongue brushed against the sensitive pebble while imprisoned in her mouth. Harrison's startled moan was reward for a job well done. But just as she was about to torture the other bud, Harrison reversed their positions and securing her hands within one of his own, he raised them high over her head. The position forced her breasts to aim for the sky. And like a seeking predator circling overhead, Harrison spotted his prey, and swooped down to seize it. The right nipple fell victim to his talents as he sucked the delectable blackberry into his mouth. He applied just enough pressure to make Jillian clamp her legs tight from the sensation. She writhed and moaned as he treated the left breast to similar delights.

As Harrison repeatedly lowered his mouth to her brown breasts, Jillian watched fascinated. The scene wasn't as strange as she had once imagined. This wasn't just some white man loving her, this was Harrison—her man—loving her and oh, what a job he was doing. Jillian arched in agony as his free hand replaced his mouth on her breast. It squeezed and caressed the already sensitive nipple.

Harrison's heart raced wildly as his mind thought of ways to love Jillian. He wanted to erase all memories of other men. He released her arms while his mouth went lower down her torso. His tongue flicked in her small navel and detected the faint scent of peaches. Going lower he parted her thighs as he savored her like the plump sweet fruit. With his mouth tormenting her so deliciously, Jillian ached her back and released a satisfied moan.

Her body was on fire. She tangled her fingers in his thick dark head of hair and held on. The pleasure was so sweet that Jillian began to cry. It had been three long, lonesome years and the feeling overwhelmed her.

Harrison kissed his way back up Jillian's body, then flipped her over onto her stomach. A bolt of lightning caught the surprise in her eyes. He swept her hair to the side as he kissed his way down the back of her body. His hands kneaded and caressed the flesh of her body; all the while Jillian squirmed in anticipation. Harrison didn't disappoint her. His hand slid between her thighs. Jillian's breath caught at the initial invasion. Soon the fire Harrison was so carefully building became a raging inferno requiring attention. But despite her sounds of pleasures and words of encouragement to take the next step, Harrison continued to stroke her, while his mouth tormented the flesh behind her ear.

Jillian was throbbing with need. She begged, twisted, and asked for what she wanted, but Harrison continued to deny her. Then in another quick move, he had her on her back again. But instead of just lying there waiting to be pleasured, Jillian administered a little pleasure of her own. She leaned forward caressing Harrison's chest and further down his body. She returned the favor and dipped her tongue into his navel while sliding down his body. But as she tried to go lower, Harrison hauled her back up. He could see the confusion in her eyes.

"I don't need that from you. What I gave you was a gift, an expression of my love that I don't expect nor need returned."

Jillian nodded as tears formed in her eyes. She drew his head down to hers and expressed her love for him with a scorching kiss.

Harrison reached into the nightstand and removed a condom. He quickly tore it open and with Jillian's assistance rolled it on. The feel of her small hands on him had him hard and heavy. He grabbed her legs and pulled them apart. The object of his desire beckoned him. Positioning himself at her entrance, he tensed as Jillian guided him home. Harrison was a large man, and feeling the evidence of Jillian's three-year inactivity caused him to go slow. He gently slid inside of her and went deep. He found and nudged that spot which made Jillian cry out in ecstasy.

Their eyes met and held as they finally became one. The pleasure of their union was sweltering hot. With each stroke Harrison made into her body, Jillian rose to meet it. Quickly the pace escalated into a maddening tempo as perspiration bathed their bodies and the sound of their lovemaking drowned out the raging storm. But they didn't stop. The pleasure was too great. Jillian contracted around Harrison as he came into her with a powerful thrust. The pressure she applied nearly stole his breath away. He groaned from the bottom of his gut up to his chest and eventually the back of his throat. He sucked in much-needed air as Jillian contracted around him again. He cursed, releasing her thighs and lowered his body on to her. He buried his head in the bend of her neck while fighting the urge to pump till completion. "Sweetie, another move like that and I'm going to nail you to this bed."

But Jillian wasn't afraid to be loved by him. She locked her legs around his hips and teased his back with her nails. An arch of her spine sent him even deeper and he groaned again, but kept a hard rhythmic pace going. Jillian's nails went lower to scratch his bottom at the same time she undulated her hips and squeezed. Harrison's groan was as loud as the thunder rumbling overhead. He humped his back and delivered on his promise. The panting sound of Jillian in his ear spurred him on and when the sound turned to a keening noise, he knew it wouldn't be much longer. Two final thrusts later, he and Jillian screamed the house down as their bodies arched and convulsed with pleasure.

Harrison rolled onto his back and sucked in a much-needed breath. He stretched and sighed deeply before glancing over at Jillian. She was watching him with tears in her eyes. It alarmed him. "Did I hurt you?" his voice was filled with panic as he turned and reached out to her. "I know it got a little rough, but..."

Jillian silenced him with a kiss. She stared into his worried eyes, knowing that she had never loved any man the way that she did Harrison. "These aren't tears of pain, but of joy." She blinked and a tear rolled down her cheek. "The joy I discovered in making love with you."

"Oh, Jillie." he pulled her against him.

"You've never called me that before." Jillian leaned back slightly to look at him.

"I know. I figured you-know-who probably called you that and I didn't want to do anything like he did." He shrugged a shoulder. "But I recalled Faye calling you that and liked it. It just slipped out."

Jillian forced Harrison onto his back then proceeded to crawl on top of him. She traced his hairline and kissed the bridge of his nose. "I like it when you call me sweetie. It makes me feel special inside." She undulated her hips against his recovering member. "And lover boy, you did nothing like him." To prove her point, Jillian rose and sat back on Harrison. He filled every pulsating inch of her as she began to rock against him. Their eyes were locked in the moment as Jillian created another firestorm. Unable to stand the pleasure, Harrison closed his eyes and threw his head back into the pillow. His hands clamped around her waist and assisted with her provocative efforts. The pace increased and the prize was just in sight. Jillian arched her back and slid down on him with a final move and hurled them both over the edge into ecstasy.

For the longest time neither of them moved. Jillian remained sprawled out on top of Harrison, while he stroked her damp hair. Their heart rates were finally returning to normal as the storm outside died down. Harrison glanced down his body to where Jillian lay. The experience of loving her was the most beautiful in his life and also the most frightening. In the back of his mind he was constantly reminded that someone wanted her dead. He could lose this love if he didn't get back and locate the responsible party. His body tensed with anger.

Jillian registered the change in Harrison. She raised her head to meet his dark brooding eyes. There was no need to ask what was on his mind because she knew. It was always in the back of hers as well. But this was their moment and she didn't want it interrupted with bad thoughts. She slid from his body to stand at the foot of the bed.

"Where are you going?" Harrison whispered alarmed.

She smiled like the seductress she was feeling. "Now that it appears the storm has passed, I'm going to run us a bath, then proceed to bathe you. Is that all right with you?" Her eyes were heavy with desire.

Harrison didn't answer right away. His own eyes were too busy taking in the full view of Jillian in the soft glow of candlelight. Her breasts were high and firm, the nipples berry-size and dark, her waist curved perfectly down to hips made for holding on to and her long legs were beacons of desire sheltering her hidden treasure. They had made love equally and just as heatedly to the other. She held nothing back and demanded what she wanted. And he had given it freely over and over again. As he began to harden for the third time, Martin's words tripped across his mind. Jillian was indeed inflicting damage on his body, but he was more than willing to allow her. "Quite all right," he responded getting out of bed.

He followed Jillian into the bathroom and watched as she lit the candles around the bathtub. When she bent over to sprinkle bath salts into the water, he grabbed her around the waist and positioned her over the vanity. The box of bath salts fell to the floor as she reached out grabbing the marble counter top. Their eyes met in the mirror over the vanity as he eased in behind her and loved her once more. The pace was maddeningly slow as he took his time loving her. He watched the play of emotion in her face as he eased in and out. Then when neither could take the pace any longer, he drove into her increasing the tempo. They climaxed together and collapsed onto the floor. Eventually they made it into the tub.

"I've never done that before," Jillian whispered from her side of the tub. Her foot teased the juncture of his thighs.

His eyes were on her. "What haven't you done before?"

"The vanity deal."

Harrison's eyes widened as he realized what Jillian was saying. "Never?"

She shook her head no, as she continued to play under the water. "I've only been with two men and you're one of them."

"I thought as much." He caressed her foot. "Did you like it?" Harrison watched her. "If you didn't, I'll never do it again." He didn't want to do anything that made her uncomfortable.

Jillian laughed, then bit her lip shyly. Her eyes sparkled in the candlelight. "Don't you dare. I enjoyed it very much." She smiled over at him. "My marriage and marriage bed was very traditional. I wanted the passion that I saw between my parents and Faye and David. I wanted the secretive glances and the gentle caresses. I wanted to cuddle and whisper in the dark. I remember as a child hearing my parent's hushed voices and then their laughter. It always made me feel safe and secure because I knew they loved each other. But our marriage was just the opposite. It was cold and restrictive. Everyone had a role to play and no deviations were allowed."

From what they had shared tonight, Harrison knew Jillian hadn't been satisfied in bed or in her marriage. "I just want to please you, Jillian." He whispered and grabbed her leg, pulling her down to his end. Water spilled onto the floor, but no one paid it any attention. Harrison claimed her mouth in a passionate kiss while his hands went on underwater maneuvers.

Another line of storms moved in just before dawn. Jillian and Harrison were asleep. They lay spooned together as the first clap of thunder followed by lightning shook the house. Jillian jumped and tensed beside Harrison. He awoke and didn't give Jillian a chance to panic. His hand resting on her belly slipped lower and soon had her melting around him. He whispered erotic words in her ear while his hands demonstrated. The rhythm in bed escalated with the storm outside.

Jillian closed her eyes and leaned against Harrison as he stoked the fire inside her once more. The brightness of the lightning could still be detected behind closed lids, but the activity going on below was far more demanding. She curved an arm around Harrison's head as she arched against him.

The pressure was building and just in reach, when the most blinding lightning flashed in the sky and turned the whole world white. Her eyes were open, but not to the room. In the backseat of the parked sedan, she saw him. He was in profile, but she would have recognized him anywhere.

"Josh!" Jillian screamed and convulsed.

"What the hell?" Harrison roared and practically leaped from the bed. He towered over Jillian hurt.

Jillian sat up in bed as Harrison's words brought her back to the present. She blinked and stared at him excited. "Harrison..."

He cut her off. "It's too late, Jillie, you've already called his name."

Shaking her head in confusion, Jillian tried to make Harrison listen. "No, listen to me..."

"I heard you, Jillian. People don't lie in the throes of passion. They call the name of the one they love." His face was hard with suppressed rage. He was nude and didn't care. His heart was breaking and he felt like a damn fool.

Jillian finally understood what Harrison was talking about. Desperate to make him understand, she sprang from the bed and kissed him passionately. When he tried to push her away she held on tighter. He was quiet and glaring at her when she released him. She finally got the chance to speak. "I love you and only you. But I remember now. It was Josh I saw in the backseat of the sedan. A bolt of lightning flashed and lit up the parking garage, like the one a moment ago, and I saw him. He was in profile, but I would know Josh anywhere." As the words left her, the realization of what she had just said, set in on her. She collapsed onto the bed and began to cry. The man she had once loved and created a child with wanted her dead. Her shoulders shook with racking sobs.

Harrison eased down beside Jillian finally understanding. He wrapped her in his arms only imagining the pain she must be experiencing. Although she had made wisecracks about Josh wanting her dead, neither of them had believed it or taken the comments seriously, but now it appeared that maybe she was right.

"Jillian, I'll nail his hide to the wall before he gets another chance at you." He scooped her into his arms and repositioned her in bed. Easing in beside her, he could only hold her and tell her that he loved her. For the time being, this moment was the most important and he intended to get her through it. He would focus his attention and mounting rage on the man responsible for Jillian's pain in the morning.

Josh William's backside belonged to him and he intended to collect full payment on behalf of Jillian and Travis.

CHAPTER 13

Jillian began preparing breakfast the next morning while Harrison retrieved the backpack from his bedroom closet. He entered the kitchen and began spreading the faxed documents from Martin over the kitchen table. He was searching for a connection to Josh. There was a list of clients and corresponding account numbers. There was also paperwork from a bank down in the Cayman Islands. Martin had contacted the bank and received a printout of the last six months transactions. The activity on the account belonging to Melvin was frequent and the balance in the millions. Harrison was quite sure he had found the motive for the accountant's murder. Now all he had to do was find a connection between Melvin and Josh.

He spotted his father's name on the client list. A Touch of Italy was his father's newest restaurant, which opened in Birmingham last year. But nothing to connect Josh to Melvin. Harrison became disappointed and tossed the papers in a kitchen drawer. He joined Jillian over at the stove. Wrapping an arm around her waist, he nibbled on her earlobe.

"How are you doing this morning?"

Jillian laughed as she pressed into him. "A little exhausted."

"Yeah, but it's a good exhaustion," Harrison commented, turning her around in his arms to kiss her. The sound of a boat motor caught their attention. Harrison released her to peek out the kitchen window and spotted his father's boat docking.

"It appears my father couldn't wait a couple of days."

Jillian turned off the stove and moved to the window in time to see Antonio step out onto the pier. "I'm glad he's here actually. I can get my apology out of the way."

"It's going to be fine." Harrison squeezed her shoulders reassuringly. "Come on, let's go meet him."

The couple walked down the pier to meet their guest halfway. Harrison and his father shook hands, then Harrison made proper introductions.

"Mr. DeMarco," Jillian greeted the older version of Harrison with an outstretched hand.

"Antonio, please." He clasped Jillian's hand and brought it to his lips in an old-world greeting. "I apologize for upsetting you yesterday."

"I'm the one who owes you an apology. I'm really sorry for my behavior and words."

Antonio still held Jillian's hand. He covered it with his other hand affectionately. "Let's call it even." He gave her a broad smile similar to Harrison's.

"I was just placing breakfast on the table," Jillian said to him. "Will you join us?"

"I'd be delighted." He smiled down at her, then at his son. The three of them returned to the villa with Jillian and Antonio walking arm in arm.

Over breakfast Harrison informed his father of how he and Jillian met. He told him about the sniper at her office and the attack on the cabin. He expressed his suspicion about someone associated with the police department working with the person responsible. Lastly he informed Antonio about Jillian remembering seeing Josh at the scene of the murder.

"I remember Mr. Williams from his opposition to your being a member of the police force," Antonio added. "He also opposed my opening the restaurant."

"What restaurant?" Jillian asked, looking at Harrison then his father.

"A Touch of Italy," Harrison answered, pointing at his father.

Jillian's eyes widened at the news. "You took me to your father's restaurant?" Jillian looked at Harrison. To Antonio, she said, "I love that place."

"Well I'm glad to hear it," Antonio responded proudly.

"It was Josh who told me that you were responsible for the murder and the attempt on my life," Jillian told him.

Antonio nodded as he took it all in. "After Harrison phoned for help, I did a little checking into Mr. Williams' past." He gave Jillian a meaningful glance.

Jillian could feel her face muscles stiffen as Antonio looked at her. She knew that if he investigated Josh, then it was inevitable, that he had investigated her as well. She didn't know him well enough to read. No longer comfortable in his presence, she rose from the table to walk over to the window. Glancing out she said, "So you know that I was married to Josh and that I killed our child?"

Harrison was out of his seat in a flash. He embraced Jillian. "You did not kill your child."

"You love me, Harrison. But your father doesn't know me and may see things differently. Let's hear what he has to say." They both turned to look at Antonio who now stood.

"Jillian, I didn't mean to upset you again, but Harrison is my child and I had to know what was going on." He ran a hand through his hair.

Jillian noticed the habit and smiled to herself. Father and son were so much alike and yet so different. "I understand."

He advanced and took her hands within his. He gave them a fatherly squeeze. "Josh cheated on you because he was jealous of your intelligence and legal talent. He's the type of man who has to be center stage, and with you, he had to share it. You deliberately tried to remain in the background, though you are by far the more talented one. You turned down several prestigious job offers so as not to outshine your husband."

"Is that true?" Harrison asked touching her shoulder.

Jillian cringed just remembering the arguments they had had over the job offers. "I really wanted that teaching position at Cumberland School of Law, but they hadn't approached Josh with an offer and he saw everything as a competition. Now we're on opposing sides again."

Antonio released Jillian's hands and returned to his place at the table. The next bit of news he had to deliver wouldn't be easy. "Harrison."

"Yeah, Pop?" Harrison returned to the table as well.

"The police have issued a warrant for your arrest."

"What?" Jillian shouted and hurried over to the table.

"I'll be damn," Harrison roared. "What is Josh accusing me of doing?"

"He's claiming that the cabin incident was staged to cover up the fact that you delivered a police witness to your father, the suspect."

"I don't believe this," Jillian wailed as she took a seat. "Josh is accusing you." She pointed to Antonio, "of a crime he knows he committed." She then looked at Harrison. "And he's trying to ruin your career."

"I don't give a damn about my career. Right now I'm worried about saving your life and clearing my father's name." Harrison walked over to the kitchen drawer where he had stashed Melvin's papers. He came back to the table and stood between his father and Jillian, spreading them out. "Martin faxed me these papers from Melvin's personal computer. These documents came from a password-protected file. There's a client list and some online banking records of transactions. From what I can tell, he was skimming money from all of his big clients. You included, Pop."

"Which is a definite motive," Jillian commented.

"You're right, but only if we can find a link between Melvin and Josh," Harrison responded.

Jillian and Antonio crowded together examining the list while Harrison looked on. Nothing stood out as the names of clients were read off the list. Jillian was growing disappointed. Then near the end of the first page, three items from the bottom, a name leaped off the page to her.

"I know this one," she called out pointing to the business.

Harrison and Antonio strained to see the company she was pointing to. "Magic City Construction," Antonio read out loud.

Jillian took off running out of the kitchen to both men's surprise. "Where are you going?" Harrison called behind her.

She paused just long enough to answer. "I have documents on this company. I'll be right back." She continued on to her room and located the cargo shorts she had been wearing the day they were attacked on the floor in the closet. Releasing the button on the pocket, she withdrew the folded documents and headed back to the kitchen. When she arrived, both men looked at her curiously.

"I have a client who works for this company as a foreman. He suspected the owner of the company of using inferior building supplies and made a formal complaint to the city's building inspector, Thomas Lynch. When nothing happened, he went to the police with his suspicions about Harold Compton. But the next day, he received a package in the mail at home. Inside the package were supply invoices with his signature at the bottom."

"They sent him a message," Antonio stated coolly. "He would be the one implicated if he continued to talk."

Jillian eyed the man curiously. There was no doubt in her mind that he had sent a couple of messages in his day. "Exactly. So he comes to me for legal advice," Jillian picked up her story. "After hearing what he had to say, I wanted to know who this Compton guy was and as much as I could about Magic City Construction."

"I take it you found your answer?" Harrison asked.

Jillian answered by spreading the documents on the table for both men to examine. Harrison whistled as he read over the information, then looked hard at Jillian. She knew that glare didn't mean anything good, so she waited.

"This information alone will get you killed," Harrison bellowed angrily. "Why didn't you show it to me?"

Jillian returned his heated stare and raised her chin defiantly. "At the time I didn't know that the two were connected and I sure as heck didn't want to draw attention to the fact that I had such incriminating information in my possession."

Antonio watched the fire between the two. He knew passion when he saw it and Jillian and Harrison were a perfect match for each other.

"All right, I can understand that," Harrison reluctantly admitted.

"I also recognize the name now," Antonio added. "This company has been building all over the southeast. They have undercut bids and effectively placed other companies out of business. There were rumors about materials, but the building inspectors didn't find anything."

"Of course not. According to these documents, they have paid off inspectors all across the southeast," Jillian told them what she knew.

Harrison began pacing the kitchen while putting all the pieces together. "Okay so we have Josh at the scene of Melvin's murder. And we know Melvin was stealing from Magic City Construction which has been paying off city building inspectors.

"But why would Josh kill Melvin is the question." Harrison put forth.

Antonio shuffled papers on the table. He finally pulled one from the bottom of the stack out. He read over it for a moment before placing it on the table. "This is a record of banking accounts and transactions that Melvin made." He glanced down the list. "Here it is, Magic City Construction."

Harrison grabbed the paper. "There are deposits made on behalf of Magic City Construction to an account in the Cayman Islands."

"No doubt where they're stashing the profits from cutting corners," Antonio commented. "Whose name is listed on the account?"

Harrison located the page before that one and began reading off the names. "Actually there are four names listed."

"Four?" Jillian remarked confused. "So there are four people who make up Magic City Construction?"

"It appears that way," Harrison responded. "But Josh's name isn't listed."

"If his name isn't listed, then what's the motive?" Jillian asked baffled.

"I don't know, but the names listed on this account are Harland Chandler, Wayne Miles, Trent Long, and Travis Brown."

Jillian collapsed into the nearest chair as she exclaimed, "Oh my God!"

Harrison and Antonio looked at her expectantly. Harrison came and crouched in front of her. He could see that she was stunned by something that she had heard or read. "What is it, sweetie?" Harrison encouraged her to answer.

Jillian's eyes were void of emotion. She looked completely shell-shocked. "Travis Brown is Josh's real name," she whispered disbelievingly.

Harrison's brow furrowed as he tried to make sense of Jillian's words. "What do you mean his real name?"

She clutched his hand resting on her knee. "Josh's mother was a teenager when he was born. She named him Travis after his father and Brown was her maiden name. When he was seven, she married a man named Joshua Williams. Josh adores him and as a child he wanted to carry his father's name, but of course Mr. Williams wasn't his father. So when he turned ten, Mr. Williams legally adopted him and had his name changed from Travis Brown to Joshua Williams."

"I'll be damn," Harrison whispered, not believing what he was hearing.

"Well you have your motive," Antonio pointed out. "Melvin was stealing from the company and Josh as one of the owners had him killed."

Jillian shivered. How could she have been married to a man capable of cold-blooded murder? "But Josh was with me when the attempt was made on my life." She looked at Harrison. "He could have been killed also."

Antonio could see that Jillian was extremely disturbed by this new information, but there was no nice way to describe a contract hit. "Think about it, Jillian. What better way to throw off the police than being with you? If the sniper had succeeded, he would have been considered lucky to be alive. If the sniper failed and you remembered seeing him at the murder scene and pointed a finger in his direction, then everyone would be saying, but Josh was with her. His bases were covered either way."

She still was doubtful. "But I remember him telling me to stay close."

Harrison listened while she and his father debated Josh's involvement in her murder attempt. There was another possibility. "Josh could have been the target as well," he stated drawing both their complete attention.

"Why?" Jillian asked.

"Because he left a witness," Antonio answered knowingly. "And it didn't help his case any that the witness was his ex-wife. These other men could have felt that Josh was now a liability."

"So they would kill two birds with one stone," Jillian finished the thought. For some foolish reason, that explanation caused her to feel better.

Harrison picked up the list of owners and studied it closely. "They all changed their names." He placed the list back on the table so that everyone could see. "Harland Chandler, H. C. is Harold Compton, Wayne Miles is really Willie Melvin, and Trent Long is Thomas Lynch."

"And Josh simply had to use his real name," Jillian added.

"That's it all neatly wrapped," Harrison told Jillian coming back to her. "I have to give it to them. They had a smooth operation—builder, building inspector, district attorney, and accountant all in cahoots together to defraud. And from their bank balance it appears that their operation was quite successful, until Josh made a crucial error. He offs Melvin and you witnessed it, which Josh reports back to the other two. These guys don't believe in taking chances so they make an attempt on both your lives. But the sniper missed and now you're in hiding after a second attempt. Alive you can place Josh at the scene of the crime, which will have a domino effect. And these documents are evidence enough to lock all three of them up for a long time."

"If you're right, Josh's life is in danger," Jillian stated quietly.

Harrison didn't respond right away. He studied Jillian's face, seeing the concern for a man who had inflicted so much pain upon her. For a brief moment he was jealous, then he realized that her concern was for a man that she had once loved. She was an incredible woman and he was thankful to have her love now. "You're right. The only way to protect him is to have these guys arrested as soon as possible."

"Then do it," Jillian ordered. "Despite the way our marriage ended, I don't want to see him hurt or, worse, dead."

"I understand that and I'll do what I can to keep him safe. However, we're going to need help," Harrison told her.

"Martin?" she asked.

"Can you trust him?" Antonio asked them both.

Harrison ran a hand over his head thinking. "I want to believe that we can, but I'm not sure. We'll be taking a gamble."

"We can trust him," Jillian replied without hesitation.

Harrison took her hands in his as he looked deep into her eyes. He saw her conviction. "If you're sure."

"I am. Martin risked a bullet in the back for testifying against a fellow cop. He knew the risk but he still did it. A cop like that doesn't suddenly turn bad." She looked at Harrison waiting. "But, I'll respect your decision."

He smiled appreciating her faith in him. "You're one heck of a defense attorney. However, in this case I trust him too."

"Well then, let's do it."

CHAPTER 14

"Hello," Martin answered his phone on the first ring. He was praying to hear from Harrison and had been keeping his cell phone close. Despite what the DA had been saying to the media, Martin had faith in Harrison and knew that his friend and partner would contact him eventually.

"It's me."

"Where are you? Williams has been telling the press that you kidnapped Jillian to deliver her to your father. There's an all points bulletin out on you," Martin rushed to fill him in.

"So I've heard, but believe me Josh has reason to throw a spotlight on me."

"What's going on?"

"Jillian's memory returned. Josh was present at the murder. She saw him sitting in the backseat of the gunmen's car."

Martin cursed. "Are you telling me that her ex tried to off her?"

"No, but one of his partners did."

"What partners?" Martin asked interested.

So for the next few minutes Harrison brought his partner up to date on the case. When he finally finished, he prayed he hadn't made a mistake in trusting Martin. "Two things, partner. Someone inside the division gave these guys the security layout of the cabin. Do you have any ideas about who it could be?"

"I noticed the same thing," Martin told him. "My suspect would be Hart. I told you he has been holding a grudge against Jillian since the trial."

"Okay, I trust your instincts. Check him out and make sure he doesn't know what's coming down because with the documents in Jillian's possession, we'll be able to round these guys up in no time and get a conviction."

Martin listened and agreed with him. He would get the ball rolling on his end. "Fax me the documents so that I can get things moving."

"I will, but I tell you up front, you won't be able to trace me by them," Harrison supplied.

Martin understood what wasn't being said. "You're not sure if you can trust me."

Harrison sighed before answering. "As a cop I had to ask myself that question. But as your friend, I didn't hesitate, and Jillian was adamant about your honesty."

Martin smiled to himself. “I knew I liked her for a reason.” He listened and laughed as Harrison used a colorful expletive. Then just before disconnecting he said, “I’ll call later to see where we stand.”

“Harrison just phoned his partner like I told you he would.”

“Did he say where he was? Were you able to get a phone number?”

“No, he didn’t and the number was scrambled.”

“I guess he did learn something from his old man. So what do we do?”

“Get rid of Josh like we should have, then that lady lawyer like I wanted to do a long time ago.”

“I don’t know. We’ve been friends for years, it doesn’t seem right.”

“Josh is weak. I told him not to marry that woman, but he had to have her. Now look at this mess. He should have killed her in the garage as well.”

“Why don’t we just cut our losses and leave the country?”

“No lady lawyer is going to make me run!” he bellowed angrily.

“What do you want us to do?”

"Pick up Josh and go to the rendezvous point. Wait for my instructions."

"What are you going to do with Josh?"

"What he should have done to his ex-wife in that garage."

Antonio left the island later that afternoon to return to his bed and breakfast on a neighboring island. Harrison had walked with his father down to the boat launch. They had taken the time together to discuss the latest developments of the case and Harrison's feelings for Jillian.

"You're in love with her," Antonio had stated knowingly.

"Do you disapprove?" Harrison asked, ready to defend their love.

"I'm the last person to tell someone who to love. Your mother loved me despite her parent's objection and what she knew about me," Antonio answered and looked over at his son. "I get the impression that you would behave similarly."

"Yes." Harrison stared into eyes so much like his own.

"Then your love will withstand life's ups and downs."

"Jillian doesn't need any more downs. She's had it pretty rough."

Antonio slid his hands into his pockets as he recalled what the detective had produced on Jillian. "Losing a child is a parent's worse nightmare."

"I can only imagine." Harrison looked past his father as he debated his next words.

"What is it, son?" Antonio asked seeing his struggle.

Harrison sighed, then looked back at his father. "I wonder if she wants other children?"

Antonio admired the man his son had become. A man of his own making and highly respected in the community for his actions and not his power to terrorize. "You want to marry her?"

"Yes."

"Then you should ask Jillian that question."

"You're right." Harrison embraced his father before the man climbed back into his boat. He headed back to the villa once his father's boat pulled away from the pier. His mind was occupied with thoughts of Jillian and the future he wanted with her. As he approached the villa he could see Jillian lounging on the patio. She glanced up as he approached. Their eyes met and held. There was a powerful force surging between them that he hoped would always be present in their relationship.

Jillian loved to watch Harrison walk. He moved gracefully and yet commandingly. His broad shoulders were always held erect and his head held high. His long muscular legs produced just enough swagger to his walk to make a woman breathless. The dark moodiness of his eyes could set her on fire with one glance. She felt a surge of passion as he continued to look at her. When he came to where she lay, she opened her arms to welcome him. She raised her mouth to his and expressed the love she felt through her kiss. When they finally came up for air, Harrison's body was humming with need.

"Let's take a swim," Harrison suggested pulling Jillian up from the lounge. He needed the cool water to quench his thirst for her.

The mood was broken. Jillian's eyes grew large with fear as she pulled free of his grasp. "No swimming. I'll sit on the beach with you, but I'm not getting in the water."

Harrison saw her fear. "Do you swim?"

"Yes. I mean I used to."

"You haven't been in the water since the accident, have you?" Harrison asked.

Jillian started to walk away. "I don't want to talk about it."

Harrison reached out stopping her from leaving. It was his guess that she had been running from her fears since the accident. It was time to put an end to it and help Jillian reclaim her life. "I'll be with you every step of the way."

"I was with my son and I couldn't save him," she shouted in response.

Gently and unhurriedly, Harrison pulled Jillian into his arms. He stroked her back lovingly as he spoke in a nonthreatening tone. "You're a strong woman, Jillian. You faced a gunman and survived. Now it's time to face this hurdle in your life."

Jillian buried her face in the side of Harrison's neck fighting the rising fear inside of her. She knew that he was right, but she couldn't make herself go willingly. "I'm scared."

"I know, sweetie, but I'm right by your side."

Taking a deep breath and placing her trust in Harrison, Jillian finally pulled away to look into his eyes. "Promise to stay close?"

"Every step of the way."

"I'll go change into a swimsuit."

Harrison wrapped an arm around Jillian's waist. "We're on a private island in the Caribbean. There's no need for a swimsuit."

She smiled with disbelief. "I've agreed to get back in the water and now you want me to swim nude?"

Harrison's smile was purely male. "I've seen you nude before, darling."

Jillian blushed. "But not outside," she squeaked.

"Come on, sweetie," Harrison crooned as he led the way down to the beach. He began unbuttoning his shirt. His lightweight pants were next.

Jillian looked on as he stood now in formfitting boxers. The man could make a fortune in underwear modeling. "Well don't stop now." She smiled at him.

Harrison released a deep laugh as he pulled his remaining garment down and stepped out of it. He stood before Jillian gloriously nude and semierect. The heat in her eyes as they traveled the length of his body was about to make him forget about the swim.

"Your turn."

Jillian bit her lip not believing she was about to strip down naked to swim outside. What was Harrison doing to her? She had made love with him in places and positions she had never done before and now she was actually contemplating swimming in the nude. But as she took in his beautiful body and the instrument of his desire rising, she didn't want to be left out on the fun. Slowly she inched up the hem of her sundress and clasped the band of her panties. She looked at Harrison while she slid them slowly down her legs and stepped out of them. His eyes had darkened and his member stirred. The favorable reaction spurred her own.

Harrison could feel the blood and pressure building at the juncture of his thighs as Jillian removed her clothes. She was by far the sexist woman he had every met. It wasn't what she did that turned him on. It was her obvious comfort with her body. Yes, she wasreluctant about swimming outside in the nude, but he knew it was convention and not personal insecurities that caused her to hesitate. As the straps to her dress were lowered and the dress pulled down to reveal her beautiful bare breasts, Harrison's mouth watered with a need to taste them.

Jillian saw the raw hunger in his eyes and laughed. She held the dress in place with a hand. "You said swimming, nothing else."

His dimples winked at her. "But you don't want to swim," he reminded her.

For a moment Jillian thought about accepting the easy out, but then changed her mind. It was now or never for her and the water, and if she was going to face her fears, she would rather do it with Harrison by her side. "You talked me into it," she said releasing the dress and allowing it to pool at her feet.

Harrison hissed an expletive as he advanced on her with a purpose. As he neared, Jillian ducked and took off running down the beach. She couldn't believe she was parading around nude and having the time of her life doing it. But at the water's edge she stopped. Harrison walked up beside her after a while.

The playfulness was gone. Jillian stared at the ocean as though it were an enemy and she its next victim. "I don't know if I can do this."

Harrison came to stand in front of her. He took her hands in his and slowly backed into the water. It was at their ankles and pleasantly warm. "It's okay," he crooned to her.

"Please don't let go," Jillian whimpered as the water now rose to around her knees.

"I'm not letting go."

However, as they moved into deeper water the ground beneath their feet disappeared and they both went under. Jillian fought and clawed her way to the surface. Her eyes were huge with fear as she realized that Harrison still held her.

"Swim, Jillian. That's all you have to do. I'm right here with you."

Jillian stared at him as though he had lost his mind. "I don't want to swim. I told you that back on the patio," she was screaming at him in anger. She followed as he inched away from her.

"Doesn't the water feel good on your body?" Harrison asked ignoring her anger and placing distance between them.

"Who cares how the water feels? I don't want to swim," Jillian continued to close the distance between them.

"Stop complaining." Harrison splashed her playfully.

Jillian screamed as water splashed into her face. She couldn't believe he had done that. Quickly she returned the favor as he tried to escape.

Harrison splashed more water and ducked underneath the surface to resurface behind her. Jillian was in fast pursuit making threats. Soon they were laughing and splashing like kids. Jillian dove under the water and pulled him under. She laughed breaking the surface knowing that he would be seeking revenge. As he came up behind her, she increased her strokes to get away, but wasn't successful. Harrison grabbed for her around the waist and carried her under with him. When they broke the surface of the water together, he claimed her lips in a long, slow, drugging kiss.

"I love you," he whispered as their mouths separated.

"I love you too," Jillian replied. "Don't think I don't know what you've been doing."

"I knew you'd catch on eventually." Harrison smiled lovingly.

"I almost forgot how much I love the water. It had become my enemy."

"It was a tragic accident, sweetie, nothing more."

Jillian shook her head realizing that. Everyone had told her the same thing. Her parents, her sister, and friends, but guilt had made her see that moment in time as something more sinister. But today, Harrison had given her back a part of herself. She loved the water and had always enjoyed swimming.

"Thank you," she told him as she swam away on her back for the simple pleasure of it.

Harrison didn't pursue. He floated in the water watching her reclaim a piece of herself. She swam well. Her love for the water was evident in her skill. He decided to allow her to enjoy it alone. He swam to shore and lay back on their pile of clothes enjoying the view.

Jillian swam on her back for several minutes before she realized that Harrison was no longer in the water. She searched and found him watching her from the beach. Feeling her love for him expand she swam to shore. The blood pulsing in her veins was hot and needy. She could feel her nipples harden as her feet touch the soil beneath her. Walking from the water, she felt bold and daring.

He saw the look in her eyes as she emerged from the water. They were heavy with desire as were her breasts. God she's exquisite.

Jillian walked from the water to where Harrison lay watching her. Her body dripped with water and glistened in the evening sunlight. She allowed her eyes to travel up the length of his gorgeous body. When she reached the juncture of his thighs, she knew how the day would end. She smiled with womanly satisfaction as their eyes connected.

Harrison was like a man on drugs. No matter how much or how often he had her, he would always crave more of Jillian's loving. He watched as a drop of water left her hair and fell onto her shoulder. It made a slow track toward the swell of her right breast and down to the nipple. It pooled there for a moment, tempting him as it dangled, then just as he thought about licking it away, it fell and landed on her lower abdomen. The sight of it trailing down into the dark curls nearly drove him crazy.

Jillian knew he was barely hanging on as she spread out atop him. She licked his lips, tasting the salt. As she kissed him and applied slight pressure, Harrison's hand came up and forced her head firmly against his. His lips parted as he sucked her in. Their tongues twined and mated in a passionate fashion as his other hand caressed her pleasing backside. Jillian sighed with pleasure as he opened his legs and she settled between them.

Harrison thought he would lose his mind if he didn't get inside of her. He rolled pinning her beneath him. His mouth worshiped her neck, the swells of her breasts and further down her abdomen. But at her thighs he stopped. He parted her legs to enter her. He located his discarded pants and removed his wallet. In the side slit was a condom. He ripped it open and rolled it on. In a wanton thrust, he entered her and went deep.

Jillian gasped from the pleasure and raised her legs to lock around his waist. She didn't think about where they were. She simply allowed herself to feel Harrison's love and he hers. They made love slow, yet highly passionately as the waves played love tunes in the background. As their passion reached increasing heights, Harrison braced himself over Jillian as he thrust harder inside of her. His eyes were closed as the feelings inside his heart expressed themselves through his hips. He wanted Jillian to feel the need and the depth of his love for her.

Jillian received the message loud and clear every time he came into her. His passion seemed without end as they rocked together. Then he touched that place in her that set off rockets in her head. She moaned and pressed further into the sand as the sensation began to take center stage. Her fingers clutched his backside as he continued to move inside of her. Then all of a sudden the feeling was too good and she tightened around him to intensify their pleasure. Harrison groaned deep in his chest and thrust harder, deeper, until he could no longer hold back his release. With his eyes fixed on hers, he thrust one final time as the condom broke and he spilled into her. The convulsions of his body went on and on as he laid sprawled between her thighs gasping for air.

Jillian was trembling from the experience. They had reached a new height in their lovemaking and things between them would never be the same. She stroked his back lovingly as she savored the weight of his body against her. Her mind thought of what they had done and where.

"What are you smiling about?" he asked looking down into her face. His eyes were still heavy with passion.

"I was thinking how much I love you and how you always seem to get your way." Her smile widened.

"I'm a cop." He kissed her quick. "I'm supposed to be persuasive."

"I'm a lawyer, lover boy." Jillian moved her hips against him, "and it's my duty to make one believe they are in control all the while leading them where I want to go."

Harrison laughed. "Is that what you did?" His eyes were bright with laughter.

"You're here aren't you?"

They both broke out into laughter. Harrison separated from Jillian and realized that the condom had broken. He glanced at Jillian, aware that she knew what had happened. "I'm sorry."

Jillian looked at the torn condom and realized the possibilities that their actions carried. She smiled as she imagined that possibility looking like Harrison. "There's no reason to be sorry, so stop frowning."

Harrison nodded and swept his concerns away for the moment. He led her out into the water to rinse. Their frolicking soon led to making love and Jillian added a new location to her list. Eventually they returned to the villa and after a long eventful shower, they made a light meal and carried it to the bedroom to enjoy. Afterwards, they were exhausted and snuggled under the covers together. Tomorrow held many uncertainties and so tonight they pushed them aside and concentrated on the moment. Harrison spooned Jillian. His hand stroked her abdomen, remembering that the condom had broken and that they hadn't used a condom later. He wondered if Jillian was thinking about that.

"We didn't use protection," he whispered.

Jillian covered his hand. "I know. I've been tested."

Harrison stroked her face with his. "So have I, but what if you're pregnant?"

Jillian smiled at the thought. "Then I'll thank God for the second chance at being a mother and do my best not to fail this time."

Her answer made him love her more. She would welcome his child. He tightened his arms around her. "You didn't fail. God just needed another angel," he whispered.

Harrison's words caught her off guard. They were so beautiful and inspirational. She flipped over so that she could see him. "You believe that?"

He shook his head, yes. "My faith tells me that it's true."

Jillian watched his eyes, seeing his conviction. "What faith are you?"

"Born and raised Catholic. I've slipped, but I haven't forgotten."

Jillian snuggled further into his arms finding comfort in his faith. "I believe and pray, but I haven't been back inside a church since the funeral. I felt angry because it was his life taken and not mine or Josh's. My baby was a good boy and he didn't deserve to die like that."

"God understands your anger. But he hasn't left your side. He brought you through the tragedy stronger, and look what he has laid before you. A new chance at life and love."

Tears rolled down Jillian's face as she realized that he was right. "I loved being a mother," she whispered.

"Then you'll be again. I promise." He lowered his mouth to hers and tried to make good on the promise.

CHAPTER 15

The next morning Harrison was more focused and determined to end this case. He and Jillian were going to have a life together, and the sooner this case was behind them, the sooner they could get on with living. He phoned Martin from the patio.

"Martin, it's me."

"You aren't going to believe this, but Josh is gone."

"What do you mean he's gone?" Harrison's voice rose with concern.

"He's disappeared. I went to his home and the place had been tossed. No one's seen him. He hasn't phoned in to his office." Martin rushed to fill Harrison in.

"What about the others? Did you pick them up?"

"They're all gone, Harrison. However, their places were in order which leads me to believe they're chasing Josh."

"I agree with you, and if they find him before we do, they'll kill him."

"So what's next?" Martin asked.

Harrison thought for a moment then answered. "Next, we're off to the Cayman Islands. Josh is going for the money and will probably disappear afterwards. I need the captain to clear the way for me with the local authorities," Harrison explained.

"You can't go after these guys alone. I'll meet you down there tomorrow. Tell me where to meet you."

Harrison realized that he was happy to have his partner and friend working with him again on this case. "I'll have to phone you back when arrangements are made."

"I'll be waiting to hear from you."

The men disconnected and began making arrangements for travel.

Antonio hung up the phone from speaking with his contacts in the Caymans. Arrangements had been made for their arrival later tonight. They would fly into the country under the cover of darkness and lodge at a friend's estate. People were already scouting the island for Josh on their behalf.

"Everything is set for our arrival," Antonio informed Jillian and Harrison in the living room. Our plane leaves at eight o'clock tonight. We'll be staying at Gino's place. You remember Gino, don't you, son?"

Harrison smiled with fond memories of the man he had called uncle. "Of course I remember Gino," he replied.

Gino Giattina was a large formidable man from the old country with a heavy accent. He and Antonio had grown up together on the streets of little Italy in New Jersey. Their friendship had lasted through the years into both their retirements from the family. Rooming at his estate would ensure them the security they required.

Jillian laid on the sofa listening to the conversation. It was obvious from the stories exchanged that this man Gino was like family to the DeMarcos. At the moment she was finding it very difficult to take pleasure in their storytelling. Her mind was on Josh and how their lives had changed so drastically in three years.

Harrison glanced in Jillian's direction and noticed the sadness in her eyes. He promptly excused himself from his father and joined her on the sofa. He ran a hand up her thigh as he sat on the cushion beside her. "You're worried about Josh?"

She smiled lovingly at him, amazed by his intuitiveness. "Does it bother you?" she asked softly.

Harrison shook his head. "Not at all. I know you two had a life before us and I wouldn't expect anything different of you."

Jillian shifted on the sofa so that she could place her head in his lap. "I'm frightened for us as well. I want this case solved so that we can get on with our lives."

"It will be soon," Harrison tried to reassure her. He stroked her hair.

"Do me a favor?"

"Anything," Harrison responded without question.

"Send your father home to your mother. I couldn't stand it if something happened to him."

"Antonio DeMarco never ran from a fight, Jillian, and I'm not starting now," Antonio responded after overhearing her request.

Jillian promptly sat up facing the man who looked like the man that she loved. "Antonio, this isn't your fight."

The older man looked at her through dark thoughtful eyes, so like his son's, Jillian knew that he was going to put up a fight.

"Do you love my son?" he asked watching her closely.

"Very much," Jillian responded without hesitation. "But I don't see what that has to do with my request."

"Is there a chance that you might be carrying a DeMarco?" Antonio asked her point-blank.

Jillian glanced at Harrison who looked as shocked by the question as she did. Then giving her attention back to Antonio she answered. "There's a chance."

His eyes held hers with an intensity that caused Jillian to hold her breath expectantly. "DeMarco men protect and defend our women and children. Now will be no different," he stated forcefully. "Now, I'm going to lay down for a couple of hours before our trip. I suggest you both get some rest as well, because when we arrive it will be nonstop until this case is wrapped up." He headed to the master suite down the hall.

Jillian rose from the sofa as she called after him. He stopped and turned facing her; she walked over to him and embraced him with a daughterly hug. "Thank you for the kind words and the wonderful man that you reared."

Antonio glanced at Harrison with the pride of a father. He then focused back on Jillian, knowing that her family must be very special to have produced such an outstanding young woman. "The words were true and it is I who should be thanking you."

"For what?" she asked.

"For loving my son despite who his father is. That means a great deal to me," he said kissing her head lovingly.

Jillian watched as he headed down the hall then returned to Harrison on the sofa. "I understand what you meant about judging a person based on their actions."

"It can get difficult sometimes," Harrison admitted as he drew her down beside him.

"So what's the plan once we reach the Cayman Islands?" Jillian asked changing the subject.

Harrison looked at her long and hard. "I really wish you would stay here on the island with some of Pop's men," Harrison voiced.

Jillian faced him with fire blazing in her eyes. "Not a chance. I go where you go. If you're going to place your life in jeopardy because of me, then my place is beside you, not hiding out like a coward."

"Do you agree to stay at Gino's estate?" he demanded with raised brows.

Jillian rolled her eyes angrily. "All right, I agree," she said defeated.

"Thank you." He gave her a light peck before getting up to call Martin with the details.

Later that night under the cover of darkness the threesome arrived in the Cayman Islands and were driven to the estate of Gino Giattina. Desmond, the hulking black man that had met them at the private airstrip was now showing them around the property. He led them in through the front door and into the foyer. White ceramic tile covered the area and ran throughout the house. Healthy green plants decorated the sparsely furnished space. They were shown the all-white kitchen, then led into the living room. The furnishings were rattan and wrought iron in an off-white stain. The cushions of the sofa, loveseat, and chair were in a tropical coral pattern with shades of green. An off-white entertainment center was placed against the far wall. Coffee and end tables were in an off-white wrought iron and glass. More green plants filled the empty spaces.

There were four bedrooms in the house: two downstairs and two upstairs. Desmond led them upstairs to examine the bedrooms. Each room came with its own bathroom. The two rooms facing the back of the house had a view of the turquoise waters of the Caribbean and a sliding door that led to the outside verandah. Jillian and Harrison chose the upstairs room, which overlooked the water, while Antonio chose the room across the hall.

Back downstairs he flipped a light switch and took them out onto the all-white verandah with hammock and wooden swing. Patio table and chairs were off to the right. Steps led down to the lawn. To the right was a brick patio surrounded by shrubbery. On the patio itself sat a hot tub big enough for eight. To the left of the yard was a kidney-shaped swimming pool surrounded by a brick walkway. A cool breeze was blowing off the ocean as they stood examining their surroundings. Jillian could hardly wait to see the place in the light of day.

Antonio excused himself to his room, leaving Jillian and Harrison with their escort. He informed them that they were to make themselves at home. Harrison walked Desmond out while Jillian climbed into the hammock. On the front porch, Desmond filled Harrison in on the search.

"Our people are scouting the island for this man Williams. The moment we get a lead, we'll contact you." The man went to the trunk of the vehicle and returned with ammunition and weapons.

"Thanks for all your help," Harrison told Desmond as they shook hands. "Tell Gino, I'll never forget this."

Harrison returned to the verandah after stashing the ammunition and weapons in the front closet. He found Jillian swinging gently in the hammock. He grabbed the webbing to stop the sway and climbed in beside her. He wrapped her in his arms as he set the hammock to swinging once again. They swung for several minutes with neither speaking. The warmth of their bodies and tender caresses were all they needed. But eventually the real world had to be discussed.

"Gino's people are looking for Josh, but have yet to find him. So we'll sit tight until in the morning. I'll make contact with the local authorities and alert them to the situation. While I'm in town I'll do a little looking around myself before driving over to the airport to pick up Martin."

Jillian leaned into Harrison, meeting his eyes. "I don't want you out there looking for these people without proper backup. Speak with the authorities, but please wait for Martin to assist you in the search." Her eyes were filled with worry.

Harrison hated to bring more stress to Jillian, but time didn't allow for him to sit around and wait. "Sweetie, I have to move quickly if I'm to find Josh before his partners do. I may get lucky and find him on my first try," he tried to explain.

She knew that he was right and tried to rein in her fears. "I'm sorry for complaining. I just don't want anything to happen to you."

Harrison watched as Jillian closed her eyes and settled back against him. Even in the dim lighting, he could see the signs of stress marring her face. He kissed her head tenderly and continued to hold her. Several minutes later he heard her soft snore and knew that she had drifted off to sleep. As gently as possible, he eased from the hammock and slid his arms beneath her. He returned to the house with Jillian in his arms. He used his hip to close the door. Turning the lock, he then proceeded to set the alarm. He carried Jillian up to their room where he placed her in bed and helped her out of her clothing. She mumbled goodnight when he was settled beside her and went back to sleep. It wasn't long before Harrison followed.

The next morning Jillian woke up in bed alone. She felt the side of the bed and found it cold. Obviously, Harrison had been gone for some time. The clock on the side of the bed read a little after seven. Then a thought occurred to her and she was out of bed in a flash. She quickly found her robe and went tearing downstairs. He wasn't in the kitchen. The verandah was empty too. She ran to the front door as Antonio walked in. Their eyes connected and she knew that she was too late.

"He left without saying good-bye," she whispered.

"He wanted to get an early start." Antonio secured the door behind him.

Jillian stared at Antonio without speaking. She allowed herself to be led into the kitchen where Antonio poured her a cup of coffee. The warmth of the cup felt good in her suddenly cold hands. Taking a sip, she settled back in her chair and nailed Antonio with a glare.

"Why didn't you make him wait for Martin?"

"He's a man, Jillian, I can't make him do anything," he said looking at her. Then he smiled and continued. "I did send Desmond with him."

A smile slid across Jillian's face. She sat her coffee down and sprang from her chair. She hugged Antonio affectionately. "Thank you.

"No need to thank me. I love him too."

In town the two men stopped first at the police department where Harrison introduced himself and discovered that the captain had cleared the way for him. Two local police officers were assigned to assist in the search. Martin had faxed photographs of all the men to the station and so they broke up into pairs and went off into different directions. They began by checking all the local hotels in the area with no luck which led Harrison to believe that Josh was either staying at a bed and breakfast, or had rented a villa. The local tourist spots were checked next, again with no results. They checked store after store for anyone who had seen Josh and the two men. By the time he was due at the airport to pick up Martin, Harrison was beginning to think that maybe Josh was on one of the other islands.

He brought Desmond back to his home and headed straight for the airport. Fearing that he was late, he checked the time on his watch and saw that he was indeed on time. Harrison pulled the Jeep up to the curb in front of the airport and was surprised to see Martin and the captain waiting for him. He parked the car quickly and rushed to greet his friends.

"It's good to see you, partner." Harrison embraced Martin in a bear hug.

"You too, buddy," Martin replied boisterously. He slapped Harrison on the back.

The captain extended his hand when the men separated. Harrison pumped it vigorously, happy to be surrounded by people he could trust.

"Captain, I wasn't expecting you." Harrison smiled at the broad-shouldered black man who had welcomed him into the division without reservations. He was genuinely pleased to see him.

"Well, I couldn't leave my best detectives to have all the fun chasing down these guys." he returned the smile. "I thought my being here would make things easier with the local authorities."

"I appreciate that. Your phone call paved the way already, but I'm sure glad to have you both here to help me." He shook his head with frustration. "All this running and hiding is beginning to take a toll on Jillian and I'm worried about her."

Martin and the captain exchanged knowing glances. It was the captain who thumped Harrison on the shoulder. "Dammit Blake, you've fallen in love with your witness," he bellowed.

Harrison looked first at the captain then Martin who was smiling foolishly. "Guilty as charged, Captain."

Martin erupted into laughter. "That woman has turned you inside out, buddy," Martin commented while slapping Harrison on the other shoulder. "Not that I can blame you. The lady is a looker and a terrific cook as well."

Harrison couldn't help the smile that spread across his face. "Captain, I know it's not a wise move getting involved with a witness, but Jillian and I simply happened. Hell, I even tried to deny my feelings for her, but you know what, it didn't work. She was still all I wanted or thought about."

The captain looked at Harrison long and hard. He could see that the man was a goner. "I can't wait to meet the lady lawyer that has your nose wide open," he said, then broke out into laughter. "I thought the lady hated cops. She's some type of police watchdog."

"More like an advocate for good policing," Martin chimed in.

Both men glanced in his direction. The captain's expression was one of curiosity while Harrison's was one of knowing.

"Jillian likes you too, buddy," Harrison told his friend.

"She's a good woman," Martin responded.

A car behind them blew. Harrison quickly opened the hatch and placed they're bags in the back. The captain climbed up front while Martin sat behind Harrison. He drove slowly through town pointing out the police station. While driving, he informed the new arrivals about his morning search of the local hotels and shops. He told them of his suspicion that Josh might be on Cayman Brac or Little Cayman.

"Where is the bank their using?" Martin asked.

"Here on the Grand Cayman about two blocks from here." He turned at the next block and drove by the bank Magic City Construction was utilizing. "I know eventually they will have to return here."

"So why don't we stake out the bank and just wait for them to come to us?" the captain suggested.

Harrison looked over at the man as he turned right onto the main road leading to the villa. "Jillian and I believe Josh's life is in danger from his partners. He messed up the hit on the accountant and left a witness alive to testify."

"So Martin tells me that you both believe the attack at her office was meant for him as well."

"Yes, we do. That's why we have to get to Josh first," Harrison stressed. "Besides I don't think it will take much persuasion by us to get him to testify against the others."

The captain made an annoyed face. "Blake, I know you're in love with the lady, but Jillian isn't the cop here, you are," the captain reminded him. "The three of us will sit down and decide the best course of action to take."

Harrison didn't appreciate the remark about Jillian and chanced a glance at Martin who shrugged his shoulders in the rear view mirror. The three men rode in complete silence back to the villa. Harrison now wished that the captain had remained back in Birmingham. He was such a stickler for following the book and could hamper the timeliness of this case. He turned off onto the drive that led to the villa. He stopped in the driveway and braced himself for Jillian's fury. No doubt she would be angry about his leaving before Martin's arrival and without saying good-bye. He opened the car door as the front door swung open.

Jillian stepped out to greet the new arrivals. She met Harrison's questioning gaze with a smile and saw him visibly relax. She then turned to welcome their guest. Martin came to stand in front of her and received a friendly hug.

"Martin, it's good to see you again," she whispered for his ears only.

"And you too." He returned her embrace. "You and Harrison scared the hell out of me when I didn't hear from you, and the devastation at the cabin took a couple of years off my life."

"It took a couple off mine as well." Jillian stepped out of his arms and turned her attention to the captain watching her closely. "Captain, how are you?" she greeted the first black police captain in the city. She had never met him in person. At the precinct it had been Harrison and Martin she dealt with. But now in person she was surprised by his good looks. He was just shy of six feet, but just as broad in the shoulders as Harrison. She guessed him to be in his midforties. His nut-brown face was slim and enhanced by a neat goatee. Green eyes with short curling lashes were clear and assessing.

Captain Warren Morton had to admit that Jillian Newman was indeed a beautiful woman. But he wasn't pleased that one of his best detectives was thinking with the wrong part of his anatomy and allowing a non-cop to interfere in their case.

"It's good to see you're alive, Ms. Newman."

"It's good to be alive and please call me Jillian." She extended her hand. She knew that the captain wasn't a fan of hers. Her watchdog efforts on behalf of the community had pitted them against each other several times during the course of his command.

"Jillian it is then." A movement behind her caught his attention. Antonio DeMarco came into view as he stepped out onto the porch. The men exchanged challenging glances before Antonio nodded in greeting.

Jillian watched the silent glances, thinking this was going to be a long couple of days. She affectionately wrapped an arm around Antonio's waist and made introductions. Martin greeted Harrison's father warmly. It was apparent to her that the two men had met before.

The captain gave Jillian and Antonio a stony glare before stepping forward. "There's no need for introductions. Your reputation precedes you, Mr. DeMarco."

For a moment everyone held their breath while the two men assessed each other. Then in true DeMarco style, Antonio smiled with a cockiness designed to relax.

"Haven't you heard that I'm retired?" The smile on his face and the challenge in his eyes dared the captain to say otherwise.

Captain Morton studied the cool, unruffled demeanor of Antonio DeMarco knowing instinctively that the man must have been a challenge to law enforcement. "Of course, it's just that I never thought we would be working on the same side," the captain responded, then laughed dryly.

Jillian jumped in before anything else could be said. "This way, gentlemen." She led the small party into the villa. "Harrison, will you show them to their rooms while I place the food on the table?" She turned to the men. "I'm serving a late lunch on the verandah in ten minutes." She left the men in Harrison's hands while she returned to the kitchen. Antonio was there brooding.

"I can't stay here with a house full of cops," he said meeting her gaze.

Jillian laughed as she laid a hand on his folded arms. "Ignore Morton. I hear he's a by the book type of guy. It's in his nature to give someone of your career choice a hard time. And besides, I really believe his foul attitude is directed at me."

"You've had run-ins with him?" Antonio asked. His brown eyes were dark with concern.

She weighed his question not sure how to answer. "Not really run-ins, more like differences of opinions. I accused his staff of being heavy-handed, and he labeled me a troublemaker who doesn't understand the workings of a police force."

"In other words, the guy has a grudge against you."

She was thoughtful. "I guess you could say that. But in his defense his personal track record is above reproach."

Antonio nodded. "Just as long as Harrison can trust these two men."

She met his intense gaze. "He can. Stop worrying. You're going to ruin that reputation of yours."

Antonio unleashed a laugh so like Harrison's. "I sure don't want to do that, now do I?"

She smiled as Antonio left the kitchen.

CHAPTER 16

After lunch the men sat around the table discussing the case. Martin was sandwiched between Jillian to the left and Antonio on the right. Jillian sat next to the captain and Harrison was between him and his father. He was busy outlining what they knew about the case and describing the attack at the cabin. Both men agreed that there was a mole inside the detectives division. When Harrison concluded, Martin turned toward Jillian.

"I hope you don't mind, but I called your sister after speaking with Harrison. I knew with Josh all over the news broadcasting that Harrison had kidnapped you and turned you over to his father, that your family would be sick with worry."

"No of course not, I'm grateful to you." Jillian grabbed his arm anxiously. "How are they? You told them not to worry about me, right?"

Martin smiled and covered her hand with his as he met her concerned stare. "I spoke with your sister because I remembered that's where Harrison took you the night of the shooting. What surprised me was that she asked me point-blank if I was sure you were with Harrison. And when I told her that I had heard from him and that yes you were with him." He paused smiling at his partner. "She said the strangest thing."

Jillian looked expectantly at him. "What did she say?"

"She said that as long as the two of you were together, she wasn't worried because Harrison would take care of you."

Jillian glanced across the table at Harrison who was trying pitifully to look innocent. "You and my sister had a conversation about me, didn't you? But when would you two have spoken?" Jillian was perplexed.

He smiled guiltily as he squirmed. "At the hospital." His smile faded as the fear he had experienced that day came flooding back to him. "Faye and I were both scared to death. You were all covered in blood and our emotions were running high. Things were said that we probably never would have shared before that moment."

"Blake, you mean to tell me that you and this woman were involved before you were assigned to protect her?" Morton bellowed, drawing everyone's attention. "You never should have accepted that assignment. I should bring your sorry behind up on charges."

"Captain Morton," Antonio's commanding voice drew everyone's attention. "There's no one better to protect a woman than the man who loves her and DeMarco men always protect their women."

Harrison and Martin exchanged glances. Finally Harrison entered the conversation. "Look, Captain, perhaps I was wrong, but no one was going to fight for Jillian any harder than me."

Captain Morton turned the words over inside his head. Maybe if he were in the same situation he would do the same thing. But as the captain of detectives, he was responsible for the adherence of policy. "Look everyone, I do understand, it's simply that protecting someone you love isn't good policing."

Jillian and Harrison both recalled his earlier concerns about that very thing. They could no longer be angry when the man was only saying what they both knew to be true.

"You're right, Captain," Harrison conceded. "I must admit I questioned my decision to protect Jillian a time or two myself, but I couldn't leave her life in someone else's hands."

"Well, it seems Jillian is in one piece, so I guess we can forget this as long as we don't make a habit out of breaking rules." He shot Harrison and Martin warning glances.

He fell silent for a moment. His mind was still processing the details of the cabin attack. "Harrison, I assume you capped the body back at the cabin?" He watched his detective closely.

Jillian nearly jumped out of her skin at the mention of the man she had killed. Her eyes were wide as she met Harrison's cool gaze. He was trying to send her a message. What it was she wasn't sure, but she knew him well enough to remain quiet and follow his lead.

"Why do you ask?" Harrison wanted to know.

"The angle of the wound was odd."

"Oh," Harrison sighed in relief. He went on describing exactly where they were in the room and how they were positioned. But when it came to who shot the man, he lied smoothly and stated that he did.

As an attorney the desire to tell the truth was eating away at Jillian. However, she knew if Harrison was lying, there had to be a very good reason for him doing so. She would have to ask him later. As for right now, she tried to control the slight trembling in her hands.

Captain Morton took a long look at Jillian. She was the picture of innocence. Only the slight shake to her hands gave her away. But he understood Harrison's reason for lying. It would be easier to close that portion of the case if it was a cop who fired and killed the man. However, the woman next to him was far more than a pretty face. He filed that thought in the back of his mind for another day.

"That explains it," he responded satisfied.

Harrison chanced a glance at Jillian. He was thankful that she had remained silent. He could feel her need to confess to the shooting, but there was no point in dragging her through an investigation when the killing was in clear self-defense. Not to mention it wasn't standard policy to provide a witness with a weapon.

Captain Morton turned with assessing eyes to Jillian. "Now a question for you, Ms. Newman," he spoke with authority.

Jillian hiked a brow as she returned the look. "Yes?"

Captain Morton leaned in her direction, demanding her complete attention. "What I'm about to ask will no doubt anger you, but I would be derelict in my duty if I didn't ask."

"Go ahead, I've nothing to hide."

"Are you sure?"

"Captain," Harrison cautioned the man.

Jillian took a quick glance at Harrison and silenced him with a hand. "It's all right." To the captain, she met his eyes with directness. "Ask your question."

The captain gave her a slight smile and nodded. "You aren't falsely accusing Josh of being the man you saw in the parking garage as a way of getting back at him?"

There was no doubt in anyone's mind about what he was referring to. Jillian suddenly felt very exposed. In a textbook defensive response, she folded her arms across her chest as she looked him deep in the eyes.

"No, Captain Morton, I'm not falsely accusing Josh because he divorced me. Despite the death of our child, which led to our divorce, he and I have managed to have a civil relationship. As a matter of fact, Josh led me out of my office when it was being sprayed by bullets."

"And this is the way you're repaying him?" he asked sarcastically.

"I'm doing what I must because it's right and I'm telling the truth," her voice rose with annoyance. She was growing very tired of this man and his suspicious attitude.

"Tell me some more truths, Jillian," he barked, his demeanor growing more confrontational by the moment. "Were you a part of this scheme when you and Josh were married?"

"Captain," Harrison roared angrily.

But Captain Morton ignored him as he kept pressing Jillian for answers. "It was okay to look away while the two of you were together, but Josh boots you out and all this time you have just been waiting for the perfect moment to stick it to him."

"No," Jillian shouted in response. Her eyes were wide and desperate. She looked to Harrison for help.

"Women always know what their husbands are into," he kept pressing.

Jillian was out of her chair. She stared down on the man with fire blazing in her eyes. "You're absolutely right, Captain, women do know what their husbands are into. I knew that Josh was sleeping around, I knew a little too late that he didn't love me and that he only married me because I represented everything he wanted in a mate. And yes I chose to remain in that marriage because I believed in the vows. But I did not at any time know of his illegal activity. To be honest with you, I don't believe he was involved with these people while we were married."

"Come on, Jillian, surely you aren't that naive? Our investigation shows that he was involved with these people during your marriage." He stood regaining control.

"Back off, Morton," Antonio ordered with a deadly tone.

"Call me what you want," she half screamed. "I didn't know. I wouldn't have known if I hadn't remembered seeing him in that parking garage and his name being on those documents."

"About those documents." He kept firing questions at her. "How did you come by them?"

Her head was swimming from the barrage of questions. She was beginning to feel like a criminal rather than a victim. "A concerned citizen provided them and that's all I'm telling you," she glared at him.

"And you just happened to recognize Josh's real name? Don't you think that's a little coincidental?" He stood directly in front of her. He could see that she was angry and a little off balance, but the lady wasn't caving in. She was giving him glare for glare and not backing down.

Harrison sprang from his chair to place himself between Jillian and the captain. He was fit to be tied at the moment and desperately wanted to slam his fist into the captain's face. "Look, we all know the routine and have performed this dance, but you're off course here and I don't appreciate the way you're attacking Jillian," he roared.

"And I don't like the fact that you lied about shooting the guy at the cabin," Morton's voice rose higher. He stepped around Harrison and advanced on Jillian. "You shot that man, Jillian, didn't you?" he nearly screamed while pointing an accusing finger.

The tears were instant as the guilt of taking a human life overwhelmed her. "Yes," she screamed in response. As all eyes were on her, Jillian took off running for the beach.

"Just whose side are you on?" Martin yelled from the table.

"I'm on the side of the truth," Morton answered.

"Well, the truth, Captain, is that Jillian killed that man defending me. He had me cold and when I heard that gun discharge, I thought I was a goner. It took me a split second to realize that I wasn't hit and I owe that to Jillian. Now you do what you want with that information, but if you harm Jillian, I'll announce to the world that you have a dirty cop on your watch," Harrison threatened the stunned man.

Antonio pushed from the table and went after Jillian. Stopping at the stairs he turned toward the captain. "You wanted to break her."

Morton threw up his hands. "I wanted the truth, people. If we're about to arrest the district attorney, I have to be sure of the evidence and the person making the accusation. Blake, you're in love with the woman. Your judgment where she is concerned isn't the strongest."

Harrison's hands were planted firmly on his male hips to keep them from around the captain's throat. "You didn't have to attack her. Jillian would have answered any questions you had willingly."

"See that's what I mean about you. The woman is a lawyer, Blake. She makes a living instructing her clients on how to respond to police questioning. I had to break the lawyer in her to get to the truth."

"The truth is, those documents containing Josh's name came from Martin's investigation, not the papers given to Jillian. She didn't manufacture evidence."

"I'm convinced." Morton finally backed off. "I was only doing my job, like you should have been doing when your mind was on the lady. Now let's sit down and decide how to get these guys." Morton returned to his seat aware that Blake and Martin were still fuming.

Harrison ignored the captain as he looked down the beach to where Jillian sat with his father. It was obvious from the movement of her shoulders that she was crying. He wanted to be with her, but the sooner they got these guys, the sooner he could place the captain on a plane back to Birmingham. The man really knew how to ruin an afternoon. He reclaimed his chair and listened as the captain offered his suggestions.

Down on the beach Antonio consoled a distraught Jillian. He held her in his arms as she cried. His thoughts were on Captain Morton and what he would have done with a man like him during his day. The more he thought on the ugly scene, he knew that with one phone call he could still make things happen. But Jillian and Harrison were servants of the law and he would bring no shame or dishonor to either one.

"The man is a bully," he crooned to Jillian.

"No, he's just good at his job." She swiped at the tears on her face and sat up. "I hadn't given consideration to how the evidence might look to someone from the outside. He was right to question me."

"Perhaps, but that was an attack," Antonio commented glancing back toward the house.

Jillian smiled and leaned over kissing Antonio on the cheek. "I bet you were a force to be reckoned with in your day."

He glanced down at her and wrapped an arm around her shoulder. "With the right provocation I can still be a menacing foe."

She didn't doubt him and for some reason took great comfort in knowing that he was close if she needed him. When they finally returned to the villa, the men were gone from the verandah. Antonio informed Jillian that he wouldn't be staying on. "Where will you lodge?" she asked concerned.

"I have friends on the island. Don't worry about me. I'll be by tomorrow to check on you," he promised.

Ten minutes later a car pulled out front and blew the horn. Antonio had stashed his luggage in the hall closet. Retrieving it, he kissed Jillian then opened the door and headed to the waiting vehicle.

"I hope I'm not responsible for the old guy leaving," Captain Morton's voice came from behind her.

Jillian rolled her eyes heavenward as she searched for strength. This man was wearing her last nerve thin. "Not at all," she lied. "Antonio has friends everywhere who are delighted to see him anytime."

He assessed her. "I'm really surprised that you would befriend a man like him. You're always preaching about the law and doing the right thing.

How can you tolerate a man who has made such a mockery out of the legal system?"

Jillian had pondered these questions herself, so the captain's asking didn't really bother her. "For starters the man wasn't sworn to uphold the law as your officers were. Secondly, there aren't any charges pending against the man. His restaurants are all legit operations. And as to his past, it's just that, the past. I made my position about Antonio very clear to Harrison. He assured me that his father was out of the family business."

"And Harrison's word is enough for you?"

She raised her chin slightly as she met his probing eyes. "Yes, and that's all you need to know." She stepped around the man and headed to her room in search of Harrison. When she opened the bedroom door, he was there waiting for her. His eyes were dark and worried. As she entered the room and closed the door behind her, he met her in the middle of the floor. His hands buried themselves in her hair as his mouth descended on hers. The urgency and passion of the kiss was evidence of his frustration with the earlier situation. Their mouths parted and he led her to the bed where the encounter was forgotten.

"Hello."

"It's me."

"Where are you?"

"Grand Cayman. Any luck in finding our prey?"

"Not a sign, but we'll find him."

"You better or everything will be lost."

"We've worked too hard to allow that to happen."

"I agree, but if Josh and the lady lawyer testify against us, we're through."

"We'll start the search again first thing in the morning."

"Check the other islands. They all seem to believe he may be on one of those. If all else fails, sit on the bank because we know he'll come there eventually."

"Got it."

CHAPTER 17

The next morning it was decided that the men would search the other islands for Josh. Harrison and Martin would break up and each take a different island. The captain wanted to go into town and check in with the local authorities. Antonio had returned in time for breakfast and would stay with Jillian.

Harrison chose to investigate Cayman Brac. He took the twenty-minute flight from Grand Cayman to the Brac. At the small structure that serves as an airport, he was greeted by the local Caymanians lined on the second-floor terrace. He approached the lone cabbie waiting at the curb. He introduced himself as a cop from the states chasing wanted felons. Producing photographs of Josh and his partners, he questioned whether he had seen the men on the island. When he responded no, he then pulled two crisp bills from his wallet and negotiated for the cabbie to show him around the island. The excitement of the chase seemed to be all the cabbie needed to agree. He was willing and ready to go.

Their first stop was the local police station in Creek. Harrison provided his credentials and the warrants for the men's arrest. Satisfied that his papers were in order, the authorities gave him permission to check the island. They copied the photographs of the suspects to be posted on their wanted board in their office. Back on the road, the cabbie drove around the small island while Harrison searched every face they passed. He was so desperate to find Josh before his partners did, that he failed to see the beauty of the island.

The men began their search by making stops at all the resort hotels showing the picture of Josh and his partners to guests and employees alike. Unfortunately no one had seen them. The cabbie suggested Walton's Mango Manor, a local bed and breakfast that sat on three acres on the island's north shore. Once again they struck out. With no other recourse, they began checking out the private rental cottages along the coastline. Harrison hid in the car while the cabbie pretended to be looking for a fare. By late afternoon the men were ready for a meal and a little rest. The cabbie suggested Aunt Sha's by the sea. After a meal of kingfish, rice and peas, the men began the search all over again. It was late when Harrison returned to the airstrip for the ride back to Grand Cayman. He left his phone number with the cabbie in case Josh or his partners showed up. After a hearty good-bye, he boarded his plane for the ride back to the big island.

Martin's search on Little Cayman proved just as uneventful. The island was the least inhabited and the resorts few in number. A check of the seashore cottages still produced nothing. The trip, he concluded, was a waste of time. After a day of fruitless searching he too headed back to Grand Cayman.

The captain was learning all that he could about the island from the local police. He learned the island was the most congested when the cruise ships docked. He also learned the operation of the bank in question. It opened promptly at nine, with the half hour after the opening being the busiest. It was the perfect time to slip into the bank and conduct a clandestine transaction without being noticed.

The officer with Captain Morton drove around the city of George Town pointing out the best escape routes to the airstrip or the docked cruise ships. He drove down shortcuts and back roads. They stopped by the airstrip to see the daily schedule as Martin's plane arrived from Little Cayman. The captain spotted his detective and flagged him over to the counter. After gathering all the necessary information to plan appropriately for an encounter with the three men, Captain Morton and Martin caught a ride back to the villa with the officer.

Antonio and Jillian had spent most of the day lounging on the verandah getting to know each other better. They sat side by side on the swing enjoying the light sea breeze as they talked. Jillian had felt quite comfortable prying into his criminal past while Antonio tried to explain the dynamics of an organized crime family. He had explained that during his day, it went without saying that the son would participate in the family business.

"But I didn't want that for my own children," he told Jillian. "I had dreams of being a chef." He laughed self-consciously. "I guess that's why when I retired I opened the restaurants."

"I'm sorry you didn't get to follow your dreams."

He patted Jillian's hand, which rested atop his right hand. "I've had a good life. I was fortunate to have met and married a wonderful woman."

"A Southern Belle no doubt." Jillian smiled over at him. "How did that go over back in New Jersey?"

Antonio laughed deeply as the memories of those days came back to him. "I thought my mother would faint when she heard my sweetheart's southern twang."

Jillian laughed just imagining the scene. Then she sobered as she prepared to ask her next question. "How do you think your wife will react to me?" she asked softly, then felt foolish for asking. It wasn't like Harrison had asked her to marry him or anything. "Forget I asked," she said raising a hand and turning away.

But Antonio wouldn't allow her to trivialize their relationship. He grabbed her chin and forced her to look at him. "My wife can't wait to meet the woman our son loves."

"I can't wait to meet her as well," Jillian said as she wrapped her arms around his neck for a hug.

"Is this what happens when I leave you two alone?" Harrison joked as he joined them out back. His face was lit with a smile as his eyes landed on Jillian. He admired the way the teal sundress caressed her body as she came to him with open arms. They embraced and shared a quick peck before Jillian led him over to his father. He dragged one of the wrought iron chairs from the table over to where they were sitting. He quickly brought them both up to date on his search. When he concluded passing on the details, Jillian excused herself to place dinner on the table. Antonio made his apology for not staying and quickly left the villa.

Harrison joined Jillian in the kitchen after seeing his father out. "I don't think Pop likes Captain Morton," he said waiting to see how she responded.

"The man isn't easy to like," she answered quickly and rolled her eyes.

Harrison couldn't help laughing. "I know his style is rough and antagonistic, but he is a very effective law officer."

"He may be, but he isn't easy to like." She continued to reheat food in the anticipation of the others' return. And right on cue there was a knock at the front door. Jillian made a face as Harrison went off to answer it. She could hear his laughter all the way to the door. Minutes later all three men could be heard discussing their search out on the verandah.

"Little Cayman was a waste of time," Martin informed the other men. "It's a beautiful island with some really nice cottages for rent. I think I'd like to return here one day."

"The entire Caribbean is beautiful," Harrison replied.

"Well unfortunately, detectives, we aren't here on vacation," Captain Morton injected. "I did get a chance to ride around with one of the officers and learn the layout of the city, as well as the operation of the bank. I say we give Grand Cayman one more search tomorrow, but if we haven't located these men by tomorrow evening, then we sit on the bank."

Inside the telephone was ringing. Jillian appeared at the door, eyes bright with excitement. She ran over to Harrison. "Your cabbie from Cayman Brac phoned to say that Josh was spotted getting in a boat headed for Grand Cayman. He said that he was positive it was Josh and that he was alone."

The three men listened intently as they processed the new information. Finally Captain Morton spoke up. "At least we now know that he's in the area. Any idea where he's headed?" He looked at Jillian.

"No," she answered, shaking her head. "All he said was that Josh was on a boat headed toward Grand Cayman."

"Do we dare check the local piers?" Martin asked.

"I doubt if Josh is traveling at night that he'll use a public pier," Harrison offered. "My guess is he's docking wherever he'll be spending the night."

"Which could be almost anywhere," Jillian added.

The captain stood up and began pacing the length of the verandah. He stroked his goatee while he paced, unaware of the three sets of eyes watching him. Finally he came back to the assembled group. "Josh has come to the island to collect his money and possibly to catch a flight out to anywhere in the world."

"How do we know he hasn't already collected his money?" Jillian interrupted him.

"An officer and I made contact with the bank president and verified that no money had been withdrawn."

"So, I take it we are sitting on the bank and the airport," Harrison commented.

"That's what I'm thinking unless one of you have a better plan?" Captain Morton asked.

When no other plan was offered the men began mapping out their strategy while Jillian returned inside and placed dinner on the dining room table.

She called the men in when she was ready to serve. She asked Harrison to say the blessing to which he agreed. Afterward, while the food was being passed around, the men continued to iron out their plans. They discussed observation positions, the pattern and flow of bank traffic as well as outside traffic. It was amazing to Jillian to hear all the technical details about daily living that each man had picked up while venturing into the city. She gained a new respect for law enforcement officers, and reluctantly had to agree with Harrison that Captain Morton was indeed good at his job.

"Listen, I don't have much time. Josh is somewhere on this island and we had better find him before they do or it's our butts. The plan is to stake out the bank and airport, so I suggest you both discover a way to enter that bank unnoticed. Instead of leaving from the airport, take a boat over to the other island and board a plane there."

"What do you want us to do with Josh?"

"We have no choice but to kill him."

"But you two are like brothers."

There was a heavy sigh. "I know but he didn't stick to the plan. He chose that lady lawyer over us and left us with no choice."

Jillian and Harrison laid in bed talking in soft whispers. Both knew that tomorrow could possibly be the end of the nightmare. Harrison expressed his confidence that they would get their men, while Jillian expressed this gnawing feeling inside of her that something would go very wrong.

"We've planned for every conceivable outcome, sweetie." Harrison tried to allay her fears.

Jillian snuggled closer to him in an attempt to ward off the chill, which was fast moving over her body. She just didn't feel as confident about tomorrow as he did. "Promise me that you'll be careful," she asked, raising her face to his.

Harrison could see the fear in Jillian's eyes and had learned through the years to trust human intuition. He made a mental note to caution the captain and Martin in the morning. But for right now he had to settle Jillian's raw nerves.

"Sweetie, we're prepared, please stop worrying," he whispered while stroking her hair.

"How can I stop?" she practically screamed at him. "The three of you are risking your lives for me and I'm terrified. My whole world is hanging by a precarious thread and at any moment it could give way. If something were to happen to either of you because of me, I would never forgive myself."

He held her body close to his while rubbing her back soothingly. He searched for the magic words to ease her fears, but came up empty-handed. "Hopefully by tomorrow this time, it will all be over and we can began to make plans for a future together," Harrison stated without further explanation. He waited for Jillian to respond. He had wanted to bring up the subject before now but hadn't, and now with all their lives hanging in the balance, he felt the need to explore the possibility.

Jillian pushed herself up against the headboard and looked at him for several minutes trying to decipher the meaning in his words. "What type of plans are we talking about?" She looked at him closely and moved over as he too sat against the headboard.

Harrison reached down and threaded his fingers with Jillian's. He held them up in front of them. "The world may see us as black and white and I'm sure we will probably face some opposition. And my father's reputation may interfere with your career plans." He looked her directly in the eyes. "I guess what I'm asking you, Jillian, is whether or not your love for me is strong enough to face the world as my wife, and mother of my children?"

Jillian's heart overflowed with love as she met Harrison's beautiful brown eyes. They were open and honest and windows into his soul. She didn't hesitate to respond. "As you once told me, I'll be your shelter through any storm, be it natural or man-made." She brought their joined hands toward her and placed a kiss on his hand. "The world may see us as black and white, but in the eyes of God, we'll be man and wife, father and mother. Our love, Harrison, is strong enough to face any opposition and if you haven't guessed, I would be honored to be your wife." Tears of joy slowly ran down her face, as his love for her was visible in his eyes. He smiled with joy, displaying those enticing dimples.

Damn if he didn't feel like crying himself, Harrison thought as he drew Jillian into his arms. They held each other tightly as the love between them surged throughout their bodies. Harrison pulled away just far enough to lower his mouth to Jillian's. Their kiss was tender and loving. The passion they normally felt and shared was overshadowed by the purity of their love. Harrison turned off the bedside lamp, then lay back down with Jillian nestled in his arms. They discussed children and where they would live. Jillian suggested a wedding date with no regard to tomorrow. For right now they were a couple in love making plans for a marriage.

CHAPTER 18

Jillian watched as Harrison dressed for the stakeout. He was dressed in all black with his gun holstered across his shoulders. His appearance was identical to the first night that they met, and she was suddenly in awe of how far they had come in such a short time. She loved him. And because of that love, she wanted to beg him to stay with her. However, being the man that he was, she knew that there was no way he would send his friends into danger alone.

That haunting feeling was still with her, but she didn't speak of it. She wanted Harrison's mind clear to concentrate on the job at hand. Josh and these men would be desperate and desperate people sometimes do desperate things and she wanted Harrison focused and prepared. It still amazed her how one single moment in time had changed her life so drastically. In one way, it had brought her nothing but misery and yet without it, she would have missed Harrison's love.

Through the mirror Harrison watched her. She sat on a wicker chest at the foot of the bed watching him with fear clouding her beautiful whiskey-brown eyes. Her lip was clamped between her teeth as though preventing herself from saying something. He wondered if she still had that feeling of dread from last night. He wished that he could remove it, but the only way to do that would be to arrest Josh and his friends. With any luck, by the end of the day, there would be nothing more for her to fear. Josh and his buddies would be behind bars and he and Jillian would be free to return to their lives.

Harrison turned around and walked to where Jillian sat. He hunched down before her and caressed her cheek. It overwhelmed him how much he loved her. "Pop should be arriving soon to stay with you while I'm gone. I want you two to prepare a feast tonight for the announcement of our engagement." He gave her his best smile, but Jillian knew what he was up to.

She leaned forward and placed a tender kiss to his lips and held his gaze. "Nothing will keep me from worrying about you."

"Sweetie, I don't want you sitting around here today worrying. This case will probably be over with by tonight and we'll be heading home. So take advantage of this beautiful island. See if you can get Pop to swim with you."

Jillian couldn't help the smile that spread across her face as the mental image of Antonio swimming popped into her head. "I get the message. Now, stop worrying about me. I want you back here in one piece ready to celebrate."

"Yes, ma'am," he replied with a smile.

They came down the stairs hand in hand. The captain was seated in the living room talking on the telephone. It was apparent from his end of the conversation that he was speaking with the local authorities. As they reached the last step, a gut-wrenching noise reached them. Jillian and Harrison exchanged glances as they realized the sound was coming from down the hallway. Together they went to investigate. The sound was coming from Martin's room. Harrison knocked but didn't wait for a response. The door to the bathroom was closed as well, but the sound of retching could be heard.

"Martin, I'm coming in," Harrison yelled through the door.

There was a flush and the sound of running water. Just as Harrison opened the door, Martin appeared in the doorway white as a ghost. His posture was slumped as he weakly tried to make it back to the bed. Harrison grabbed his arm and assisted his efforts while Jillian straightened, then turned back the bed.

As Harrison laid him down, Jillian placed her hand against his head.

"You've got a slight fever," she said softly.

"My stomach is killing me," Martin moaned as another cramp set in.

Jillian looked at Harrison as Martin moaned. "We need to get him a doctor," she told him.

In a weak grip, Martin grabbed her arm. "I don't like doctors. I'll be okay. I think it must have been something I ate."

"I hope it wasn't my dinner last night." Jillian looked genuinely concerned.

"Of course it wasn't," Harrison reassured her. "The rest of us aren't sick."

"He's right," Martin whispered. "I ate some type of fish dish from a roadside vendor on the island yesterday."

"That probably did it," Harrison remarked.

Jillian headed for the door. "I'm going to check the medicine cabinet upstairs. I'll be back with a glass of water for you. You've got to stay hydrated," she said rushing from the room.

"You can tell she was a mother," Martin whispered, drawing Harrison's attention.

Harrison eased down on the bed beside his friend. "With any luck she will be again."

Martin rolled his head to the left to look at him. He could tell that Harrison was serious. "You're planning on marrying her?"

Harrison looked directly at Martin. "I asked her last night and she accepted."

Jillian returned with a tray. She had something to soothe the stomach and a small pitcher of water and a glass. Trailing behind her was Captain Morton and Antonio.

"What's this, a party?" Martin attempted to joke, but cringed as another cramp hit him.

"I needed to see you for myself," Captain Morton remarked with a frown. "Maybe we should call this off until tomorrow. We can get the locals to watch the bank for us."

"No, you and Harrison go as planned. We can't risk these guys getting away," Martin tried to persuade him.

"Martin's right, Captain," Harrison told him.

"I don't leave a man down, Harrison," the captain explained.

Martin struggled to push up. "Hey, Captain, I'm sick not dead. Go on get these guys. Jillian and Harrison have a wedding to plan."

Jillian glanced at Martin, then Harrison. "I thought we were going to announce it tonight?"

Having the decency to look guilty, Harrison gave Jillian his best sad face. "I couldn't keep my happiness to myself."

His sweet words made her smile. "How can I be mad with you when you talk so sweet?"

The room burst into laughter and words of congratulations. Handshakes and hugs were exchanged before Martin reminded them about the stakeout. "Business first, gentlemen," he told the captain and Harrison.

"If you're sure, Martin?" the captain asked once again.

"I'm sure. Now go."

After the room was cleared of people, Jillian gave him the pink stuff for his stomach and a glass of water. "That should help soothe your stomach," she commented, screwing the top back on the bottle. "Get some rest and call me if you need anything."

"I will and thanks."

It was nine o'clock and the bank was just opening. Early risers and shop owners were the first in line. Harrison was hidden on one side of the street while Captain Morton was in hiding on the other. A local officer disguised as a customer had entered when the doors opened. He would sit inside and monitor the comings and goings. It was obvious from the rush of people that the bank did a brisk business.

The lunchtime rush came before they knew it. The street was bustling with people moving in all directions and the bank was a hot spot today. Men in all hues, heights, and body types went in and out. The police were having a time of it trying to check out everyone. After a while the faces began to look like blurs. Harrison was fast becoming disappointed when he spotted a guy carrying a briefcase with a large straw hat shadowing his face approach the bank from across the street. His height and body build drew Harrison's attention, as did his confident walk. He notified the captain on the radio.

"What do you think?"

"Height and body type is right, but I'm not sure. Hold your position," the captain radioed back.

So they watched as the figure grew closer to the bank and blended into the crowd going in. Just inside the doorway of the bank, he removed the hat and revealed a clean-shaven head. Harrison swore under his breath and began to turn away when two men, one black and one white, rushed down the sidewalk and sandwiched the man between them. Looking closely he recognized the two and then realized that the bald man was actually Josh.

"Captain, it's Lynch and Compton. The bald guy is Josh," Harrison spoke hurriedly into his radio.

"Are you sure it's Josh?"

"Positive."

"Okay then, let's wait for them to make their withdrawal, then take them down as soon as they come out."

The captain then radioed their man inside to keep an eye on the threesome. He reported that they were in with a bank representative who was obviously making a large cash withdrawal on their behalf. He further reported that the three appeared to be in a heated argument in the representative's absence. As they got ready to leave, the officer radioed back that the men were on their way out. He further reported that he suspected the taller of the men, Compton, of having a weapon inside his jacket pocket. All outside heard his warning and prepared for the confrontation.

On cue the three men left the bank bunched closely together. Josh still was in possession of the now laden briefcase. Lynch was to his left and Compton to his right. Compton's right hand was inside his pocket and out of the line of sight. The captain instructed everyone to hold their positions until they cleared the bank's entrance before moving in. The last thing he wanted was for the three to rush back into the bank and create a hostage situation. As the three approached the corner, the captain gave the word to move in.

"Police! Stay where you are," Harrison commanded as his weapon was trained on the three men. The local police rushed from the other directions completely circling the three men. "Compton," Harrison called. "Remove your right hand slowly so that I can see it."

All three men were paralyzed with fear as they realized that their great plan had turned out to be their worst nightmare.

Compton could feel the cool metal of his weapon and the sweat forming under his armpits. He eyed the numerous cops with their trained weapons pointed in his direction and knew that pulling his weapon was pointless. Slowly, he removed his right hand and placed it so that it was visible.

"Compton, raise both hands and take two steps back," the captain ordered and Compton complied.

Harrison rushed the man and quickly handcuffed him. The six-four blond man was quickly searched. The gun located in his right pocket was seized as evidence. The local police chief advised the man of his rights, as did Harrison. He was then led to a waiting vehicle. Lynch followed next, but was found to be clean of a weapon. Lastly, Josh was ordered to place the briefcase on the sidewalk and take two steps back, to which he complied. He too was handcuffed, searched, and read his rights, but instead of being placed in a car with Lynch and Compton, he was placed in a car by himself. The local chief secured the briefcase and led the way back to his vehicle. Harrison, Morton, and the chief discussed the best way to interview their suspects on the drive back. Once at the station, the three men broke off, each taking a suspect. The chief would interview Compton, while the captain took Lynch, and Josh was left to Harrison.

"Blake," the captain called to Harrison before he went to interview Josh. "I'm allowing you to question Josh against my better judgment mind you, only because I know you have a vested interest. Don't let that temper of yours, or your dislike for Josh, foul up this case. Remember Jillian's life depends on what we do here."

Harrison stared at Captain Morton knowing that he was right. "I know, sir, and I won't mess this up."

"Good man. Now break him down."

Harrison smiled to himself as he watched the captain disappear into the adjacent interrogation room. The man no doubt was set out to do the same with Compton. Harrison quickly opened the interrogation room door and entered.

Josh looked down at his wrists handcuffed like a common criminal. He was the District Attorney of Birmingham for goodness sakes. All his hard work and dreams were going up in smoke. Disgusted with himself, he realized that he had no one to blame for his situation but himself. He had allowed envy, jealousy, and greed to replace common sense and now look where he sat. His attention was drawn to the door as Harrison entered the tiny room. He knew the routine and decided to save them all some time by cooperating.

Harrison took the chair at the scarred wooden table across from Josh. Their eyes met and Harrison realized that Josh intended to cooperate.

"Josh, you and I both know this song and dance," Harrison opened the conversation.

"You're right, so look, I'm willing to tell everything I know in exchange for a deal."

"You carried out a hit, Josh," Harrison stated matter-of-factly. "Jillian finally remembered seeing you in the parking garage."

"I was afraid of that." Josh lowered his eyes to the table. Then raising them he met Harrison eyes. "But I couldn't kill her. Despite how our marriage turned out, I loved her in my way."

"Jillian doesn't know that. She thought you married her because she fit some image you had for the perfect wife," Harrison informed him.

"Damn, she was always too smart for her own good." He laughed dryly, shaking his head. "She was right. I did marry her because she came from the right neighborhood, social circle, school, you name it; everything about Jillian was better than where I came from. For the longest of times, I didn't know people like Jillian's folks existed."

"So you educated yourself and selected the best woman for your wife," Harrison commented.

"Yeah. Can you believe she married me?" Josh whispered.

Harrison suddenly realized that the confidence Josh exuded was one big sham. "Sure I can."

"Well I couldn't, but I had to have her. That was another way of showing that I had made it from my less than humble beginnings. So here I was with the most perfect woman and I was afraid to touch her like I did other women. Don't get me wrong, we did create our son, but you understand what I mean? And after his death I didn't see the point in pretending any more. I was angry with myself for giving Jillian a reason to run out into that storm. As I think about it, I now realize that I wanted her to leave me because I was to weak to leave her. And I knew if she found me with a woman in our bed, that that would be the final straw. But I never expected her to run out into that storm or Travis to pay for my sins." He was quiet for several minutes. Then his eyes connected with Harrison's. "You're in love with her."

Harrison returned the look. "Yes. I've asked her to marry me."

"Damn, Blake, you don't waste any time do you?" Josh laughed sadly. "I couldn't kill her and for that reason they tried to kill me with her."

"No need to worry about it, we've got all three of you now, and those guys can't hurt you."

Josh's head came up in a jerking motion. "All three? What do you mean three?" His eyes were narrow and suspicious. He was beginning to behave edgy.

Harrison didn't know what to make of Josh's reaction. "Three, as in you, Lynch, and Compton. Of course there was Melvin, before his death."

"Melvin was never a part of Magic City Construction. He was just a thieving accountant that had to be dealt with," Josh answered in near panic.

"Look, Josh, we figured out that everyone changed their names, but kept the same initials, all but you of course—Travis Brown, Harland Chandler, Trent Long and Wayne Miles, a.k.a. Willie Melvin."

"You idiot," Josh nearly screamed. "Wayne Miles isn't Willie Melvin, he's the man in charge, the one who ordered the hit on Jillian, and your police mole."

Harrison's mind was racing. There was one member of this group still out there and Jillian's life was still in danger. "Tell me who it is," Harrison bellowed. He could feel his heart racing with anxiousness as Josh prepared to speak. Then as he heard the name, it was as though he was moving in slow motion while his world came crashing down around him.

Jillian and Antonio occupied themselves with the television in the living room. It was a temporary distraction from worrying about the stakeout. Neither had eaten anything this morning and so as the noon hour passed, Jillian decided that both should eat. She had taken a tray to Martin earlier in the hopes that his stomach was settled enough for nourishment, but he had declined. And a moment ago when she checked in on him he was out like a light. She dragged herself from the sofa and stuffed her nervous hands into the pockets of her jeans. Looking over at Antonio, she caught him watching her and knew that he had seen her trembling hands.

"Harrison is safe," he said rising from his chair. "I feel it in here." He pointed to his heart.

Jillian smiled up at him. "Because I know how much you love him, I'm going to trust your heart. Have a seat while I get lunch together." She walked into the dining room and back right into the kitchen. She switched on the counter radio. A Smokey Robinson tune was playing and she hummed along. As she prepared the tray, she asked Antonio what he wanted to drink. When there was no reply, she grabbed the tray and napkins and headed back into the living room. Obviously he hadn't heard her over the radio.

"What would you like to drink?" she asked again, approaching his chair from behind. She immediately noticed his head drooping and smiled. Apparently he had fallen asleep while she prepared lunch. Easing the tray to the coffee table Jillian glanced back at him with a smile in place and received a shock to the system. The entire right side of Antonio's head was covered in blood. It streamed down his face to his chin and fell to his white gauze shirt.

"Oh my God," she screamed and dropped the tray. Sandwiches and napkins scattered unnoticed over the floor as she stumbled towards him. She couldn't tell by glancing at him whether he was breathing or not, so she extended a badly trembling hand to check for a pulse. As she located the faint beat a voice called out to her.

"He's alive, Jillian. It's you I want."

CHAPTER 19

Jillian's blood ran cold as she recognized the southern drawl and slowly turned. In the shadow of the staircase stood Martin with his gun in hand, aimed at her.

"Martin? What's going on?" she asked with a slight tremor to her voice. Her eyes were wild with fear. She didn't recognize the man pointing the gun as her friend, Martin. Gone was the fun-loving man she had gotten to know. In his place stood a figure masked in cold rage.

Martin took a long slow glance from her head down to her bare toes. A sneer spread across his face as though he smelled something foul. "Don't start playing stupid now, Jillian. It really isn't becoming."

Although her heart was slamming against her ribcage, Jillian tried to remain calm as she placed all the pieces of the puzzle together. "You're the mole."

"Right, but there's more," he taunted her. "Go on."

"I don't know what else."

"Sure you do, just think about it." He waved the gun as he spoke.

"I don't know," she screamed, not liking this game.

He laughed deep in his chest with satisfaction. "See, I told Josh you weren't all that special, but no, he believed you were and had to have you." His blue eyes were glazed over.

Jillian tossed the words around inside of her head trying to make sense of them. "You knew Josh while he was in law school?"

He laughed again, then moved out of the shadow and took a seat on the steps. "I knew Josh way before you did. There was a time when we were like brothers. Then he saw you and decided that he had to have you. He placed you on a pedestal like something special when all along I knew you were nothing but trouble."

"How long have you known Josh?" Jillian asked to buy herself some time.

"The four of us were suitemates at the university. We met our freshman year and bonded."

"Four?" Jillian stated to herself confused. "There's Lynch, Compton, Josh, and you." She paused, beginning to get a clearer picture. "Melvin wasn't a member at all. Wayne Miles was a pseudonym for...Wade Martin," she whispered amazed. "You just aren't the mole, you're a member of Magic City Construction."

"Give the lady a hand." He laughed again, then narrowed his eyes. "You always were too damn smart for your own good."

Jillian picked up on the obvious resentment towards her. The least said by her at the moment the better.

"I don't believe it. The lady lawyer has nothing to say?" Martin screamed, startling Jillian. He smiled with pure satisfaction at her obvious fear. He was in control now.

"You do know that your marriage to Josh was pathetic? He loved you, but was too afraid to be himself with you. In his twisted mind, he couldn't picture making love to you the way that he did with other women. You were Miss Perfect not to be touched just any way." He rose from the steps closing in on her. Jillian ran behind the wicker and wrought iron coffee table, placing it between them, but Martin simply pulled it out of his way effortlessly and grabbed her around the neck. With his gun hand, he caressed the side of her face as he searched her eyes for fear. It was there, although she was trying her best to hide it.

"I bet Harrison touches you any way he chooses and you like it," he whispered into her ear as his hand trailed down to her breasts.

"Stop it," Jillian shouted and shoved against his chest. He released her with a laugh. "Oh yes, there's plenty of passion inside of you." He gave her a lascivious once-over. "I bet my Italian friend has been keeping you pretty busy at night."

"Why don't you get to the point, Martin," Jillian shouted with anger.

"The point, Jillian," Martin said, waving the gun at her, "is that you're going to die today." He leaned over and checked Antonio. Removing handcuffs from his pocket, Martin slipped one cuff onto the unconscious man's wrist, then secured the other around the iron of the chair. All was done in a practiced fashion while maintaining an eye on Jillian.

"Please let me see if I can stop the bleeding?" Jillian pleaded. Her eyes were drawn to the ever-increasing bloodstain on Antonio's shirt.

"He's all right. Head wounds just bleed a little easier than others. It'll stop soon." He returned to the steps and resumed his position. "Aren't you curious about our little group? I know that legal mind of yours has to be clicking away, trying to process everything."

"I am curious about one thing," Jillian spoke up.

"Just one?"

"Why did you help me win my case?"

Martin tipped his head back and released another one of those deep laughs. "Everything isn't about you. I had worked too hard to position myself for our cause to allow some overzealous cop to ruin my efforts. I testified for me."

Jillian stood beside Antonio's chair trying to figure her way out. Maybe if she could keep Martin talking it would give Harrison and Morton a chance to return. "We do what we have to do," she stated flippantly. "So tell me about the members of Magic City Construction." She looked directly at Martin.

He pointed a finger at her. "I knew you were curious about more than that trial." He laughed, pleased with himself for forcing her to ask. He leaned back against the stairs with his elbows resting on the steps behind him. The image he presented was one of carefree relaxation.

"The four of us were suitemates at the university. We connected instantly considering we all grew up in poor neighborhoods. We would watch people like you parade around in fancy clothes and shiny new cars, never working an hour for any of it. It made us sick. Here we were working our tails off to stay in school and people like you looked down your noses at us. But we were smart. We earned our degrees, then devised a plan to get all the wealth we wanted.

Compton used his architectural degree to start the construction business. Lynch was an engineer and secured a position as a building inspector, eventually working his way up to the top position. Josh as you know was the legal mind. It didn't take long for him to reach the DAs office."

"And you the police detective who squashed any investigation against Magic City Construction," Jillian filled in the last piece of the puzzle.

Martin smiled proudly. "You have to admit it was a damn good plan. And it was working until you and Josh got married. With you in the picture we didn't see each other as often as we used to. Josh always had to get back to the little wife. His mind stayed preoccupied with thoughts of you. I could see trouble coming and tried to persuade him into divorcing you, but he couldn't. Where you were concerned, the man was weak." He grew quiet and glanced off into the distance before casting Jillian with an accusatory glare. "The times Josh didn't follow my advice were all centered around you. So imagine how surprised I was to discover there was a witness to Melvin's murder. I wondered why Josh hadn't mentioned it to me, or why the witness wasn't killed at the scene. Then Harrison gave your name as our witness and I knew why he hadn't told me."

"So you thought you would do it for him," Jillian spat as her eyes narrowed angrily.

"Yeah, and unfortunately Josh became a liability that the three of us could no longer tolerate. I decided to kill two birds with one stone, so to speak.'

Jillian knew if she was going to stand a chance of getting away from him, that she had to get closer to the open sliding glass door. She took small steps in its direction while they talked. The hope was that he was too distracted with his recital that he wouldn't notice.

"Why the elaborate scheme? Why did you provide Harrison with actual documents?"

"That was a little risky." He looked at her and smiled with cockiness. "To tell you the truth I didn't believe you two would put the pieces together. But, then I didn't know you had documents on the company."

"Why didn't you kill us at the cabin when you came to visit?" she asked while calculating the steps it would take to get to the door.

Martin's blue eyes were glacier as they examined her. The gun was still pointed in her direction, but was held a little relaxed. "I'll nail you before you can reach the threshold," Martin growled out in a voice that sent goose bumps down Jillian's spine.

"I don't know what you're talking about." Jillian tried to appear innocent. "I was interested in your story."

Martin was up and in her face before she could take two steps. His free hand came down hard across her face and sent her reeling backward from the force of the blow. She collapsed to the floor. The taste of blood filled her mouth while the ringing in her ears appeared to go on forever.

"Liar!" he screamed coming apart at the seams. "That's your problem. You think you're so smart. Well let me tell you something, lady lawyer," he hissed down at her. "I had no intention of killing Harrison. Those men were ordered to wound him, but to make sure you were dead." His lips thinned as he made the point.

"Did you know that I requested to be Harrison's partner?" Martin glared down on her. "I was hoping he would introduce me to his father which he did. Antonio and I have been cultivating a relationship that was about to become lucrative until you came along and ruined my plans to approach him."

"Antonio wouldn't work with you, Martin. He wouldn't do anything to bring shame or cast doubt on Harrison." She slowly made it to her feet while wiping away blood with the back of her hand.

"Why don't you worry about Jillian?" Martin roared in anger. He didn't like being talked down to and would give her another taste of discipline if she didn't keep quiet. However, this time when he reached out toward her, Jillian was prepared. She remembered what her military father had taught her in case a boyfriend got too touchy-feely." She slid out the way of the gun and grabbed his arm, applying pressure to a specific point. The movement caught Martin completely off guard and caused him to fall to a knee and release the gun at once. She shoved it across the room with her bare foot and headed for the door. As she closed in on it Martin lunged for her. They both hit the floor with a thud, but Jillian's hands were now gripping the doorframe. As the air rushed out of Martin's lungs, from the impact of her legs with his chest, Jillian struck out. She pulled her legs free and began kicking at him with the heel of her foot. She made contact with Martin's face twice before he released her. She scrambled to her feet and hit the door running.

Martin got to his own feet and retrieved his gun and then out the door in pursuit of Jillian. She didn't make it very far before he was upon her once more.

"You witch," Martin raged as he grabbed Jillian around the waist. He dragged her down the back steps onto the lawn. "I've had enough of you," he spewed.

Jillian struggled against the strength of Martin's arm. She scratched and gouged his flesh, but he failed to release her. Tears streamed down her face as she sensed he was at the end of his rope and she at the end of her life.

"Martin, please let me go. I won't testify. I'll tell them that I made it all up to get back at Josh," she rambled while searching for the right words to say.

"You won't testify all right," Martin said with alaugh. "You'll be dead by the time Harrison gets back here. A pool accident."

God, he intends to drown me. Jillian fought with all the strength that she had. She did manage to cause him to stumble to the ground and temporarily release her, but Martin was all over her in a flash. Elbows swung and feet kicked as she tried to fight him off, but it was of no use. Once again imprisoned in his arms she was led to the swimming pool.

"Martin, please don't do this," she cried as they drew closer. "Please," she wailed.

"Be quiet!"

"You won't get away with this. Harrison will know it was you. Don't you think Josh is filling him in right now?"

His response was to laugh. "I'll be long gone before he gets back here. I electronically transferred money from the bank before coming down here. My flight awaits me. Now all I have to do is get rid of you." He dragged Jillian into the gated area of the pool. As she struggled against him, he slapped her once more, then dropped her to the ground. He grabbed a handful of hair before she could regain her senses and led her to the pool's edge. Then kneeling down beside her, he held her upper body out over the water and stared at her in the watery reflection.

Jillian sobbed uncontrollably. She tried scratching at his hand in her hair, but Martin was unaffected. "Please, Martin, don't do this," she continued to beg.

"I'm sorry, Jillian, but you leave me no choice," he told her. With his hand still buried in her hair, Martin plunged her forward, until water came up past her shoulders and to his elbow. He focused on the task at hand and tried to ignore the thrashing body bumping up against him. Then as an afterthought, he pulled her out the water with a violent jerk. In her eyes he saw raw natural fear and felt a surge of strength he hadn't felt in along time. The smile on his face was that of a person intent on rendering the most pain. "Do you think this is how your Travis felt?" When he saw the anguish then rage in Jillian's eyes, Martin laughed with satisfaction.

Water streamed down Jillian's body. Her lungs burned from the lack of oxygen rendering her weak. She breathed deep and rapidly trying to replenish her oxygen supply. His cruel words about her son's death made her realize how ironic life could be. She had survived the floodwaters only to die later by drowning in a pool. But before she could respond to his question, Martin submerged Jillian once more. She could sense the rage in his strength this time as she struggled against his grasp and knew that this was it. Her mind was in a state of panic as her lungs began to burn in agony from oxygen deprivation. The sunlight from up above was warm on her back, but no longer visible in the water of the pool. Slowly everything around her grew quiet then eventually all was dark. A calm settled over her as she took a fatal breath.

Martin's face was a mask of rage as he held Jillian submerged under water. His clothes were wet from her thrashing, but he didn't even notice it. His mind was racing through the years with his friends and how Jillian had ruined all their plans. He wanted her dead. Without her testimony to the murder, Josh would be spared from the death penalty. He tilted her further into the water as another wave of anger washed over him. So preoccupied with drowning her, Martin didn't notice that she no longer moved or that there was movement behind him.

"Let her go, Martin!" Harrison ordered in a booming voice, which managed to penetrate his thoughts.

"It seems we're both too late," Martin said in a resigned voice as he realized that he wouldn't be making that flight. He released Jillian and watched as she tumbled into the pool.

"Noooo!" Harrison screamed at the top of his voice and went running towards the pool. He forgot all about Martin as he dove in the pool and brought Jillian to the surface.

Captain Morton's weapon was trained on Martin. "You know the position, Wade, assume it," he ordered with authority. However, as Martin rose from his hunched position he reached for his weapon tucked in the front of his pants. Like a scene from a movie, both men exchanged gunfire, but it was Captain Morton who remained standing. Detective Wade Martin fell forward into the pool fatally wounded. Captain Morton lowered his weapon quickly then radioed for the paramedics to come back to the pool area. Soon the backyard was flooded with people running in all directions.

CHAPTER 20

Harrison sat quietly beside the still body lying in bed. His blood ran cold every time he recalled the image of Jillian's lifeless body falling into the pool. He didn't remember running to the pool or diving in, pulling her out. He also didn't remember the wails of anguish he released in between administering CPR. But what he would remember for the rest of his life was the sudden breath she took before the water rushed from her body and her eyes opened. Their whiskey-brown beauty was clouded with fear and exhaustion. They had blinked in his direction several times before slowly giving in to exhaustion and closing.

He reached out touching Jillian's hand atop the sheet. She was warm now and resting comfortably. When he had pulled her from the pool, she had been lifeless and so very cold. His head tilted forward as the feeling of fear and loss engulfed him once more. He had come so very close to losing her.

"She's alive and you're both going to have a wonderful life together," Antonio said to his son as he placed a reassuring hand on his shoulder.

"What are you doing out of bed?" Harrison asked. He rose from his chair beside Jillian and led his father to the vacant seat. "You should be resting."

The sound of voices penetrated through the darkness. Jillian recognized Harrison's voice and struggled to open her eyes. She tilted her head in the direction of his voice and managed to crack her lids open. There to the right at the foot of the bed stood the man she loved. His head was tilted down and his shoulders slumped. She shifted her head to the immediate right of her and spotted Antonio. His brown eyes were looking back at her.

"Look who's finally awake," he said in a whisper.

Harrison's head came up and swung in Jillian's direction. A smile spread across his face on seeing her awake. She had slept what remained of yesterday away and half of today. He eased beside her, taking her hand. It hurt to see the swelling in her face where Martin had struck her.

"Welcome back," he said through the tears clogging his throat.

Jillian tried to speak but had to clear her raw throat first. "I thought I would never see you again."

Tears streamed from the corners of her eyes. "It was Martin all along." She began to get upset as the horrible scene replayed inside her mind. Tears washed down her face as a sob tore from her lips. "He wanted to kill me."

Harrison hushed her fears with a soothing croon. "It's all right, sweetie, he won't be harming anyone ever again." He stroked her hair, then leaned forward and lightly kissed her swollen lips. "I'm so sorry I let you down."

Jillian searched his face. "You've never let me down."

"I was supposed to protect you."

A weak smile of understanding spread across Jillian's face. She reached out touching Harrison's cheek. "He was our friend. Neither one of us knew we had to protect ourselves against Martin."

Harrison nodded, although he would never forgive himself for not being there to protect her. He kissed her sweetly once more. "I love you."

Theirs eyes met as he withdrew. "I love you too," Jillian said back. "How's your father?"

"Better men than Martin have tried to put me out of commission," Antonio remarked lightheartedly and moved in closer. "We've been worried about you."

Jillian smiled weakly over at him. He too had become quite important to her. "I'll be okay as long as Martin's behind bars."

Antonio and Harrison exchanged glances. "Martin is dead, sweetie. He pulled his weapon on the captain and Morton fired back killing him."

"Oh my God! I'm sorry, love. I know he was your friend."

"A friend wouldn't try to kill the woman I love."

Jillian raised a hand to his face. Stubble darkened his complexion even more and he had never looked more handsome. "He told me everything."

"Josh did likewise. By the way, he's responsible for your being alive. He confessed to everything, then realizing that Martin was on the island, he told me about their operation and Martin's involvement." He lowered his eyes as he thought about the man he really didn't know. "It still amazes me as to how long their little setup worked."

"When can we go home?" Jillian asked.

"The doctor said you would be released tomorrow and Pop has a flight all lined up for us."

Jillian smiled at Antonio. "Thank you. I just want to put this whole nightmare behind me and get on with my life."

Harrison sat back. He ran a hand over his head in thought as a moment of insecurity washed over him. "What about our life together?"

The true meaning of his words didn't escape Jillian. Her whiskey eyes read his masked expression, not believing that he could still possess doubts about her love. She forced herself up on an elbow. With her left hand she drew his head to hers as their eyes met and held. "You are my life and if you believe you're getting out of a wedding that easily, you're mistaken."

Harrison released a sigh of relief and laughed heartily. "I wouldn't dream of it."

EPILOGUE

Harrison pulled into the driveway of their new home after a day of work. He surveyed the neighborhood with pride. This was the type of life he had dreamed of having and now it was a reality. His parents now lived in the city, and between Jillian's parents and sister there was always someone visiting the house. But he loved the closeness and wouldn't change a single thing. As he walked up the sidewalk, he admired Jillian's green thumb. Flowers bloomed in a profusion of colors all across the front of the house and down the sidewalk. He let himself into the house and felt the troubles of the day melt away. He opened the hallway closet and removed his service weapon. Taking down the metal case, he placed it inside and locked it. Then he went in search of Jillian with no other concerns than that of his family.

She sat on the floor in the family room, leaning against the sofa while breastfeeding their three-month-old daughter. The sight of her nourishing their child stole his breath away. It was the most pure and loving scene. Jillian was staring down at Arianna with love in her eyes. He could stand there watching the two ladies in his life forever. But the desire to be close to them drew him away from the doorway.

Jillian's head came up as Harrison walked into the room. Her eyes lit with love as he came and sat down beside her. She was happy being a wife and mother.

"Hi," she greeted him as he joined them and offered a kiss.

"How's my big girl doing today?" Harrison asked teasingly. Since the birth of their daughter he had begun to refer to her as such. He reached out stroking Arianna's silky black hair. He had fallen head over heels in love with his daughter from the moment she emerged from her mother's body.

"Your big girl and little girl have had a wonderful day." She removed her breast from the now sleeping baby's lips. "And just as soon as I place your daughter down, I plan on making sure your evening is equally as wonderful." Her eyes smoldered with passion.

Harrison's own brown eyes were alight with desire. "Why don't I place Arianna down and meet you in the bedroom?" He rose from the floor and gently took their daughter from her arms.

"Who said anything about the bedroom?" Jillian asked saucily and laughed with satisfaction as she gained his complete and undivided attention. She eased her breast back inside her bra and closed the clasp. "I was thinking a candlelight bath with chilled wine for you and ginger ale for me with chocolate dipped strawberries and grapes."

His smile was wicked as he took in her appearance. She wore a simple dress with a row of buttons down the front. He made plans to passionately torture Jillian button by button before they climbed into that tub. "You remember what happened the last time you planned a rendezvous in the bathtub?"

"How could I forget, she's lying in your arms."

"Well, just as long as you know what you're getting into." He winked.

Jillian tilted her head up to him as her eyes darkened with mounting passion. "You forget, love, that I'm a lawyer. I always know where I'm headed, but it's my job to lead others to where I want them to go." Her lips brushed his.

"Then lead the way, sweetie, because I'm ready."

2008 Reprint Mass Market Titles

January

Cautious Heart
Cheris F. Hodges
ISBN-13: 978-1-58571-301-1
ISBN-10: 1-58571-301-5
$6.99

Suddenly You
Crystal Hubbard
ISBN-13: 978-1-58571-302-8
ISBN-10: 1-58571-302-3
$6.99

February

Passion
T. T. Henderson
ISBN-13: 978-1-58571-303-5
ISBN-10: 1-58571-303-1
$6.99

Whispers in the Sand
LaFlorya Gauthier
ISBN-13: 978-1-58571-304-2
ISBN-10: 1-58571-304-x
$6.99

March

Life Is Never As It Seems
J. J. Michael
ISBN-13: 978-1-58571-305-9
ISBN-10: 1-58571-305-8
$6.99

Beyond the Rapture
Beverly Clark
ISBN-13: 978-1-58571-306-6
ISBN-10: 1-58571-306-6
$6.99

April

A Heart's Awakening
Veronica Parker
ISBN-13: 978-1-58571-307-3
ISBN-10: 1-58571-307-4
$6.99

Breeze
Robin Lynette Hampton
ISBN-13: 978-1-58571-308-0
ISBN-10: 1-58571-308-2
$6.99

May

I'll Be Your Shelter
Giselle Carmichael
ISBN-13: 978-1-58571-309-7
ISBN-10: 1-58571-309-0
$6.99

Careless Whispers
Rochelle Alers
ISBN-13: 978-1-58571-310-3
ISBN-10: 1-58571-310-4
$6.99

June

Sin
Crystal Rhodes
ISBN-13: 978-1-58571-311-0
ISBN-10: 1-58571-311-2
$6.99

Dark Storm Rising
Chinelu Moore
ISBN-13: 978-1-58571-312-7
ISBN-10: 1-58571-312-0
$6.99

2008 Reprint Mass Market Titles (continued)

July

Object of His Desire
A.C. Arthur
ISBN-13: 978-1-58571-313-4
ISBN-10: 1-58571-313-9
$6.99

Angel's Paradise
Janice Angelique
ISBN-13: 978-1-58571-314-1
ISBN-10: 1-58571-314-7
$6.99

August

Unbreak My Heart
Dar Tomlinson
ISBN-13: 978-1-58571-315-8
ISBN-10: 1-58571-315-5
$6.99

All I Ask
Barbara Keaton
ISBN-13: 978-1-58571-316-5
ISBN-10: 1-58571-316-3
$6.99

September

Icie
Pamela Leigh Starr
ISBN-13: 978-1-58571-275-5
ISBN-10: 1-58571-275-2
$6.99

At Last
Lisa Riley
ISBN-13: 978-1-58571-276-2
ISBN-10: 1-58571-276-0
$6.99

October

Everlastin' Love
Gay G. Gunn
ISBN-13: 978-1-58571-277-9
ISBN-10: 1-58571-277-9
$6.99

Three Wishes
Seressia Glass
ISBN-13: 978-1-58571-278-6
ISBN-10: 1-58571-278-7
$6.99

November

Yesterday Is Gone
Beverly Clark
ISBN-13: 978-1-58571-279-3
ISBN-10: 1-58571-279-5
$6.99

Again My Love
Kayla Perrin
ISBN-13: 978-1-58571-280-9
ISBN-10: 1-58571-280-9
$6.99

December

Office Policy
A.C. Arthur
ISBN-13: 978-1-58571-281-6
ISBN-10: 1-58571-281-7
$6.99

Rendezvous With Fate
Jeanne Sumerix
ISBN-13: 978-1-58571-283-3
ISBN-10: 1-58571-283-3
$6.99

2008 New Mass Market Titles

January

Where I Want To Be
Maryam Diaab
ISBN-13: 978-1-58571-268-7
ISBN-10: 1-58571-268-X
$6.99

Never Say Never
Michele Cameron
ISBN-13: 978-1-58571-269-4
ISBN-10: 1-58571-269-8
$6.99

February

Stolen Memories
Michele Sudler
ISBN-13: 978-1-58571-270-0
ISBN-10: 1-58571-270-1
$6.99

Dawn's Harbor
Kymberly Hunt
ISBN-13: 978-1-58571-271-7
ISBN-10: 1-58571-271-X
$6.99

March

Undying Love
Renee Alexis
ISBN-13: 978-1-58571-272-4
ISBN-10: 1-58571-272-8
$6.99

Blame It On Paradise
Crystal Hubbard
ISBN-13: 978-1-58571-273-1
ISBN-10: 1-58571-273-6
$6.99

April

When A Man Loves A Woman
La Connie Taylor-Jones
ISBN-13: 978-1-58571-274-8
ISBN-10: 1-58571-274-4
$6.99

Choices
Tammy Williams
ISBN-13: 978-1-58571-300-4
ISBN-10: 1-58571-300-7
$6.99

May

Dream Runner
Gail McFarland
ISBN-13: 978-1-58571-317-2
ISBN-10: 1-58571-317-1
$6.99

Southern Fried Standards
S.R. Maddox
ISBN-13: 978-1-58571-318-9
ISBN-10: 1-58571-318-X
$6.99

June

Looking for Lily
Africa Fine
ISBN-13: 978-1-58571-319-6
ISBN-10: 1-58571-319-8
$6.99

Bliss, Inc.
Chamein Canton
ISBN-13: 978-1-58571-325-7
ISBN-10: 1-58571-325-2
$6.99

2008 New Mass Market Titles (continued)

July

Love's Secrets
Yolanda McVey
ISBN-13: 978-1-58571-321-9
ISBN-10: 1-58571-321-X
$6.99

Things Forbidden
Maryam Diaab
ISBN-13: 978-1-58571-327-1
ISBN-10: 1-58571-327-9
$6.99

August

Storm
Pamela Leigh Starr
ISBN-13: 978-1-58571-323-3
ISBN-10: 1-58571-323-6
$6.99

Passion's Furies
AlTonya Washington
ISBN-13: 978-1-58571-324-0
ISBN-10: 1-58571-324-4
$6.99

September

Three Doors Down
Michele Sudler
ISBN-13: 978-1-58571-332-5
ISBN-10: 1-58571-332-5
$6.99

Mr Fix-It
Crystal Hubbard
ISBN-13: 978-1-58571-326-4
ISBN-10: 1-58571-326-0
$6.99

October

Moments of Clarity
Michele Cameron
ISBN-13: 978-1-58571-330-1
ISBN-10: 1-58571-330-9
$6.99

Lady Preacher
K.T. Richey
ISBN-13: 978-1-58571-333-2
ISBN-10: 1-58571-333-3
$6.99

November

This Life Isn't Perfect Holla
Sandra Foy
ISBN: 978-1-58571-331-8
ISBN-10: 1-58571-331-7
$6.99

Promises Made
Bernice Layton
ISBN-13: 978-1-58571-334-9
ISBN-10: 1-58571-334-1
$6.99

December

A Voice Behind Thunder
Carrie Elizabeth Greene
ISBN-13: 978-1-58571-329-5
ISBN-10: 1-58571-329-5
$6.99

The More Things Change
Chamein Canton
ISBN-13: 978-1-58571-328-8
ISBN-10: 1-58571-328-7
$6.99

Other Genesis Press, Inc. Titles

A Dangerous Deception	J.M. Jeffries	$8.95
A Dangerous Love	J.M. Jeffries	$8.95
A Dangerous Obsession	J.M. Jeffries	$8.95
A Drummer's Beat to Mend	Kei Swanson	$9.95
A Happy Life	Charlotte Harris	$9.95
A Heart's Awakening	Veronica Parker	$9.95
A Lark on the Wing	Phyliss Hamilton	$9.95
A Love of Her Own	Cheris F. Hodges	$9.95
A Love to Cherish	Beverly Clark	$8.95
A Risk of Rain	Dar Tomlinson	$8.95
A Taste of Temptation	Reneé Alexis	$9.95
A Twist of Fate	Beverly Clark	$8.95
A Will to Love	Angie Daniels	$9.95
Acquisitions	Kimberley White	$8.95
Across	Carol Payne	$12.95
After the Vows (Summer Anthology)	Leslie Esdaile T.T. Henderson Jacqueline Thomas	$10.95
Again My Love	Kayla Perrin	$10.95
Against the Wind	Gwynne Forster	$8.95
All I Ask	Barbara Keaton	$8.95
Always You	Crystal Hubbard	$6.99
Ambrosia	T.T. Henderson	$8.95
An Unfinished Love Affair	Barbara Keaton	$8.95
And Then Came You	Dorothy Elizabeth Love	$8.95
Angel's Paradise	Janice Angelique	$9.95
At Last	Lisa G. Riley	$8.95
Best of Friends	Natalie Dunbar	$8.95
Beyond the Rapture	Beverly Clark	$9.95
Blaze	Barbara Keaton	$9.95
Blood Lust	J. M. Jeffries	$9.95
Blood Seduction	J.M. Jeffries	$9.95

Other Genesis Press, Inc. Titles (continued)

Bodyguard	Andrea Jackson	$9.95
Boss of Me	Diana Nyad	$8.95
Bound by Love	Beverly Clark	$8.95
Breeze	Robin Hampton Allen	$10.95
Broken	Dar Tomlinson	$24.95
By Design	Barbara Keaton	$8.95
Cajun Heat	Charlene Berry	$8.95
Careless Whispers	Rochelle Alers	$8.95
Cats & Other Tales	Marilyn Wagner	$8.95
Caught in a Trap	Andre Michelle	$8.95
Caught Up In the Rapture	Lisa G. Riley	$9.95
Cautious Heart	Cheris F Hodges	$8.95
Chances	Pamela Leigh Starr	$8.95
Cherish the Flame	Beverly Clark	$8.95
Class Reunion	Irma Jenkins/ John Brown	$12.95
Code Name: Diva	J.M. Jeffries	$9.95
Conquering Dr. Wexler's Heart	Kimberley White	$9.95
Corporate Seduction	A.C. Arthur	$9.95
Crossing Paths, Tempting Memories	Dorothy Elizabeth Love	$9.95
Crush	Crystal Hubbard	$9.95
Cypress Whisperings	Phyllis Hamilton	$8.95
Dark Embrace	Crystal Wilson Harris	$8.95
Dark Storm Rising	Chinelu Moore	$10.95
Daughter of the Wind	Joan Xian	$8.95
Deadly Sacrifice	Jack Kean	$22.95
Designer Passion	Dar Tomlinson Diana Richeaux	$8.95
Do Over	Celya Bowers	$9.95
Dreamtective	Liz Swados	$5.95

Other Genesis Press, Inc. Titles (continued)

Ebony Angel	Deatri King-Bey	$9.95
Ebony Butterfly II	Delilah Dawson	$14.95
Echoes of Yesterday	Beverly Clark	$9.95
Eden's Garden	Elizabeth Rose	$8.95
Eve's Prescription	Edwina Martin Arnold	$8.95
Everlastin' Love	Gay G. Gunn	$8.95
Everlasting Moments	Dorothy Elizabeth Love	$8.95
Everything and More	Sinclair Lebeau	$8.95
Everything but Love	Natalie Dunbar	$8.95
Falling	Natalie Dunbar	$9.95
Fate	Pamela Leigh Starr	$8.95
Finding Isabella	A.J. Garrotto	$8.95
Forbidden Quest	Dar Tomlinson	$10.95
Forever Love	Wanda Y. Thomas	$8.95
From the Ashes	Kathleen Suzanne Jeanne Sumerix	$8.95
Gentle Yearning	Rochelle Alers	$10.95
Glory of Love	Sinclair LeBeau	$10.95
Go Gentle into that Good Night	Malcom Boyd	$12.95
Goldengroove	Mary Beth Craft	$16.95
Groove, Bang, and Jive	Steve Cannon	$8.99
Hand in Glove	Andrea Jackson	$9.95
Hard to Love	Kimberley White	$9.95
Hart & Soul	Angie Daniels	$8.95
Heart of the Phoenix	A.C. Arthur	$9.95
Heartbeat	Stephanie Bedwell-Grime	$8.95
Hearts Remember	M. Loui Quezada	$8.95
Hidden Memories	Robin Allen	$10.95
Higher Ground	Leah Latimer	$19.95
Hitler, the War, and the Pope	Ronald Rychiak	$26.95
How to Write a Romance	Kathryn Falk	$18.95

Other Genesis Press, Inc. Titles (continued)

I Married a Reclining Chair	Lisa M. Fuhs	$8.95
I'll Be Your Shelter	Giselle Carmichael	$8.95
I'll Paint a Sun	A.J. Garrotto	$9.95
Icie	Pamela Leigh Starr	$8.95
Illusions	Pamela Leigh Starr	$8.95
Indigo After Dark Vol. I	Nia Dixon/Angelique	$10.95
Indigo After Dark Vol. II	Dolores Bundy/ Cole Riley	$10.95
Indigo After Dark Vol. III	Montana Blue/ Coco Morena	$10.95
Indigo After Dark Vol. IV	Cassandra Colt/	$14.95
Indigo After Dark Vol. V	Delilah Dawson	$14.95
Indiscretions	Donna Hill	$8.95
Intentional Mistakes	Michele Sudler	$9.95
Interlude	Donna Hill	$8.95
Intimate Intentions	Angie Daniels	$8.95
It's Not Over Yet	J.J. Michael	$9.95
Jolie's Surrender	Edwina Martin-Arnold	$8.95
Kiss or Keep	Debra Phillips	$8.95
Lace	Giselle Carmichael	$9.95
Last Train to Memphis	Elsa Cook	$12.95
Lasting Valor	Ken Olsen	$24.95
Let Us Prey	Hunter Lundy	$25.95
Lies Too Long	Pamela Ridley	$13.95
Life Is Never As It Seems	J.J. Michael	$12.95
Lighter Shade of Brown	Vicki Andrews	$8.95
Love Always	Mildred E. Riley	$10.95
Love Doesn't Come Easy	Charlyne Dickerson	$8.95
Love Unveiled	Gloria Greene	$10.95
Love's Deception	Charlene Berry	$10.95
Love's Destiny	M. Loui Quezada	$8.95
Mae's Promise	Melody Walcott	$8.95

Other Genesis Press, Inc. Titles (continued)

Magnolia Sunset	Giselle Carmichael	$8.95
Many Shades of Gray	Dyanne Davis	$6.99
Matters of Life and Death	Lesego Malepe, Ph.D.	$15.95
Meant to Be	Jeanne Sumerix	$8.95
Midnight Clear (Anthology)	Leslie Esdaile Gwynne Forster Carmen Green Monica Jackson	$10.95
Midnight Magic	Gwynne Forster	$8.95
Midnight Peril	Vicki Andrews	$10.95
Misconceptions	Pamela Leigh Starr	$9.95
Montgomery's Children	Richard Perry	$14.95
My Buffalo Soldier	Barbara B. K. Reeves	$8.95
Naked Soul	Gwynne Forster	$8.95
Next to Last Chance	Louisa Dixon	$24.95
No Apologies	Seressia Glass	$8.95
No Commitment Required	Seressia Glass	$8.95
No Regrets	Mildred E. Riley	$8.95
Not His Type	Chamein Canton	$6.99
Nowhere to Run	Gay G. Gunn	$10.95
O Bed! O Breakfast!	Rob Kuehnle	$14.95
Object of His Desire	A. C. Arthur	$8.95
Office Policy	A. C. Arthur	$9.95
Once in a Blue Moon	Dorianne Cole	$9.95
One Day at a Time	Bella McFarland	$8.95
One in A Million	Barbara Keaton	$6.99
One of These Days	Michele Sudler	$9.95
Outside Chance	Louisa Dixon	$24.95
Passion	T.T. Henderson	$10.95
Passion's Blood	Cherif Fortin	$22.95
Passion's Journey	Wanda Y. Thomas	$8.95
Past Promises	Jahmel West	$8.95

Other Genesis Press, Inc. Titles (continued)

Title	Author	Price
Path of Fire	T.T. Henderson	$8.95
Path of Thorns	Annetta P. Lee	$9.95
Peace Be Still	Colette Haywood	$12.95
Picture Perfect	Reon Carter	$8.95
Playing for Keeps	Stephanie Salinas	$8.95
Pride & Joi	Gay G. Gunn	$8.95
Promises to Keep	Alicia Wiggins	$8.95
Quiet Storm	Donna Hill	$10.95
Reckless Surrender	Rochelle Alers	$6.95
Red Polka Dot in a World of Plaid	Varian Johnson	$12.95
Reluctant Captive	Joyce Jackson	$8.95
Rendezvous with Fate	Jeanne Sumerix	$8.95
Revelations	Cheris F. Hodges	$8.95
Rivers of the Soul	Leslie Esdaile	$8.95
Rocky Mountain Romance	Kathleen Suzanne	$8.95
Rooms of the Heart	Donna Hill	$8.95
Rough on Rats and Tough on Cats	Chris Parker	$12.95
Secret Library Vol. 1	Nina Sheridan	$18.95
Secret Library Vol. 2	Cassandra Colt	$8.95
Secret Thunder	Annetta P. Lee	$9.95
Shades of Brown	Denise Becker	$8.95
Shades of Desire	Monica White	$8.95
Shadows in the Moonlight	Jeanne Sumerix	$8.95
Sin	Crystal Rhodes	$8.95
Small Whispers	Annetta P. Lee	$6.99
So Amazing	Sinclair LeBeau	$8.95
Somebody's Someone	Sinclair LeBeau	$8.95
Someone to Love	Alicia Wiggins	$8.95
Song in the Park	Martin Brant	$15.95
Soul Eyes	Wayne L. Wilson	$12.95

Other Genesis Press, Inc. Titles (continued)

Soul to Soul	Donna Hill	$8.95
Southern Comfort	J.M. Jeffries	$8.95
Still the Storm	Sharon Robinson	$8.95
Still Waters Run Deep	Leslie Esdaile	$8.95
Stolen Kisses	Dominiqua Douglas	$9.95
Stories to Excite You	Anna Forrest/Divine	$14.95
Subtle Secrets	Wanda Y. Thomas	$8.95
Suddenly You	Crystal Hubbard	$9.95
Sweet Repercussions	Kimberley White	$9.95
Sweet Sensations	Gwendolyn Bolton	$9.95
Sweet Tomorrows	Kimberly White	$8.95
Taken by You	Dorothy Elizabeth Love	$9.95
Tattooed Tears	T. T. Henderson	$8.95
The Color Line	Lizzette Grayson Carter	$9.95
The Color of Trouble	Dyanne Davis	$8.95
The Disappearance of Allison Jones	Kayla Perrin	$5.95
The Fires Within	Beverly Clark	$9.95
The Foursome	Celya Bowers	$6.99
The Honey Dipper's Legacy	Pannell-Allen	$14.95
The Joker's Love Tune	Sidney Rickman	$15.95
The Little Pretender	Barbara Cartland	$10.95
The Love We Had	Natalie Dunbar	$8.95
The Man Who Could Fly	Bob & Milana Beamon	$18.95
The Missing Link	Charlyne Dickerson	$8.95
The Mission	Pamela Leigh Starr	$6.99
The Perfect Frame	Beverly Clark	$9.95
The Price of Love	Sinclair LeBeau	$8.95
The Smoking Life	Ilene Barth	$29.95
The Words of the Pitcher	Kei Swanson	$8.95
Three Wishes	Seressia Glass	$8.95
Ties That Bind	Kathleen Suzanne	$8.95

Other Genesis Press, Inc. Titles (continued)

Tiger Woods	Libby Hughes	$5.95
Time is of the Essence	Angie Daniels	$9.95
Timeless Devotion	Bella McFarland	$9.95
Tomorrow's Promise	Leslie Esdaile	$8.95
Truly Inseparable	Wanda Y. Thomas	$8.95
Two Sides to Every Story	Dyanne Davis	$9.95
Unbreak My Heart	Dar Tomlinson	$8.95
Uncommon Prayer	Kenneth Swanson	$9.95
Unconditional Love	Alicia Wiggins	$8.95
Unconditional	A.C. Arthur	$9.95
Until Death Do Us Part	Susan Paul	$8.95
Vows of Passion	Bella McFarland	$9.95
Wedding Gown	Dyanne Davis	$8.95
What's Under Benjamin's Bed	Sandra Schaffer	$8.95
When Dreams Float	Dorothy Elizabeth Love	$8.95
When I'm With You	LaConnie Taylor-Jones	$6.99
Whispers in the Night	Dorothy Elizabeth Love	$8.95
Whispers in the Sand	LaFlorya Gauthier	$10.95
Who's That Lady?	Andrea Jackson	$9.95
Wild Ravens	Altonya Washington	$9.95
Yesterday Is Gone	Beverly Clark	$10.95
Yesterday's Dreams, Tomorrow's Promises	Reon Laudat	$8.95
Your Precious Love	Sinclair LeBeau	$8.95

Order Form

Mail to: Genesis Press, Inc.
P.O. Box 101
Columbus, MS 39703

Name ____
Address ____
City/State _________________________ Zip _______________
Telephone _________________________

Ship to (if different from above)
Name ____
Address ____
City/State _________________________ Zip _______________
Telephone _________________________

Credit Card Information
Credit Card # _______________________ ☐Visa ☐Mastercard
Expiration Date (mm/yy) ______________ ☐AmEx ☐Discover

Qty.	Author	Title	Price	Total

Use this order form, or call 1-888-INDIGO-1

Total for books ______________
Shipping and handling:
$5 first two books,
$1 each additional book ______________
Total S & H ______________
Total amount enclosed ______________

Mississippi residents add 7% sales tax

Visit www.genesis-press.com for latest releases and excerpts.